Twice Dead

Eleanor Sullivan

HILLIARD HARRIS
PUBLISHER

Published by

HILLIARD HARRIS
PUBLISHERS

P.O. Box 3358
Frederick, Maryland 21705-3358

Twice Dead Copyright © 2002

First Edition   ISBN   1-59133-005-X

Cover Designed by

HILLIARD HARRIS

Manufactured/Printed in the United States of America

2002

In memory of my grandmother,

Alice Ricker Reed Clore, RN

Acknowledgements

This book would not have been possible without help from many people. Elaine Level, RN, supplied hands-on information about intensive care nursing in today's busy hospitals and made many helpful suggestions. Roger Jackman, MD, provided medical information and tirelessly answered my many questions. A native of South St. Louis, Francis Buehler explained details that no outsider could have known. U. S. Postal Inspector Scott Sullivan knows more about bombs than most of us want to know, and he generously shared that information with me. St. Louis Police Officer Nancy Lorino Stelmach told me what life on the streets of St. Louis is like, and St. Louis Police Detective Tom Wiber explained investigational techniques. Former Army Ranger Brad Sullivan recreated the camaraderie of off-duty soldiers, lending realism to their interactions in my story. I appreciate all of the information they provided. Any errors of fact, however, are my own.

Colleen Daly, editor extraordinaire, became my teacher, coach and cheerleader as I was learning the craft of writing mystery fiction. Mary Dolan, who shares the vision, offered friendship and encouragement along with other Sisters in Crime. To these people and the many other nurses, friends and family members who offered information, ideas and support, I give my heartfelt thanks.

Eleanor Sullivan

"There is something so physical about sisterhood; some body-memory, too deep for words."

Kennedy Fraser

Prologue

The surgery—if you could call it that—didn't last long. The time it actually took was probably less than it seemed since she didn't know how long to expect it to take. The doctor didn't say much. Just told her to lie still.

Soon all remnants of him were gone—every sign that he had entered her body and left his telltale deposits. She felt washed clean as she sensed, rather than heard, the last piece of him drop into the stainless steel basin.

Chapter 1
Saturday, 17 March, 1227 Hours

Hope died.

With no warning.

I should have been there. But, as I told Tim when he'd phoned that morning to tell me two nurses had called in sick, I'd promised to take the twins to the St. Patrick's Day parade. Tim had said they could manage; he and Laura would work double shifts.

I've spent all of my career at St. Teresa's Hospital. They offered me my first job after graduation from nursing school, I stayed to get some experience and I'm still here, nurse manager of the intensive care unit, a job that expanded when the medical and surgical intensive care units were combined. Actually, my recently-changed title is patient care manager because someone figured out we were supposed to be managing patients, not nurses.

The rain had let up conveniently right before the parade started although a saturated blanket of clouds hung over downtown St. Louis. It wasn't enough to dampen the spirits of the several hundred thousand rowdy spectators, all celebrating their Irish heritage,

2

even if they happened to be German like us or Dutch or Scandinavian or Italian. St. Louis, like many cities home to descendants of European immigrants, celebrated St. Patrick's Day in a big way. Outdoor decorations festooned most city streets, especially on the Southside. At the very least, an Irish flag hung suspended from a pole on the front porch. One home we'd passed on the way to the parade had green Christmas lights draped on its shrubbery and giant shamrocks plastered on front windows and door. Parade-goers, too, were decorated with green clothing and hats covered with shamrocks; some partyers even sported green hair. The green beer was flowing. Rambunctious spectators partied to the tunes of marching bands and bagpipes. A group of green- and white-dressed dancers, arms rigid and feet spinning to an Irish jig, were passing us when my cell phone rang. I tried to answer it but it cut off in mid-ring.

"Damn," I said under my breath. The hospital provided cell phones to all the supervisors, but chose the cheapest, and most unreliable, service. I tapped Tina on the shoulder. "We have to go."

Her face fell. "Not now, Aunt Monny."

Monny is short for Monika and, strictly speaking, I'm not their aunt. Their mom is my cousin and we are both only children of twin brothers. So growing up Hannah and I had pretended we were sisters. Her children were the nearest thing I had to progeny.

"The clowns haven't come yet!" Tina said. A favorite with the children, the clowns tossed candy to the crowds near the end of the parade.

Gena, sitting on the curb, cried, "Look, it's a green Santa Claus!"

"That's a leprechaun," her sister told her authoritatively as the helium-filled character bobbed past.

"I have to find a phone booth. I have to call the hospital. It's an emergency," I told them.

"We can stay here." Tina, older by fifteen minutes, put her arm around her sister. "We're old enough. We're not little kids any more." A blond pony tail, pushed through the opening in the back of her Cardinal baseball cap, bobbed up and down emphatically. Gena's pony tail nodded in agreement.

"All right. You stay right here. On our corner." Like many native St. Louisans, we always arrived early to claim a spot on the same corner. Ours was at Market and Eleventh Street.

"Okay?"

Two heads bobbed again.

"Don't move, and stay together."

They had turned to see the firetrucks, sirens blaring over the raucous sounds of the crowd, go by. A Dalmatian, green spots competing with black ones, sat calmly atop.

I pushed through the crowd in search of a pay phone and found one a block down the street. A heavy-set woman sat in the phone booth, cracking the door open with her foot. A young man with a bucket of green beer swinging precariously from his hand lounged against the open door. The woman inside was telling someone to do something before she got home. Or else. I tapped my foot impatiently.

My phone gave another short ring and shut down again. The young man turned at the sound; his unfocused eyes indicated that he'd already had more than one bucket of beer. I smiled apologetically.

"I need to call the hospital," I explained.

He didn't look impressed.

"I'm a nurse. They need me."

A blank face.

"Can I get ahead?"

He shrugged, splashing drops of beer on his jeans, and moved away.

I tapped on the glass.

The woman shut the door in my face.

I tapped again harder. She looked up, scowling. "Hold on," she told person on other end. "Someone's pestering me."

"It's an emergency. I have to call the hospital. I'm a nurse. Please. You can have it right back," I assured her.

Someone in the line that had formed behind me coughed pointedly. The woman glanced up briefly, then took her time ending the call.

She squeezed out of the booth, moving her considerable weight with difficulty, and slammed the door open behind her. It rattled against the frame as thunder rumbled in the distance. Dark clouds were rolling in.

"Monika, you better come in," Tim said when I reached the ICU nurses' station at St. Teresa's. Tim had been a nurse for more than ten years, the last two working for me.

"Why? What's happened?"

"It's Hope. She's dead."

"*Dead?*"

Several heads turned toward me.

I closed the door. "How could she be? I thought she was improving."

"Just get here. Laura's gone to pieces and I'm shorthanded." His voice was clipped and hard, unlike Tim.

I checked my Minnie Mouse watch. The hospital was about a ten-minute drive from downtown and I'd need five minutes to get to my car in the garage a block away. And I had to collect the twins.

"I'm on my way."

I dialed again, turning my back on the angry looks from the line outside the booth. Hannah agreed to meet me at the hospital in fifteen minutes to pick up the girls.

The parade was almost over and people had already started to leave. Traffic would be impossible soon. Thunder rumbled and the wind picked up, scattering plastic beer cups, soda cans and bits of paper in swirls through the street.

I tried to push by some boisterous partiers noisily singing "Danny Boy" off key. One of men swung his arm around my neck, crushing me in a cloud of beer-soaked smells and rain-dampened jackets. The song came to a sloppy end as I slipped out unnoticed from under his arm, irritated by their revelry while a young woman lay unexplainably dead a few miles away.

I pushed through the rest of the crowd to the corner where I'd left the twins. There were plenty of children there, but not Tina or Gena.

My throat felt dry.

"Tina, Gena," I shouted impotently into the noise. I pushed my way around the corner against the crowd of more people leaving. No twins. I turned back to the corner, checking the street sign. Eleventh Street. They weren't there. I struggled to see through to the curb but at four feet eleven, I couldn't see over the crowd. I worked my way down the street, pushed through the throng and stepped into the street, looking back toward the corner to see the girls sitting on the curb almost where I had left them. Relief, then anger, flooded through me as I started toward them.

"Where were you?" I asked in a low, tight voice as I grabbed two sticky hands and jerked the girls to their feet. Four eyes filled with tears.

"We just wanted some candy," wailed Gena. Several clowns were tossing paper-wrapped treats to children just ahead. "We were just gone a minute," Tina said swallowing her tears.

"It's okay. You're here, but we have to hurry. Let's run." A loud clap of thunder made us all jump. "See how fast we can get to the car." Tears forgotten, they pulled me along, each yelling she was going to get there first. The thunder boomed louder. Giant drops hit us just as we made it into the garage. The girls were still arguing about who had won the race as I pulled into the stream of cars heading west.

✦ ✦ ✦ ✦

Hannah's van was parked under the canopy in front of the hospital as promised. I gave the girls quick kisses, waved to Hannah, and then swung my car into the hospital's garage, steeling myself to deal with yet another unexpected death in ICU.

Chapter 2
Saturday, 17 March, 1310 Hours

As usual after a code, the room was a mess. The floor was smeared with blood. Wrappings from ripped open packages and blood-streaked IV tubing were scattered everywhere. A blood-stained blanket lay crumpled under the bed.

Hope had been a beautiful young woman with long blond hair. In death, she looked younger than her twenty-three years. Her gown was bunched up around her neck. Her breasts lay flat against her chest, scarred by burn marks from defibrillator paddles. Above her left breast I noticed a tiny butterfly tattoo I hadn't seen before. Her legs were spread open, and blood had pooled where her body depressed the mattress, filled the space between her spread-open legs and spilled onto the floor. Now the dark pool of blood under the bed was turning brown on the cream-colored tile.

"We haven't had time to clean up," Tim said, coming up behind me. "Mr. Bettelman coded after you called. We brought him back, but it took awhile."

I squeezed my eyes shut and took a breath. After more than twenty years in nursing, I had seen plenty of deaths.   Some slow, some painful, some quick and merciful.   But I want to scream at God, or the Fates, or whatever Power there is.   Afterward it's always the same: an overwhelming sadness slips over me like a gray fog.   I feel paralyzed, afraid to move, almost afraid to take a breath, as if it is not right that I am able to breathe when my patient can't.   Eventually the horror fades, and I go back to work.

"I'll give you a hand."   As I reached for the sheet to cover Hope's naked body, my foot slipped in the blood and I fell forward, landing on Hope's bare chest.   I jerked back, pushing Hope away.   The butterfly tattoo appeared to flutter as her head sank onto her chest and rolled off the pillow.

"You okay?" Tim asked.   "Any on you?"

Blood—anywhere—is a nurse's worst nightmare. AIDS.

"I just slipped.   I'm fine."   My voice sounded shaky.   I yanked the sheet loose from the end of the bed. It, too, was blood-stained.

"What happened to Laura?" I asked Tim as I grabbed some gloves out of a carton on the bedside table.

"She just walked off," he said.

I stopped with my hand half into a glove.   "Left the patient?   Where'd she go?"

"Serena found her in the restroom.   Sobbing."

"I don't get it.   This isn't her first death.   Was Laura Hope's nurse?"

"Technically."

"Technically?"

"Laura had Hope today, but Serena's making up a clinical for school and she was assigned to her."

"Where's the instructor?"

"She didn't want to come in on a Saturday."

"Maybe if I'd come in instead of taking the twins to the parade—"

"You don't know that," Tim said. "This could have happened no matter who was here. Or not. I doubt we could have stopped a hemorrhage this bad."

"You see this?" I asked Tim, pointing to the tattoo. "I always wonder why people get them," I said as I straightened her head as if she were a live patient I was trying to make comfortable. "You have them for life."

"And after," Tim added, studying Hope's arms.

"Something wrong?"

"I guess she got stuck twice." He pointed to the needle mark and bruising on the inside of her left arm. IV tubing dangled from the needle still inserted in the inside of her right arm. "Do the parents know?" he asked. "About the abortion?"

Hope had been admitted about ten the morning before with vaginal bleeding of unknown origin. She'd stopped at a service station and collapsed. An ambulance delivered her to St. Teresa's shortly thereafter. Before her father and their minister had arrived, I'd coaxed the information out of her that she'd had an abortion.

"Anyone call her parents?" I asked, ignoring Tim's question for the moment.

"Haven't had time. Between taking care of everyone, and dealing with Laura's hysterics. . . ." He pinched the bridge of his nose and squeezed his eyes shut. A loop of dark brown hair flopped down between his eyebrows.

"You're tired. I'll do it," I told him. Telling the family is the nurse's least favorite job.

"Thanks," he said with a sigh. He stared a moment at Hope, and then gathered some clean towels, wet them in the sink and began wiping the dribble that had trickled out of the corner of Hope's mouth. I started on Hope's legs and genitals, folding the towels between her legs as they became soaked with blood and the urine and feces that had been expelled when she died. Tim attached an identification tag on her toe as I slid a duplicate tag on a string around her neck. We turned her, expelling air from her lungs in one long sigh. Dark blood dribbled from between her legs.

Tim pointed to her lower back. "Ever see one of these? A retroperitoneal bleed?"

Hope's backside was mottled with purple splotches visible through her pale skin where the blood had pooled.

"Nope," I said. "Read about it but never saw one."

"I saw one once on a GYN patient, also with a diagnosis of vaginal bleeding of unknown origin," he said as we finished cleaning up and spread a clean sheet over Hope's body.

I turned to go, squishing in the blood.

"Stop," Tim ordered. "You're tracking more blood. Stand still."

He wet a towel in the sink, tossed it next to him and, using his foot, started to mop up the floor. When he finally reached me, after using a few more towels, he said, "You sure have tiny feet. What are they? Size four?"

The staff liked to tease me about my size, calling me "shorty" or "shrimp." Most of the time I didn't mind. It helped keep the barrier down between them and me, as management.

"Five. And growing." My habitual response to the "short" jokes.

"Here, wipe the bottom of your shoes on this." He threw another clean towel on the floor.

"I'll call housekeeping and have them finish up the room," I said.

"Good luck. Their budget's been cut, too, and this is Saturday."

"They have to. Administration wants the room filled." I reached down to pick up a tangle of used tubing. A round strip of plastic was caught in it. It would be a while before the room was cleaned, but I could make a start.

"Look at this, Tim. Hope's ID bracelet." Tiny drops of blood dotted the band.

We looked at each other and stepped back to the bed raising the sheet to check Hope's wrists. Neither one had an ID band.

"How'd that happen?"

Tim shrugged. "Someone probably cut it off during the code."

"I wonder why they'd do that," I said, but Tim had already left. I gathered up the bloodstained towels, tossed them into the contaminated laundry bag, peeled my gloves off and dropped them into the empty trash basket as I left the room, pulling the curtain closed behind me.

Our unit was actually one big room with twelve cubicles clustered in a semi-circle around the nurses' station. The cubicles didn't have doors, just privacy curtains to shield them from the traffic that went through the unit. There were glass windows between the rooms, and on the side opposite the nurses' station were a window and door to the outside corridor, all screened by curtains. The nurses' station had a counter running the length of the unit that shielded a long desktop. Patient monitors, computers, telephones, patient charts, and books on critical care, drugs, and equipment added to the general clutter. Ruby's large, insulated cup, labeled with her name and DO NOT TOUCH in bold, black indelible ink, sat beside the phone.

I picked up the phone and dialed reluctantly.

"Hello?" a hesitant female voice answered.

"Mrs. Shepheard?"

"Yes?"

"Mrs. Shepheard, this is Monika Everhardt, from the hospital."

"Yes?"

"Mrs. Shepheard, is there someone there with you?"

"My husband just came in." She spoke slowly, spacing her words.

"Are you sitting down?"

"Well, not now. I answered the phone."

"Please sit down and ask your husband to sit next to you."

I heard her call to him. "Earl, it's the hospital. They want to talk to us. Bring me a chair." She didn't seem at all concerned by my phone call. Then to me, "What is it?"

"I have some bad news. It's Hope. We tried everything." I waited, letting the information sink in.

"She's better, though, isn't she?"

"I'm afraid not, Mrs. Shepheard. She didn't make it."

I head a series of loud noises I couldn't decipher. "Mrs. Shepheard, are you all right?" I shouted.

"Who is this?" a male voice demanded over the phone. "And what did you say to my wife?"

"Mr. Shepheard, this is Monika Everhardt at St. Teresa's. I'm afraid I have bad news about Hope." I took a breath. "She just died."

"What?" he screamed. "She just had a little bleeding! What did you do to her?"

"Mr. Shepheard, take care of your wife."

The phone slammed in my ear.

Serena was standing by the nurses' station, arms crossed in front of her small body. Serena worked part time for us as an assistant and was just finishing her first year of nursing school. "What happened to her?" she asked me, tears clouding her eyes. She wiped at them with stubby fingers, smearing mascara onto her cheeks.

I remembered my first death as a nurse. An elderly woman I had cared for. I had barely kept my composure as I readied her body for the morgue and then, ashamed of feeling so grief-stricken over someone I hardly knew, I'd held in my emotions until I got home.

"I didn't do anything wrong." Serena's lower lip jutted out defensively.

I shook my head. "I'm sure you didn't. It just happens. We don't know why."

"Will they find out?"

"They will if they do an autopsy."

"What if the family doesn't want one?"

"Usually they do in cases like this." I checked my watch. "It's been more than twenty-four hours since she was admitted, so it's not a medical examiner's case," I explained to the young student. "As far as I know."

"She was so young," Serena said, sniffing.

I put my arm around her shoulder. "It's hard on me, too, even after all I've seen. But we have to go back to work, take care of all the others."

Mrs. Ritenour pulled back the curtain to her husband's room and motioned for help. "He just doesn't look right," she said.

"Can you see what she wants?" I asked Serena.

Serena nodded. Mrs. Ritenour grabbed her arm as she went through the curtain.

I was glad Serena was upset. She needed to feel for her patients. Without compassion, the work is just mechanical and the nurse, a machine.

✦ ✦ ✦ ✦

"I'm going to the Shepheard's," I told Tim as we were walking through the tunnel to the parking garage. I'd changed back into my street clothes—a green sweater and blue jeans—from the bloodstained scrubs and lab coat that had been clean when I'd put them on more than four hours ago. "I can take Hope's purse to them so they don't have to come in."

I had stayed and worked the rest of the shift, taking over Laura's patients. Laura had been admitted to the psych unit after an evaluation in the emergency room.

Tim had finished the lengthy reporting required after a death, especially an unexpected one. I'd finally convinced someone from housekeeping to come up and clean the room.

"It's on my way home," I went on. "Her father hung up on me and so I think I should make some personal contact. After that risk management seminar we had last week. . ."

"Yeah, personal attention." Tim's voice had a tired sneer. "Fewer lawsuits." Dark hair fell over his wearied eyes. "I think I've given about all the personal attention I can right now."

I patted his shoulder. Tim was a good nurse, but everyone has a limit. With the recent budget cuts our staff had been reduced and double shifts were becoming more common, exhausting even the best nurses. Rumor had it the new chief nurse had been hired to trim expenses even more.

"One more thing gone wrong," Tim said.

I nodded.

The repair budget had been eliminated a year ago, and lately equipment breakdowns were becoming more frequent. And more dangerous. Just last week an X-ray tech was moving an overhead machine when a pin came loose and the machine fell, smashing the exam table below. Luckily, no one was on it.

We stepped onto the garage elevator and it jerked upward.

"By the way, who pronounced her?" I asked Tim.

"Jake Lord."

"He admitted her, too, didn't he?"

"Yes, that's why I called him."

The elevator doors swung open on the fourth level. I stepped out and took a moment to remember where I'd parked my car.

Tim was holding the door open and looking out at the rain falling steadily outside.

"Isn't this your level?" I asked him.

The elevator buzzed, signaling the doors had been open too long.

"I was just thinking," he said stepping out.

"What?"

"Pads. There weren't any pads in her trash."

"Hope's?"

"Yeah."

"Um. Should have been, with her bleeding."

We keep track of vaginal bleeding by checking perineal pads, known as sanitary napkins to the public. The number used, the amount of discharge on the pad and its color, odor and consistency tell much about the patient's condition—whether bleeding is fresh from an open wound or old just sloughing off the last of a bleed. We can tell how much the woman is bleeding or if infection is developing. Examining and counting disposed of pads are important assessments for nursing care.

"Maybe they'd already picked up her trash," I said. "Do you remember?"

He shook his head. "I didn't see them." Like most of us, Tim seldom noticed the housekeeping staff, except when they didn't do their job, which was more frequent now with the staff reductions. "But that's probably it," Tim said as we walked toward our cars.

17

"Tim, if housekeeping was in the room to collect the trash, they would have noticed—"

"—the blood," Tim finished.

"So, Hope was alive when they were there. When did you find her?"

"About 11:15."

"You called the code then?"

He nodded.

"And when did Lord pronounce her?"

"You can check, but I think it was 11:35. There wasn't much hope from the start."

"And Laura's last note on the chart was at 10:15."

"That narrows it down."

"To an hour."

"Plenty of time to bleed to death."

✦ ✦ ✦ ✦

The Shepheards lived in South St. Louis, where I'd lived all my life. Known as Dutchtown, the area had been the site of the original German settlement built near the turn of the century. Narrow streets were lined with look-alike brick houses or two-family flats, all with wide front porches. Large trees—their leaves just beginning to bud—marched down well-kept lawns of still-brown zoysia grass edged by straight, even sidewalks. The area was changing, though. Urban blight was creeping south. The neighborhood was looking shabbier than I remembered it.

Unlike most Southsiders, the Shepheards weren't Catholic. Mr. Shepheard had brought their preacher, a Reverend Eden, with them when they'd come to see

Hope the evening before. I had walked in to see Mr. Shepheard and the preacher on each side of Hope's bed, like two jailers holding her captive. I'd moved to the head of her bed quickly and asked how she was. She'd given me a little smile and said she was fine. Reverend Eden and her father had stared at me and, with no other reason to stay and many other patients needing attention, I'd turned to go. As I went through the curtain I'd heard Reverend Eden beg Hope to "repent of her sins" and "admit her guilt to God." I'd glanced back to see Mr. Shepheard nodded self-importantly. Hope had cried.

It was difficult to find the house numbers in the rain. Delor Street was the address on Hope's admission form where she'd listed her mother as her next of kin although she'd said she was married. I found a parking spot behind a large, black pickup truck. An empty gun rack was mounted behind the cab and an NRA bumper sticker pasted at an angle on the back window.

I had just rung the doorbell for the second time when the front door swung open.

"And this is the last time!" came a shout from inside as a man in a black leather jacket pushed out the door, bumping into me. I watched his retreating back as he bounded down the steps on worn-at-the-heels cowboy boots with playing cards stamped on the back. He was the ace of spades on the right and the queen of hearts on the left. A winning hand. He folded his long-legged frame into a fire-engine red Mazda Miata, its body glistening with raindrops.

Mr. Shepheard stood in the doorway. "What do you want?" he said, keeping the scowl in place.

Tires squealed as the Miata pulled away from the curb.

"Who is it, Earl?" a high, girlish voice asked.

"I just wanted to see that Mrs. Shepheard is okay," I said as rain continued to splatter my face and run down my neck. "And to answer any questions you might have," I added lamely.

"Just the nurse," he called over his shoulder.

"Tell her to come in."

He stepped back silently. The house was old—seventy years at least—with dark, well-kept woodwork and stucco-covered walls. My sneakers squished as water dripped off my raincoat and onto the already damp throw rug inside the front door. A tall dictionary stand held a large family Bible, its gold-edged pages incongruously regal against the stand's rough wood. My rain-soaked face looked back at me from a large oval mirror above the Bible. A double-barreled rifle—its wood glistening—was propped in the corner.

"Come in, come in," Mrs. Shepheard said, rising awkwardly from a sofa in the neat, if sparsely furnished, living room. A throw pillow retained the imprint of her head. One large chair, faded brown plaid, worn through in places and sagging in the seat, was planted firmly in front of a large television set. A fishing show was on, but the sound was turned down. A gun rack on the wall held an assortment of rifles and shotguns, mostly old; one had a bayonet attached to its barrel.

"Earl, get a towel and a kitchen chair." She waved her arms around as she talked, her head bobbing right and left. Her skinny arms looked like sticks emerging from a peach-colored silk blouse, and crisply pressed tan slacks hung loosely on her slender frame, the sharp edges of her pelvic bones protruded from her narrow hips. She motioned me into the room, fluttering pink-tipped bony fingers, and then sat down on the edge of the sofa, perching there like a bird ready to fly away.

"No, no, I can't stay. I just wanted to be sure you're all right. Here are your daughter's things." I had put Hope's large, black bag in a brown paper grocery sack along with the sweatshirt she'd been wearing when she was admitted. Her blood-soaked jeans had been cut off in the ER and thrown out. I put the rain-dampened sack on the floor.

"I don't know what happened. One minute I was talking to you and the next I was on the floor. I'm so embarrassed." She lowered her head but peeked out from behind eyelash-whispering bangs. Highlighted, blond hair framed her young-looking face with carefully applied makeup.

"Mrs. Shepheard—"

"Faith."

"Pardon me?"

"Faith. Please call me Faith." She peered at me intently through small, stylish wire-framed glasses. One temple of her eyeglasses was taped together with a piece of old-fashioned, heavy, white adhesive tape, the kind my Aunt Octavia used to bandage my cuts and scrapes with, the kind that tore the hair off my arm when she pulled it off even though she was an expert and did it quickly. A corner of the tape had come loose and flapped each time Mrs. Shepheard's head bobbed.

"I just wanted to say how sorry I am about your daughter."

Mrs. Shepheard turned toward the mantle above the imitation fireplace. Two portraits of the dead girl

21

looked down on us with innocent smiles. An end table held more pictures of Hope, younger, poised to waltz onto the stage in ballet shoes and a tutu and another of her smiling into the sun from a perch on a picnic table.

Mr. Shepheard came in with an old-fashioned chrome-framed kitchen chair, its seat covered with cracked red vinyl.

"Sit, sit." Mrs. Shepheard directed me, her hands fluttering in the air.

The plastic seat crackled as I sat down.

Mr. Shepheard stood back, leaning against the archway between the living and dining rooms. He was a large man dressed in faded gray-blue work pants and a plaid flannel shirt with its sleeves rolled up above the elbows. The shirt pulled open at the buttons where his belly hung over his belt and a dingy white T-shirt peeked out. Dark stubble shadowed his face in the half-light. He was watching the TV fisherman push a wiggling worm onto a hook.

A phone rang in another room and Mrs. Shepheard jumped up. A diamond-studded tennis bracelet slid off her bony wrist and clanked onto the floor.

"Sit down," Mr. Shepheard ordered. "I'll get it."

Mrs. Shepheard was down on the floor. "I can't reach," she said, her voice rising in near panic. Her arm waved uselessly in the air in front of the sofa. "It slid too far back," she wailed.

Mr. Shepheard yelled, "Shut up. I can't hear," from the kitchen.

A sob rose in her throat as she sat back on her heels.

"Here I'll help you," I said, taking her arm to help her stand. I slid the sofa out from the wall and retrieved the bracelet. She fondled it as she slid it over her wrist, keeping her hand wrapped around it as she carefully resumed her seat.

"We don't know what happened," I began on awkwardly. "She just started hemorrhaging and we lost her."

"You didn't give her any blood, did you?" Mrs. Shepheard asked. "Our religion doesn't allow it. Unless it's from a relative." She reached up as if to give the sign of the cross but she just fastened the tape around her glasses as her husband returned.

"*Blood* relative," Mr. Shepheard added, squinting at me.

"It's God's will," Mrs. Shepheard said, her voice matter of fact.

"Umph! God's will, my eye!" her husband said, his words spilling out fast. "It's the damn hospital." He leaned toward me. His breath smelled like coffee. "You got that n_ _ _ _ r nurse there," he said, referring to Jessie. "I'll bet . . . I'll bet she screwed up and killed my baby." He shot a clenched fist in my direction. "And by God you'll pay," he spit out, his face red with fury.

The racial slur stung like I'd been slapped. "We did everything possible for your daughter, Mr. Shepheard," I said through clenched teeth.

"She sinned," Mrs. Shepheard stated, her voice flat.

Did they know about the abortion?

"How could God want your daughter dead? And why?" I asked.

"It was her punishment." She nodded, her head loosening the tape on her glasses.

"But surely God didn't want her to die."

"Who was it?" Mrs. Shepheard asked her husband, sliding the bracelet up and down on her arm.

"Your sister. I said you'd call as soon as she left." He jerked his head toward me.

"Pretty high price if you ask me," I said getting up. I knew I was on the verge of saying something inappropriate. "I'd better go," I told Mrs. Shepheard. "I just wanted to see that you were okay and to tell you that we are all sorry you lost your daughter." I wasn't about to say "sorry she died" or anything that might be construed to mean the hospital was negligent, although I doubted we could defend Laura's actions if they decided to sue.

At the door I turned and asked about Hope's husband, wondering if they had been separated since she'd given her maiden name to admitting. He'd have the say on whether an autopsy would be performed or not.

Mrs. Shepheard answered. "They're trying to find him. He's an Army ranger, training somewhere." She glanced at her reflection in the mirror, needlessly giving her hair a pat. "They better find him soon. We've got a funeral to plan." Mrs. Shepheard said it as if she were arranging a neighborhood association meeting and the mayor was going to be late.

The rain had stopped but clouds still threatened in the west. I stood for a moment on the top step wishing somehow I'd done better with the Shepheards and hoping I hadn't made things worse.

A black car slowed in front of the house, parked behind mine, and a tall, Lincoln-like man with a full black beard matching his thick hair got out. He was dressed in a black suit complete with vest and black string tie. The only thing missing was the stovepipe hat. He walked toward the house with the lanky looseness that tall slender men have, covering the distance to the steps quickly. A well-used Bible was tucked under his arm. He paused when he saw me, and then stopped at the bottom of the steps, looking up at me.

"Hello," I said in my most professional voice. He gave me a slow smile, holding onto my eyes. I wanted to escape but he stood in the middle of the sidewalk, blocking my way. I nodded and turned sideways to edge past him. He brushed my arm as I went by, leaning toward me to do it. I ran down the walk to my car, glancing back at Reverend Eden standing on the steps as I pulled away from the curb. He was smiling.

I floored it.

Chapter 3
Sunday, 18 March, 0935 Hours

Part of the St. Louis Sunday newspaper is delivered on Saturday afternoon. Ads, mostly, with the comics and travel section, too. But the news arrives on Sunday morning.

"St. Teresa's Doctor Does Abortions" announced the headline on the front page above the fold. Dr. Jake Lord, it was reported, performed abortions at a downtown free clinic, receiving no compensation, the article went on. Anti-abortion protesters who regularly picketed the clinic were now picketing his home. Taunts had greeted his daughter, Elisa, as she left for school on Friday, reducing the first-grader to tears. A picture of the stricken girl, clinging to her mother's arm, made the story real. The article said that when Dr. Lord and his family had moved into the South St. Louis neighborhood a month ago, they'd been the first black family on the block, and someone had dumped garbage in their front yard a few days later. But no other incident had occurred until Friday. The signs carried by the protesters, however, made it perfectly clear: Dr.

Lord's efforts to provide abortion services to pregnant women were the target of this latest harassment.

At least they hadn't heard about Hope's death. That would stir up every protester, including the nuts that hang around the fringe of all such movements. Anyway, the death certificate would not say "complications of abortion," it would most likely say death was the result of hemorrhage.

I sighed and tossed the paper on the floor where Catastrophe, my white angora, promptly pounced on it. I grabbed her up and snuggled my face in her familiar fur. She struggled to break loose and return to stalking the paper. I left her to it as I got ready to go to my cousin Hannah's. I'd promised to bring donuts—the twins' favorites—before we went shopping.

✦ ✦ ✦ ✦

"I don't know where I stand on abortion," I told Hannah after the kids had scooped up several donuts and disappeared into the family room.

Hannah was standing by the counter watching as coffee dripped into the pot. She didn't say anything. Then she pulled two mugs out of the cabinet, filled them with hazelnut-scented coffee, put mine in front of me and sat down. She was using the mug I had given her last Mother's Day that proclaimed, SISTERS ARE FRIENDS FOR LIFE.

"I don't know how you can say that, Monika. It's killing. You know that." She nodded her head emphatically.

"What about the mother? What if she was raped?"

27

Hannah shivered. "The Southside Rapist?" she asked, referring to the man, now behind bars, who'd raped a couple dozen women on St. Louis' Southside.

"Yes. Or if it's incest. Or if the woman is just unfit to be a mother. Too young, too old, too many kids."

"Or just doesn't want a child? Is that a legitimate reason?" Hannah stirred her coffee rapidly, releasing its aroma. "Where do you draw the line, Monika, when you start saying under what circumstances it's okay? And, regardless, it's still killing a baby, one who's not to blame for what happened." She leaned forward. Her flushed face was sprinkled with perspiration and her breath was coming in rapid spurts. "You don't know what it's like to have a baby, Monika."

"Ouch."

"Sorry. I just mean you've never been pregnant. Even women who think they don't want a child get used to the idea when they find out they're pregnant, and then want it more than ever."

"Not all of them. Or we wouldn't have child abuse, neglect, dysfunctional adults. Believe me, I've seen some strange people in my years at the hospital. Parents who hate their kids, even grown ones. Kids who hate their parents and can't wait to get them out of the way. We have to keep them from pulling the plug on dear old mama. Just the opposite of those who want to hold on when there's no hope." I shook my head as images of patients from the past floated through my mind.

"It's life and death, Monika. And it's not ours to take. No exceptions." She put her spoon down with a clatter. Droplets of cream-colored coffee splattered on the red-and-white checked tablecloth.

"I just don't know, Hannah. I just can't give up the idea that a woman has the right to decide what happens to her own body. Especially if she couldn't control what happened—like with rape or incest. Bad enough she's been violated. Now she's forced to carry the result of it. Forever."

"I could certainly sympathize with that situation. It'd be awful. But it'd be worse to kill a baby," she said with a shake of her head. "Nothing's worse than that."

"Worse than what?" Roger, Hannah's husband, asked as he came into the kitchen.

"We're talking about abortion," Hannah told him. "That doctor in the paper today. He works with Monika at the hospital."

"What's the argument, Monika? I thought you were a good Catholic. You know what's right." Roger reached for a chocolate-covered, custard-filled donut.

"Even good Catholics disagree about this." I took a breath. "Yesterday we lost a young woman from one."

Hannah's head snapped up. "She died from an abortion?"

"Well, we don't know that for sure. That's what she told me when she was admitted Friday night. She didn't want her parents to know."

"An unmarried teenager," Hannah said with certainty.

"No, married and twenty-three."

"Then what was the problem?"

"I don't know. Apparently she was staying with her parents because her husband had some Army duty. A ranger."

"Oh, one of those tough guys. Goes out in the woods and eats snakes," Roger added, taking another bite of donut.

"Why'd she die?" Hannah asked.

I shrugged. "We don't know. She was going home that morning. She wanted to leave Friday afternoon right after we got her stabilized, but I talked her out of it, telling her we had to make sure the hemorrhaging had stopped for good. Apparently it started again, and she just bled to death."

Hannah paled.

"Oh, I'm sorry, hon. I guess I'm just so used to it, I forget you aren't."

She shivered. "You see, Monika, if she hadn't had an abortion, it wouldn't have happened."

"What's an abortion?" ten-year-old Tina asked, grabbing a donut as she came into the kitchen. As usual, Gena trailed behind, letting her sister do the talking.

"It's where you kill a baby while it's still inside the mother," her older brother, Rick, named for my late husband, told her, taking a donut and following her out the door.

"Ugh," she said, as they went out the door. "Why would anyone do that?"

I didn't hear his answer.

"Listen, Hannah, this is confidential. I could lose my job if it got out that I talked about a patient even if I didn't use her name. It could hurt the hospital."

"They didn't do the abortion, did they?" Roger asked. "Not at St. T's?"

"No, but that doctor who does them works there," Hannah answered.

"I could be in a whole load of shit, guys."

"So would the hospital," Roger mused.

"Maybe our death knell."

They both looked at me.

"St. Teresa's is in serious financial trouble. There's not enough money for repairs, and the nursing staff has been cut—"

"Nurses? Who's taking care of the patients?" Hannah asked.

"We do the best we can. Just hit and run."

"Hit and run?"

"Hit and run nursing. That's what we call it now. Go for the sickest. Do just enough to keep them alive. And now this. Please don't tell anyone, guys," I begged.

Hannah looked at me kindly. "You know we wouldn't do anything to hurt you, Monika. No matter what we thought."

"I'm not saying I disagree with you on this, Hannah, just that I wonder about the woman. Who gets to decide what happens to her body?" I made circles on the tablecloth with my spoon. "I know you don't agree with everything the Church teaches—birth control, for example. Might the Church be wrong about this?"

She shook her head emphatically. "Birth control *prevents* pregnancy; it doesn't kill a baby!"

"It isn't a baby, Hannah, not at first."

"It's a spirit, Monika." She patted her chest just over her heart. "That's there at conception."

31

"I don't know. . . ."

"Well, let's agree to disagree." I started to interrupt, but Hannah went on. "Okay, we won't disagree, but we won't talk about it either."

I sighed. "Agreed, cousin. Friend."

"Sister?" said Hannah, recalling our childhood names for each other.

We clinked our coffee cups together in a mock toast. Roger smiled at us.

✦ ✦ ✦ ✦

The rain, which had been turning itself off and on all day, had stopped by the time I got home. Cat wanted to play but I wanted to walk before the rain began again. I donned sweats and sneakers and slipped out the front door while she was still chasing a toy mouse around the kitchen floor.

In my neighborhood—known as Holly Hills— modest, well-kept homes and two- and four-family flats stretch several blocks around Carondolet Park. The park itself is bordered by huge, two and three-story houses that sell upwards of a quarter of a million dollars and help keep neighborhood property values high. For years Holly Hills was home to the city's politicians, all Democrats, who controlled the area's racial "purity" by zoning. Such obvious discrimination is now illegal, but the neighborhood has stayed more white than not, and residents still send their kids to St. Stephen's school.

Skirting puddles on the sidewalk I reached the park and was soon lost in my own rhythm. And thoughts.

Where did Hope go for the abortion? Could she have had it done at the clinic where Jake Lord works? If so, did he do it? If he did, why didn't he say he knew her when he'd admitted her? Was the hospital culpable? And all of us? Would Hope have lived if Laura had found her sooner? Could she have stopped the hemorrhage? Too many questions. No answers.

I looked ahead and saw a boy—he looked about fourteen—on a bicycle coming toward me on the sidewalk. I wondered why he wasn't riding in the street as most bikers did to avoid the jolting cracks in the sidewalk. As he passed me, I felt hard pressure on my left breast.

"Hey!" I yelled as the bicycle sped away behind me. I reached up and touched my breast. It was tingling from the crush of his hand. Over my shoulder I could see the boy standing up and peddling hard, wheels spinning as he lengthened the distance between us. I gritted my teeth and seethed inside. How dare he touch me!

I thought about what he looked like. Cropped blond hair cut straight all around. Skinny, like his bones had grown too fast for his body, stretching it tight. He was wearing a St. Louis Rams sweatshirt, and well-washed jeans. His high-top basketball shoes were partly laced, loose laces flying behind him. Maybe he'd get the laces caught in the wheel, I thought angrily.

When I got home I gathered Cat in my arms and nuzzled my face in her comforting fur, receiving contented purrs in return. Suddenly I started shivering. I dropped Cat on the floor, ran into the bathroom and turned the hot water on as high as it would go. I stripped off my clothes, climbed in the tub and stood under the shower for a long time waiting for the dirty feeling to go away. When the water turned cold I climbed out and shivered as I rubbed hard with the towel. I was scrubbing my breast with unnecessary vigor when I realized I knew—just a bit—how it felt to be violated, to have my body invaded without my permission. What if I'd been raped? This boy had only touched me. It could have been much worse. Somehow, though, I didn't feel any better.

Chapter 4
Monday, 19 March, 0550 Hours

The phone rang early.

"I just wanted you to know," Hannah began and then stopped.

Cat was sitting by her empty food dish, staring at it expectantly. I tucked the phone under my chin and reached for the Purina Cat Chow in the pantry.

"Is something wrong?" I asked, pouring food into Cat's dish.

"Yes, but it's not any of us." She took a breath. "I'm going down to St. Teresa's this morning to join the protest. I just didn't want you to be surprised when you got to work and saw me."

"Why? What are you protesting?"

"Your doctor. The one who does abortions. We want the hospital to know who they have working there. In a *Catholic* hospital." I could picture the determined set of her mouth.

I sighed. "Okay, Hannah, you do what you think is right."

"I just wanted you to know." She hung up.

I thought we had decided to end the discussion about abortion but now I felt as if I was taking a position in favor of it, in Hannah's eyes anyway. Shaking off her lingering words, I poured another cup of coffee. Two pieces of wheat toast had turned cold. I tossed them in the wastebasket and dropped two more pieces of bread in the toaster and went outside to get the newspaper.

It had been raining steadily throughout the night and a still-gentle rain fell. Back inside I hesitated before opening the paper, fearing more news about protests against Jake Lord. Maybe the rain would keep the demonstrators away from his house today.

Seeing nothing about Jake or his clinic, I turned to the obituaries. Hope's funeral was scheduled for Thursday. She was survived by her husband, Sergeant Jack Pierce of Savannah, Georgia, her parents and a sister, Mrs. Raymond (Bud) Burke of St. Louis. The Shepheards hadn't mentioned a sister.

I decided to go to the funeral, my usual practice when a patient died, a lesson my Aunt Octavia, also a nurse, taught me long ago. It's reassuring to the families, she says, that the nurse who watched over their loved one cared enough to come. Even the Shepheards might appreciate it. And be less likely to sue, I thought, somewhat selfishly.

✦ ✦ ✦ ✦

Ruby was holding court when I arrived at the hospital. An obese black woman who worked as our ward clerk, Ruby had been at the hospital for so many years that she knew everyone in the invisible subculture of people who support the work of all big institutions: janitors, cooks, maintenance people, clerks. People in that network hear things because the higher ups—doctors, nurses, administrators—don't notice they're around, and they talk about anything and everything, confidentiality notwithstanding, in front of them. Just the month before I'd learned quite a bit about my new boss, Judyth Lancelot, in advance of the official announcement. Judyth had been the chief nurse of a major university hospital in Chicago before she'd been fired, according to Ruby.

The staff were grouped around Ruby at the nurse's station.

"An' then I say, 'you better behave yourself, Dr. Jake, we don't want no protesters here.' An' he say, 'Ruby, I gotta do what's right. And helpin' poor womens what's right.' I just told him 'don't expect me to fight off those nuts for you.' Then he smiled and said I should just keep bein' my usual cheerful self."

That got a laugh. Cheerful was not what anyone would call Ruby. "Monika," Ruby called out seeing me. "You have any trouble gettin' through them people at the door?"

I had seen the protesters from a distance, but I had no desire to watch my favorite cousin demonstrating in front of my own hospital.

"No more than usual, Ruby. I fought off all those paying customers with a big stick. Just like every morning."

Several people chuckled as they moved away from the nurses' station. Our census had been steadily declining as managed care contracts sent more and more people home earlier and kept many out of the hospital completely. In order to compete, St. Teresa's had had to reduce costs. The supply budget had been reduced by half, but the nursing budget had suffered the most. Nursing service was the largest portion of the salary budget, and it was easier to fire nurses than try to reduce fixed expenses such as electricity. Even though ICU beds were rarely empty, I'd still lost two RNs and one assistant. As if to add insult to injury, a recent memo had made it clear that the now busier-than-ever employees were to consider each patient and visitor as our guest. Customer-friendly service was our motto.

"You been filling their ears with wild tales again, Ruby?" I asked sitting down at the desk and skimming the day's roster. Three new admits pushed our census to eleven, and one nurse on vacation reduced the staff to five. We'd be busy. Too busy to give proper nursing care.

"They not wild tales," Ruby said, pushing her chin out. Folds of skin wobbled underneath it. "I always tell the truth." She rolled her chair away from the desk with considerable force and pushed her heavy body out of the chair with effort. "I've told you plenty, you know."

"You have, Ruby, and I appreciate it," I admitted. "But you also gossip. Too much."

"What's too much? It livens up their day." She chuckled as she turned to walk away.

"And yours," I added, determined to get in the last word.

Jake Lord came through the swinging doors, his long strides covering the distance to the desk quickly. I had worked with Jake Lord only a short time. He'd arrived after serving as a medical missionary in Africa with his nurse wife and small daughter. Unlike many physicians who ignored what nurses knew by experience and twenty-four-hour-a-day observation, Jake really listened to what nurses had to say.

"How're you holding up?" I asked him as he plopped into a chair and grabbed a chart from the rack as he sat down. He opened the chart, flipping through the pages to the lab reports.

Jake's black face seemed darker than usual. "You mean because I'm being harassed?" He slammed the chart back into the rack.

"Big time." I nodded sympathetically.

"Thanks," he said, as if my concern wouldn't help much.

"And your little girl. No child should be subjected to that kind of treatment."

He sighed. "It's certainly made me reconsider what I'm doing."

"Really? Well, I can't say I blame you. But where would those women go if you did?"

"That's just what Althea said. She said we'd been through worse at home and in Africa, and we survived."

Jake and his wife, who worked part-time in our emergency room, had met at church when they were in college in Georgia and had married soon after. They weren't strangers to harassment. Their church had been burned several years ago, one of the targets in the rash of racially motivated arsons that had swept the South. They'd delayed their trip to Africa to help rebuild the church.

"How's Althea doing?"

"As well as can be expected. He glanced at his watch. "I meet with administration and the board chair at ten. We'd better make rounds before then."

39

Twice Dead

After we'd checked each patient, reviewed their latest tests results, and he'd written new orders for the day, Jake left for his appointment with administration, and I moved to number twelve, the last room in the corner, the room Hope had died in. Mr. Zalensky had gone to X-ray, but I wanted to see if Serena had cleaned up in his absence. I pulled open the curtain.

Hope stood before me. Alive. Pale.

Chapter 5
Monday, 19 March, 1005 Hours

"Hope?"

"Uh, we're twins. I'm Charity," said the young woman dressed in snug-fitting jeans and a green Army jacket that was too large for her. Long blond hair streamed out over her shoulders. A large, soft-sided, black leather bag that looked like the bag that I'd taken to the Shepheards' on Saturday dangled at her side.

"You look just like her."

She nodded, unshed tears glistening in her clear blue eyes that looked so much like her sister's.

"You gave me a start."

"I'm sorry." She looked around the room as if she couldn't remember where she was. I'd seen the same look on the faces of families who couldn't yet believe their loved one had died.

"What are you doing here?" I asked gently.

"I just wanted to look for something."

"What?"

"My cross. I mean, my sister's cross. She always wore it. It's mine now." She bit her lip.

"The room's been cleaned since then. I took everything to your parents."

"It wasn't with her stuff. I checked already. It must still be here. It was special. I gave it to her when we turned thirteen." She swallowed hard.

"It was in here," she said opening the drawer in the bedside table. She rifled through the few personal items Mr. Zalensky had in there—razor, shaving cream, deodorant. Then she opened the drawer further and moved her hand to the very back of it.

"Someone else has this room now. You'd better let me look for it."

"I just thought I'd . . . here it is," she said, displaying an intricate gold cross-studded with tiny diamonds and swinging from a gold chain. She snapped the clasp expertly around her neck and put her hand on the cross, holding onto it as her chin dropped down on her chest.

"Are you all right?" I moved closer, thinking she might be about to faint.

She looked up, the tears still glistening in her eyes, and nodded as she walked out, her hand still clutching the small cross on her chest.

✦ ✦ ✦ ✦

"I'm glad you could make it tonight, BJ," I told my best friend as she slid into the seat across from me at Ruggerio's, our favorite restaurant on "the Hill" in the Italian section of South St. Louis.

BJ had changed from her police uniform into loose-fitting leggings and the oversized sweatshirt I'd given her for her fortieth birthday emblazoned with NURSES CALL THE SHOTS across the front.

That BJ had ever became a police officer was something of a fluke. She'd applied for the academy using her first name, Brandon, and her middle initial, J (for Julia). Brandon was her mother's maiden name. BJ was one of the token women accepted at that time, and the only one in her class who made it to graduation, even with hassles that she still won't tell me about.

"You look wiped," she said, dropping a black leather bomber jacket on the spare chair. She tucked a loose strand of blond hair under the French braid on the back of her head.

I shook my head. "You'll never believe this."

"Try me."

Our waiter arrived and deposited water and coffee. We both ordered spaghetti and meatballs. Ruggerio's special.

"This girl—woman—died on Saturday. She had an abortion," I said, stirring cream and sugar into my coffee.

"She had an abortion at St. T's?"

"No, BJ, not there." I took a gulp of coffee and burned my tongue. After a cold drink of water I went on. "I don't know where. She started bleeding afterwards and came to us."

"So why'd she die?"

"We don't know exactly. She just started hemorrhaging again."

"Didn't anyone notice?"

"We were short-staffed that day. I knew it and should have gone in but I'd promised the twins I'd take them to the parade so. . . ." I bit my lip.

"What makes you think you could have done anything, Monika? She might have died even if you'd been there."

"I know that. In my head at least." I sipped my coffee carefully. "She shouldn't even have been in ICU."

"Why not? Not sick enough?" BJ asked. "She died. Isn't that sick enough for ICU?"

"Not the day before. I tried to transfer her to a med-surg floor but when I called, the head nurse said she only had three nurses and 28 patients. She told me I'd just have to keep her overnight. We expected to discharge her the next morning."

"Didn't they try to save her?"

"Of course, but it was too late."

"Tough."

"That's not all." I took a tentative sip of coffee. "Laura—she was the nurse taking care of her—just walked out."

"Why?"

"That's just it, BJ. Even if you freak out, the first thing you think of is what to do to save the patient. Later you can fall apart. But not in an emergency. It's something trained into us from the beginning." I shook my head. "It just doesn't make sense."

BJ pulled off a piece of Italian bread and watched the butter melt into it.

"She ran out and hid. In the toilet! She ran into the restroom and climbed onto a toilet. Jessie found her there later."

"What'll happen to her?"

"She's in the psych ward now. She'll probably get fired, maybe lose her license."

"Will she be all right?"

"I don't know. I'm going to go up and see her. One of my old staff nurses works there evenings."

The waiter returned with our food, and I busied myself with trying to roll spaghetti on the fork with a spoon, something I'd never mastered. I gave up and cut my spaghetti into bite-sized portions.

"So what do you think about abortion, BJ?" I asked.

BJ was expertly turning strands of spaghetti around her fork. She took a bite and chewed. "I don't know, Monika," she said finally. "Never gave it much thought. Not for myself. I can't imagine having one but of course I've never been pregnant, sure've never been raped. I do know these guys don't have any right to kill or maim people who believe abortion is okay."

She stopped while the waiter refilled our water glasses.

"Hey, we caught that woman," BJ said. "The one tried to steal a baby."

"You did?"

"Yep. Her husband brought her in. Said she needed help."

"Good. Maybe she'll stay away from St. T's."

"I know how she got in."

"Yeah? We've been wondering about that."

"The lock on the nursery door was broken. She just walked right in."

"They can't afford to fix anything."

"Seems pretty dangerous to me. In a hospital."

"It is, but all they say is 'It's not in the budget.'"

45

"We hear that, too," BJ said. "The city's budget's in bad shape. They're threatening to make us pay for repairs on our patrol cars."

"How absurd! They can't do that?"

"I think it's an empty threat, but it sure makes us careful driving around."

"Do you think there's anything the police can do about the abortionist?"

BJ shook her head. "I doubt it. You probably don't know who did it, do you?" she asked, scooping another fork of spaghetti in her mouth.

"She just told me she'd had one, that's all."

She swallowed. "Not married?"

I shook my head. "Her husband's in the Army and off training somewhere. They need to find him before they can do the post or release the body."

"Sounds like it would have been a surprise for him when he came home."

"Umm." I took a piece of bread and mopped up spaghetti sauce.

"What's that 'umm?'"

"I just wonder how much of a surprise," I said.

"Uh uh. You mean maybe it wasn't his."

"Maybe."

"That could explain the abortion."

"That caused her death," I finished.

Chapter 6
Tuesday, 20 March, 0106 Hours

"Did I wake you?" BJ asked after I finally figured out the ringing in my ear was the phone.

"No," I mumbled.

"Sorry, but I wanted you to know what happened at St. T's tonight."

"What?" I reached up and turned on the light.

"A woman was assaulted in the parking garage."

"Assaulted? How? What happened?" I squinted at the clock. A little after one.

"She was grabbed, pulled behind a car and raped."

"Raped?"

"It was rape. Vaginal tearing, bruises, abrasions. She fought like hell."

"You know who did it?"

"Nope. It was dark. I doubt we'll ever know unless he tries it again, and we get lucky."

Cat jumped up on the bed and burrowed under the quilt.

"I gotta go," BJ said. "I'm way into overtime, and I'm beat."

"Wait."

"Yeah?"

"How is she?"

"She'll live, the doctor said."

"Where'd you take her?"

"Memorial. She didn't want to go to your ER."

After we hung up, I sat up for a long time, stroking Cat.

Chapter 7
Tuesday, 20 March, 0735 Hours

Max Gunther stopped by my office just as I was checking the ever-increasing number of e-mail messages we were all getting since the hospital had been networked. Max was the hospital's chief of pathology and an old friend.

"Did you hear about last night?" I asked him.

He nodded. "I'm not surprised. The neighborhood isn't what it used to be." Max had come to St. T's when South St. Louis was a growing community.

"But it's not that bad. And with security around, I thought we were safe."

"Their budget's been cut, too, Monika. Jerry's been complaining about that."

I had heard our security chief in the cafeteria a few days earlier telling an administrator that he couldn't guarantee safety unless he had more help.

"We're all in the same situation, Monika. Managed care's killing us." He laid a file on my desk. "I thought you'd want to see this," he said, looking at me intently, his blue eyes magnified by coke-bottle glasses. "Post on Pierce," he said.

I moved a stack of files off the chair in my cramped office and motioned for him to sit down.

"Can't. Trying to get my slides ready for the pathologists' meeting. Starts tomorrow in Chicago and I'm first up."

"So they found the husband."

"Yeah, he okayed it."

The file had Hope's name on the tab. Shepheard had been crossed out and Pierce scribbled above it. I flipped it open. "Cause of death: Hemorrhage." I looked up. "That's what we thought."

"Read on."

"Secondary to lacerated uterine artery," I read. "Uterine artery? How did that happen?"

"Something sharp went in through the vagina. It missed the cervix, went through the cul-de-sac and severed the uterine artery, which bled into the tissue of the calix. At least that's what I think happened. The pelvis was full of blood."

I remembered the pooled blood coloring Hope's lower back.

"There was a hole this big . . ." he held up his fist, ". . . in the cul-de-sac."

I felt the blood drain from my face.

"How'd it happen?" he asked me, "Do you know?"

"I thought a doctor did it. Now I'm not so sure."

"A doctor? No licensed physician would do anything like that."

"Abortion's not illegal."

"Abortion? This girl didn't have an abortion."

"Yes she did. That's why she was admitted. Came in bleeding."

He shook his head emphatically. "This young lady was not pregnant. That's one thing I'm absolutely sure about. She wasn't pregnant, had never been pregnant, would never get pregnant."

"What?"

"Her tubes were blocked. It would have taken surgery—and maybe not even then—for her to get pregnant."

"Are you sure?"

"No doubt."

I thought out loud. "So for some reason she thought she was pregnant, went for an abortion and some unscrupulous doctor—or someone—cut on her and told her she'd had one. If we hadn't been so short-staffed. . . ."

"It wouldn't have made any difference. She would have already been in shock before anyone could do anything for her."

"What do you mean?"

"I mean she would have bled internally and been in shock before it started to leak out."

"So Laura wasn't to blame."

"Laura? Is she the one they're saying cracked up?"

I snorted. "Now there's a medical term—cracked up. The poor girl's only been out of school a few months," I said, more defensively than I intended.

"Okay, okay, Monika. Don't get so hot about it." He picked up Hope's file. "I've got to go. I just wanted you to see this before I sent it down to administration. I'm sure someone will follow up."

He left before I thought to ask him what he meant.

✦ ✦ ✦ ✦

Ruby, of course, knew all about the rape and couldn't wait to tell me. She slowed down when I told her I already knew about it. But not for long.

"Bet you don't know this," she said, a sly smile on her face.

I picked up the day's roster. "Yeah, what?" I asked, studying the list of new patients. A young trauma patient would need close monitoring.

"About the camera."

I looked up. "What camera?"

"The one in the garage. Where the woman was raped."

"Shhh, Ruby," I whispered, nodding toward a woman waiting to go into our newest patient's room. "What about it?"

"It were broke."

"I'm not surprised." I scanned the schedule for the week, praying no one would call in sick.

Ruby's voice stopped me. "On purpose."

"What?"

She nodded knowingly. "Somebody broke it on purpose."

"No. Who would do that?"

She shrugged her heavy shoulders.

"Maybe the rapist," I said more to myself.

"Nope," Ruby said. "It were done before. I heared about it las' week."

"Why didn't you tell anyone? You might have saved that woman."

"An' what would they done? Run right out and fix it? And, anyways, they knew it were broke."

She was probably right.

✦ ✦ ✦ ✦

It was after three when I finally was able to get to my computer. We had two staff off and a new admit made a full unit of twelve patients so I'd filled in doing patient care until the evening shift arrived. After clearing off the paper mail stacked on top of my keyboard, I turned on the computer, punched in the main menu and scrolled to the "dead" file, in which records of deceased and discharged patients are kept.

"Shepheard, Hope," appeared on the screen. I accessed her medication record and scrolled down the short list. "Ambien, 10 milligrams, 2300 hours, 16 March." Eleven o'clock Friday night.

"Umm," I said out loud.

"What's that?"

I jumped.

Tim was standing in the open doorway, his hands resting on the ends of the stethoscope draped around his neck. "What are you working on?" He leaned over to read the screen. He smelled faintly of antiseptic soap.

"Just checking Hope's meds."

Tim pulled the stethoscope over his head and jammed it in his lab coat pocket. Wisps of dark hair stood up where he'd caught them in the flexible tubing of the stethoscope. "How could she have slept through a bleed like that?" I said, as an explanation of why I was checking her medications.

I pulled down the chart menu and scrolled to the nurse's notes. Tim read the screen with me. Laura had charted that Hope complained of not being able to sleep, first at eleven when Serena gave her some Ambien. Hope still couldn't sleep an hour later, so Laura had given Amytal, a narcotic and more potent sleep medication that Jake Lord, Hope's admitting physician, had ordered if needed.

High heels came clicking determinedly toward my door.

"What's going on here?" our new boss demanded.

Tim looked up, surprised.

"Tim, this is Judy, our new chief nurse.

"It's Judyth, with a y.

"Judyth with a y meet Tim with an i." I knew the minute the words were out that I'd gone too far. A dark flush crept up her pale smooth face. Not a good way to start with a new boss.

I smiled, trying for sincerity. "Judyth."

Her face settled into a neutral expression.

She nodded absently at Tim and went on. "Now, what's going on here?" she asked me.

Tim waved goodbye as he escaped back onto the unit.

"Pardon me? About what?"

"You know what," she said impatiently. "Abandoning a patient. What's wrong with your nurses?" she asked in a clipped Chicago accent.

Mine?

"What kind of a unit are you running here?" she asked, looking around as if she could see through the wall into the unit.

"Not enough help is what. Sick people, overworked staff. I'll probably lose more after this." I stood up. Judyth was a full foot taller than I. "Can't you do anything?"

She sighed and swung one long leg over the corner of my desk as she sat down on the edge. "Look," she said, looking me in the eye. "I'm—we're—under pressure here. This hospital's going under if we don't cut costs. We can't compete with the big health care systems."

"We can't take care of the ones we've got. Every bed full. Right now I've got twelve patients and four nurses. What kind of ratio is that for ICU? How can we keep them all alive, much less help them get well?" I shook my head. "Disasters are bound to happen."

"Monika, if your nurse had been paying attention, none of this would have happened." She clamped plum-colored lips together. "We're going to get hit with a violation, I just know it." She stood, putting both hands on her hips. "That nurse will never work here again. And I'll see her license jerked, too!"

The phone rang. I told X-ray to hold on. I cupped my hand over the receiver. "You need anything else?"

"We're going to get hurt on this one. Patients can't be abandoned." She turned on her patent leather heel and clicked down the hall to the elevator.

"Guests," I said to her retreating back. "They're our guests," I mumbled, returning to the phone.

✦ ✦ ✦ ✦

Serena was coming out of Mrs. Redwine's room with a wheelchair when I caught up with her. "See me when you're finished."

Anxiety flashed briefly across her face. "What's wrong?"

"Just a question."

She plopped down in the chair in my office a few minutes later. Today her lipstick was almost black, her short hair bleached white, and a row of earrings marched up one ear. She fidgeted with one that dangled to her shoulder.

"How're you doing?" I asked her.

"Okay, I guess."

"I was checking Hope Shepheard's, uh, Pierce's record. "You gave her sleep meds…"

"I can give it. Laura told me to."

"Calm down, Serena. It's not scheduled."

Scheduled drugs are those controlled by the DEA, the federal government's Drug Enforcement Agency. Opoids, mostly, known as narcotics to the public. Scheduled drugs must be administered by registered nurses licensed by the state. As a student, Serena could give a scheduled narcotic if her instructor supervised her. But she was working as a nursing assistant the night before Hope's death and no instructor was there. Laura, however, might allow her to give the Ambien, which was a mild sedative and not DEA scheduled. According to the chart, Serena had administered the Ambien, and Laura had later given Hope the Amytal.

"You gave Hope Ambien at eleven, correct?"

"Uh huh."

"Laura gave her Amytal for sleep later. I guess the Ambien didn't do it."

"Uh, yeah, I guess."

"You didn't give the Amytal, did you?"

"Why would I do that?" she said, looking up.

"You shouldn't. It's a narcotic."

"I can't then."

"No, you can't. So Laura gave it."

"I s'pose. Is that what's in the chart?"

"Yes, but I wondered if you remember anything else about that night?"

"Nope. Just that they had to stab her several times."

"Stab her?"

"For blood."

"Oh. To hit a vein, you mean." To type and cross-match in case she needed a transfusion. "But wasn't that done in the ER?"

"I don't know. I just know they came up here to draw blood."

"When was that?"

She shrugged. "Sometime later. It should be on the chart." She glanced toward my desk. "I've got people waiting," she said, pulling a piece of Juicy Fruit gum out of the side pocket of her scrubs.

I waved a dismissal as she scooted out the door, tossing the gum wrapper toward my wastebasket. It missed.

Ruby called me out to the desk to talk to the Redwine family about their mother, but Jake Lord arrived and I turned them over to him to explain brain death. I doubted her daughter was ready to make the difficult decision to disconnect the ventilator. I hoped

Jake would help them understand the futility of further treatment and allow her mother's life to take its natural course.

I went into the med room behind the nurses' station where medications and solutions are kept on shelves and in a refrigerator. Drugs and IV solutions are mixed there and every narcotic is meticulously recorded in ink in a black-covered binder with the patient's name, the name of the drug, the dose, the route and time administered, and the nurse's signature. No erasures are allowed. Any errors, spills or breakage must be recorded and co-signed by another nurse. If a drug isn't needed after it's been checked out, that's also noted. At the beginning and end of each shift, the supply is counted by two nurses—the one going off and the one arriving. The drugs themselves are kept locked in a cabinet with one nurse—usually the one in charge that shift—carrying the keys to the cabinet. These procedures usually, but not always, prevent drugs from being stolen. At least they make it more difficult. We'd heard we were going to change to a computerized record system but with the current budget crunch I doubted it'd be soon.

The record of Hope's dose of Amytal matched her patient record. I started to close the book until another entry caught my attention. A second dose of Amytal was recorded after Hope's but Tim had marked it "wasted." He'd omitted a co-signer but I supposed he'd been too busy then, and later Laura hadn't been in any shape to co-sign.

"They want you," Ruby yelled into the med room.

"Don't yell, Ruby," I told her coming out. I looked up to see a tearful daughter being consoled by her husband. Jake Lord was walking out through the swinging doors. He looked upset too.

"Let's go sit down," I said, leading them down the hall to the family waiting room. The mother had spent her last weeks with us, lingering long after a stroke had rendered her comatose. The daughter had sat at her bedside every day, stroking her mother's hand and helping sometimes with her care. We'd encouraged her to talk to her mother and she had especially liked combing her hair every day after we'd bathed her. Now I let the daughter talk about her mother. She'd just decided that tomorrow the ventilator would be turned off and, if Mrs. Redwine didn't breathe on her own, nothing more would be done.

I was relieved. So often the family refuses to give up hope even in the face of a flat EEG and the doctor refuses to write a "Do Not Resuscitate" order. Sometimes, if a patient had said repeatedly that she didn't want to be resuscitated but the family disagreed, we might be a little slow in responding to the code. We had all seen too many people kept alive on a ventilator for endless weeks while their money was eaten up and their family tried to grieve but couldn't, really, until it was over.

✦ ✦ ✦ ✦

I had stayed late to finish up the paperwork on my desk when Tim stopped at my door.

"I've been thinking," he said, leaning against the doorframe.

"Yeah?"

"About what's been happening. Stuff breaking, people getting hurt."

I rubbed my forefinger and thumb together. "Money," I said. "Or lack of it."

"That Judyth. She's a pretty cold fish, isn't she?" he asked, shifting his weight.

"They hired her to cut costs; that's what Ruby says." I stared at my broken printer stashed in the corner. "You know the security camera in the garage? The one where the woman was raped?"

Tim nodded.

"Ruby told me someone disabled it on purpose."

He snorted. "That's Ruby, exaggerating again. What she doesn't know, she makes up."

"You don't think that's what happened?"

"Oh, I think it was broken, that's no surprise, but I doubt anyone did it on purpose."

He hooked his jacket on his thumb and slung it over his shoulder. "Aren't you going home?"

"Just about done," I said looking at a still-full in-box.

"It'll still be there tomorrow."

"Oh, no, by tomorrow it will have multiplied. These things copulate at night and their progeny are born in the early hours of the morning. By the time I get here, this stack will be up to here." I held my hand as far above my desk as I could.

"Multiplying faster than viruses in the lab," he said, laughing.

"The lab," I said. "That reminds me."

"Of what?"

"They drew a blood on Hope after the night shift started."

"Yeah, the vampires were up here." He nodded. "Serena was waiting outside for them to finish. She had a medicine cup in her hand."

"Really? She told me she gave the Ambien before they drew the blood."

"I don't know; it was a crazy night, I don't remember exactly. What does the chart say?"

"Just that a blood was drawn, but there's no report on it."

"Maybe they didn't run it after she died."

"But that wasn't till the next morning."

"Yeah, well I doubt they got around to it before then."

"So what if she'd needed a transfusion that night? They always run these labs first. No matter how busy they are."

Tim shrugged. "It doesn't matter now, does it, Monika? She's gone, and we've got plenty more to take her place."

"They must have run one after her blood was drawn in the ER."

"I didn't check, but why order a blood to type and cross-match if she'd stopped bleeding?"

"Beats me. Screw-up, I suppose. Someone ordered it without checking. That's why we're losing money. Just order stuff but don't think about cost." He looked at me. "What? Something else?"

"Tim," I began, "Max was in with the autopsy report this morning."

"Yeah, what'd he say? Hemorrhage secondary to abortion, I'll bet."

"Not exactly."

"Oh?"

"Hemorrhage, yes, but no abortion."

"What? Then what was it?"

"Trauma to the uterine artery."

"Sounds like a botched abortion to me."

"It would have been if she'd been pregnant."

He looked puzzled. "What do you mean? Why else would someone have an abortion? Is he sure?"

I nodded. "He's sure. Her tubes were blocked. Tim, she wasn't able to get pregnant!"

He shook his head slowly. "What do you think happened? She thought she was pregnant and had one?"

"I guess. It seems unbelievable but it's the only explanation."

"And then the guy botched it."

"Speaking of . . . mistakes."

"Yeah?"

"That morning you signed out a dose of Amytal without a co-signer."

Tim seemed to bristle. "Look, Monika, you weren't here. We were busy, and I figured Laura had wasted it. I didn't want the counts to be off when I finally got to leave so I signed it out and planned to get Laura to co-sign later." He shook his head. "Of course she was up in psych by then."

We'd all done it, I thought, watching Tim walk away. We'd just tell the next shift we'd been too busy. They always understood.

Chapter 8
Wednesday, 21 March, 0615 Hours

ABORTION KILLS ST. LOUIS WOMAN screamed
the headline in the morning paper I was reading with
breakfast before I left for work.

A young woman had died following an abortion
at St. Teresa's Hospital, the paper said, the same
hospital where a rape had occurred in the parking garage
late Sunday night. Dr. Lord's work at a local family
planning clinic was mentioned, leaving the reader to
wonder whether Jake Lord had done the abortion at the
clinic or if he or someone else had done it at St.
Teresa's. The Archbishop was quoted as saying he
planned a full investigation, as did the city prosecutor's
office. I wondered somewhat guiltily if Hannah or
Roger had called the paper. Blessedly, Hope's name
had been left out of the story.

✦ ✦ ✦ ✦

The protesters were out marching in full force in front of
the hospital in spite of the rain. Orange police tape

made a corridor down the sidewalk to keep demonstrators and their opponents apart. Placards with pictures of tiny fetuses waved to and fro while toddlers in covered strollers were walked back and forth. The protesters moved along peacefully inside the tape, and police and hospital security officers patrolled outside the roped-off area. Another line of hospital security people stood back by the doors and I recognized a couple of officers in plain clothes leaning nonchalantly against the wall calmly smoking, violating hospital policy.

A policewoman stopped traffic in front of the hospital to let a group of students go by. Hannah held a placard reading "Stop the killing." The rain mixed with the drops of painted blood on the poster and dripped onto the hood of her green windbreaker. She looked straight ahead. A heavy-set man in a yellow rain slicker was kneeling on the sidewalk, eyes closed, hands clasped in front of him, lips moving silently.

"Baby killers" screamed a protester—a fortyish woman with blond hair, perfect in spite of the rain—at a young nursing student who was heading for the entrance between the two lines of demonstrators. The student looked alarmed but a security guard guided the girl through the automatic doors as they swished opened.

The kneeling man stood and turned toward the waiting cars. It was Earl Shepheard.

A cop motioned me on and as I started up I glimpsed Jerry Wagner, our security chief, in the glass behind the door. It looked like he was smiling.

I swung into the parking garage, made my way to the top level and took the elevator to the basement tunnel that connected the garage to the hospital. I met only other employees, grateful to have escaped harassment.

My relief was short lived.

✦ ✦ ✦ ✦

The next set of elevator doors slid open on the fourth floor where I came face to face with a tall woman in a bright red suit. Her coal black hair swung loosely across her shoulders and she wore professionally applied makeup. Behind her stood a tall, muscular man with a large video camera clamped on his shoulder. The camera was pointed straight at me, its red light steadier than I was.

"Nurse, nurse." The reporter pushed a large, fuzzy-covered microphone in my face. "What can you tell us about Hope Shepheard's death? You're the . . . patient care manager," she added, squinting at my name badge. She moved closer. "Do you know the cause of Ms. Shepheard's death?"

I tried to brush past her. The microphone followed me.

"Pierce. Her name was Pierce."

"Huh?"

"Shepheard was her maiden name. And you have to see public relations. They handle all this." I waved my arm toward the camera.

"But you were here. You know more than they do," she added, lowering her voice and leaning toward me as if I were her co-conspirator.

Mrs. Redwine's daughter emerged from ICU, her husband holding her arm. She was dabbing her downcast eyes.

I pushed the reporter aside to join the couple. "Your mother?" I said as I slipped my arm around the daughter's shoulders. Even when everyone has agreed it is time, the family is rarely ready when the vent is actually turned off. I'd hoped to be there before it happened. Elevator doors slid open discharging passengers, and I helped the young couple on. I turned to see the camera locked onto the grieving couple and then swing over to the reporter.

"We just watched a nurse comfort a family leaving the intensive care unit where a young woman died on Saturday, allegedly as a result of an abortion." She paused. "Or was she left to bleed to death, unattended? This reporter has just learned that St. Teresa's Hospital, where a rape occurred in the parking garage Sunday night, is seriously understaffed. A visitor in the ICU, who refused to be interviewed on camera for fear of reprisal on a family member, reported that patients are often left alone for long periods of time, patients who are critically ill. Is that what happened to the patient of the grieving family we just saw leaving? Or to the young woman who died here a few days ago?" She stopped, letting the words sink in. "This is Kerry Madigan coming to you from St. Teresa's Hospital in South St. Louis."

"You can't say that! You're invading these people's privacy!"

"It's the news, honey. The public has a right to know."

"The right to see people in their grief?" Spit spurted out of my mouth. "Is that the public's right?"

Several visitors and arriving staff had stopped and some were gawking open-mouthed at us.

"Whatever." She turned, handed the microphone to her video-toting partner, picked up a large shoulder bag, and punched the elevator button. The cameraman was packing their gear into a large black leather bag as I reached for it.

"Whoa, young lady. This is private property." He zipped up the bag with force and swung it expertly onto his shoulder.

"So are these people's lives!"

The elevator doors opened.

"What's going on here?" Judyth Lancelot asked, stepping off and looking from the reporter to me and back again.

The reporter gave Judyth a quick glance and followed her cameraman onto the elevator. The doors slid shut.

"You want to tell me what's happening?" Judyth said, her foot tapping impatiently.

I nodded toward the hall. "My office."

She started talking before I'd closed the door. "What are *you* doing talking to reporters? We have PR to do that. What did you say to them?"

"Look, she grabbed me when I got off the elevator. Stuck that microphone in my face. But I didn't say anything!"

"I, uh, we can't take much more of this bad press." She slumped against my desk.

I cleared off a chair and she sank into it.

"I'm just worried," she said, chewing the lipstick off a corner of her lower lip. "It's easy to say too much, more than they ask. . . ." She ran her tongue over her teeth, leaving a speck of lipstick behind.

"I didn't say anything, Judyth, I didn't, really."

"Just be sure you don't. Don't talk to anyone."

"Did you come up here to see me for something?" I asked.

She looked blank for a minute. "Yes. About your budget."

"What about it?"

She drew herself up. "There's going to be another cut."

"What? How can we? We can't take care of what we've got now!"

"I know, but there's nothing I can do. Administration's ordered it."

I thought *she* was administration.

"We're being squeezed by the managed care companies, and we've got to cut another five percent."

"From the year?"

"No, just the last quarter. But next year's has to be ten percent." She looked at me steadily. "On top of the five."

"Oh, my God. We might as well shut down now. Or kill them all off."

"Monika!"

"Look, Judyth, it's either don't admit them or don't care for them. Which is it?"

She shook her head and stood up. "I'm sorry. I wish I could do something." She turned at the door. "And, Monika."

I looked up.

"I need it by the end of the month or. . . ." She hesitated, then went on. "I'll have to do it myself."

I sat for a long time after she left. The year's budget ended on June 30th, and we could meet that cut if Laura didn't come back to work. But another ten percent for next year would mean losing another position, and there was no way I could run the unit safely with so few nurses. I'd have to talk to the staff for their recommendations, but now wasn't the time to do that, what with everything that was going on. And when would I find the time?

✦ ✦ ✦ ✦

"What you been doin?" Ruby asked when I came back through the door.

"The boss," I told her with a sigh.

"I told you 'bout her." She grinned. "But not everything."

"Yeah," I said, my mind on the budget.

"Same thing happen in Chi-cago." She leaned back against the desk, balancing her hip on the edge.

"What do you mean?"

She nodded knowingly. "People dying. Lots of them."

"Oh, for Godsakes, Ruby, it's a hospital."

"But they was dying for no reason."

"Ruby, I'm sure there was a reason. Now where are those sheets from accounting?" I asked, searching through files stacked haphazardly on the desktop.

"They fired her for it."

"For what?"

"All I knows is, too many people died and she got fired." She heaved herself off from the desk and squeezed out from behind the counter. "You figure it out, Miss Smarty Pants," she said as a parting shot.

✦ ✦ ✦ ✦

He was standing at attention in the hall by my unopened office door when I stepped off the elevator after lunch, and I knew he was a police officer even before he showed me his badge. Short brown hair, slightly worn navy-blue blazer, shirt collar too tight, subdued navy-and-red striped tie. And a Sergeant Friday expression.

"Detective Harding," he said, flipping open an ID that I didn't have time to read. "Martin Harding," he added, as I motioned him into my office.

I faced him from my chair, glad the seat was cranked up high to accommodate my short stature.

He placed a small notebook on his knee and carefully twisted an automatic pencil open. "What can you tell me about your patient who died here Saturday? Were you here?"

"No, but I came in when they called me."

"Why is that?" He looked up.

"I'm the nurse, uh, patient care manager. I'm in charge of the unit."

"Who was here?"

"What business is it of yours? Patients die here all the time and the police aren't involved."

"Just routine. Can you tell me who was on duty then?"

I told him. Tim, Laura and Serena had all worked double shifts; Jessie had come in at seven.

"What can you tell me about her? The patient who died?"

I went over what I knew about Hope's admission and her care the day before her death. I didn't tell him about her bedside confession to her father and Reverend Eden.

"What was the cause of death?" he asked without looking up.

"Hemorrhage. Same thing that brought her in."

"Why is that? Is she a hemophiliac?"

"No, females only carry the gene. But sometimes the blood volume drops too fast, especially if an artery's involved."

"Wouldn't that have killed her right away?"

"Depends on the injury."

"What was her injury?"

"I don't know exactly," I told him, which was more or less the truth. After Judyth's warning, I thought it best just to say what I knew for sure.

"What would cause someone to bleed to death?"

"She told me she had an abortion." I wondered if he had a copy of the autopsy report. It didn't say she'd had an abortion, only that there was trauma to the uterine artery, which could have been caused by an abortion whether she'd needed one or not.

He frowned. "When was that?"

"Right before she started bleeding the first time, I assume."

"Could she have done this to herself?"

"Done what?"

"The abortion."

He waited while I thought about that. It would take courage, not to mention strength, to puncture the uterine artery. "No," I said finally. "I don't think so." But I wasn't so sure.

"I suppose the room's been cleaned." He nodded toward the unit.

"Cleaned, used, and re-cleaned."

"What about sheets, towels, anything we could get samples from?"

I shook my head. "Laundered."

"How about personal items?"

"I took her stuff to her parents."

"Did you do a drug screen?" he asked.

"No. She didn't die from drugs."

A younger man came to the door. "My partner," Detective Harding explained.

"Anything on the crime scene?" The partner was a younger, slimmer version of Harding.

"Cleaned already," Harding told him, standing.

"Thank you very much, Ms. Everhardt," Harding said. "If you think of anything else, would you call me?" He handed me his card, nodded politely and joined his partner.

I pulled up Hope's chart again. The record showed a blood had been drawn in the ER, and her hemoglobin was 10.2. Not quite low enough to transfuse, but the ER physician had ordered the specimen typed and cross-matched for a possible transfusion if needed later. So why had they come back for another blood? What was wrong with the first one?

✦ ✦ ✦ ✦

It wasn't until after lunch that I had a chance to go down to the lab. Mickey was on duty and let me in with a broad smile that fit her ample frame.

"What brings you down here? Lost?"

The sounds of automated equipment whirred in the background as huge machines separated blood, mostly, but also other body fluids into minute components and examined them for abnormalities. What once had taken a lab technician at a microscope hours or days to complete was now accomplished quickly by machines controlled by sophisticated computer systems. Human error only affected the results if the specimens were contaminated or if the computer was programmed incorrectly. And fewer technicians were needed. Mickey was glad to have her job, she'd told me. She was one of the few college-prepared, licensed lab techs left. Most of the work was done by assistants with only a few weeks of training.

"Can you get to a record on a patient who died?"

"How long ago?" A small frown creased her wide face.

"Last Saturday, but she came in the day before."

She squinted. "Probably. Depends on what you want to know."

"They drew bloods twice. I want to know why."

"I can tell you that without checking. Well, the usual reasons, anyway." She clapped me on the back. "Screw-up. That's what. They don't get enough the first time. They drop it. Yeah, they do," she said in response to my unspoken question. "That's why we're back in there, sticking the poor guy again. Or they forget to label it."

"Sounds like a lot of mistakes."

"Honey, all they teach 'em now is where to stick. Some of them don't even wear gloves." She shook her head. "I try and try to tell them. You'd think AIDS would scare them into it but, no. And hepatitis, too."

"Can you find out about this patient's specimen? What happened to it?"

"Why do you want to know? Isn't she dead?"

"I'm trying to find out everything that happened that night and the next morning until she died. Mickey, I'm worried. It happened on my unit. With my nurses. And with the budget cuts. . . ."

"It's okay, Monika. These things happen. Patients die. It's a hospital," she added philosophically.

"Can you find out why the second blood was drawn? And what it said?"

She sighed. "Monika, do you know how many bloods come through here in a week?"

"I'd guess hundreds," I admitted.

"Many hundreds."

"I know, Mickey, it's a lot to ask but it's important. I want to know what happened to that girl. One minute she was fine, the next, she bled to death."

"But—"

"Mickey, we're all on the line when something like this happens. It hurts all of us."

"Look, Monika, my job's hanging now."

"What? You're their best tech!"

She smiled. "Thanks for the vote, hon, but yours doesn't count. Money does. And I'm expensive." She dropped the smile. "And, expendable."

"No, you're not, Mickey, they need you!"

She heaved her large shoulders in an it-won't-matter gesture. "What the heh, give me his name." She pulled a ball point pen and a small yellow pad of Post-it notes out of her lab coat pocket.

"Her. Pierce, Hope."

"As in stab?"

"Huh?"

"Pierce. Just a little lab tech humor."

I smiled, barely. "Yes, P-I-E-R-C-E. First name Hope. When can I get it?"

"Yesterday?" she asked with a laugh.

"Yeah, yesterday." I smiled.

"As soon as I can," she added with a shake of her head. "I'll call you."

✦ ✦ ✦ ✦

Ruby was complaining to a group gathered around the nurses' station when I got back to the unit. "He asked me where I was an' I told him, it ain't none a' his damn business what I do on my day off!" She shook her head, her tight black bun of hair bobbing in agreement.

Serena glanced in my direction and moved off. Several others followed her.

Tim came out of a patient's room. "You the one who told the paper, Ruby?" he asked, reaching for a chart on the counter top. "About our . . . patient," he added, looking around cautiously.

"'A course not," Ruby said, pulling her sweater across her chest.

Tim looked at me as if to say, "Try to believe that," and then flipped through to pages of the chart to the lab report. "Mr. Zalensky's improving. Cardiac enzymes almost back to normal," he said to me. He closed the chart and shoved it into the rack.

"I ain't told no one who'd tell," Ruby said. "They can keep a secret good as me."

Tim snorted and walked away.

Ruby put her hands on her hips, fingers spread wide. "Where you been? The po-lice been here hasslin' us. Can't get nothing done." She looked around for an audience, but they had disappeared. She shrugged. "Well, they been bugged, too."

I sat in a chair and sighed. "I know, Ruby, I know. I've talked to them. Just answer their questions. Whatever you know. You weren't here when she died. That's all you have to say. You don't have to get mad about it. They're just doing their job."

She squinted at me. "Monika, you ain't never been black. If you was, you'd know their job is bad for *us*." She sat down heavily.

I couldn't think of anything to say to that.

✦ ✦ ✦ ✦

Mickey called a few hours later. "I don't have her. No record of a Pierce, P-I-E. Could it have been P-E-A?"

"Uh, no, it's Shepheard. H-E-A-R-D."

"What, she changed her name?" Mickey laughed. "After she died?"

"No, she was admitted under her maiden name. Pierce is her married name, but I guess it wasn't changed on the computer."

"The abortion case, right?"

"Not really, but, yes, that's the patient."

"Okay, I'll look it up."

"I'll be right down."

✦ ✦ ✦ ✦

"I couldn't find out much," Mickey told me when I came through the door to the lab.

"You don't know why they drew two bloods?"

"Sit down, Monika," she said, pointing to a high stool opposite her workbench. "Want some coffee?"

"What I want is some answers," I said.

"Okay, okay. Yes, they collected two bloods. It was just what I thought. They did the counts on the specimen drawn in the ER, but they didn't get enough to type and cross-match so they drew another one after she got up to the unit."

"Why didn't we get a report?"

"Whoa there, Monika, let me finish."

I clamped my mouth shut with effort.

"It was Friday night, remember? Two people called in 'sick'—party night. So it got left till morning."

"Mickey, this is terrible. That woman needed a transfusion, and nobody was here to let us know!"

She shook her head. "That's what I've been telling you, Monika. It's not safe around here anymore. People are getting hurt."

"Well, this one sure did. She's dead! Maybe if she'd had the blood. . . ." I slid off the stool. "What about drugs?" I asked, turning back at the door.

"What about them?"

"Did you do a screen?"

"I don't know. Why?"

"The cop asked me."

"The police are here?" She looked around.

"No, Mickey, but they were. It's hot, politically. An abortion death at a Catholic hospital."

She nodded.

"They'll probably ask you if a drug screen was done."

"Even so, we send them out."

"You don't do them here?"

"Not any more. Too many drugs, and the testing's too sophisticated for us. We'd need more equipment."

I looked around the room. Every inch of wall space was filled with the giant machines. One of them started beeping.

"Just a sec," Mickey said heading toward it. She moved lightly on her feet in spite of her weight. She punched a large red button on one of the machines and moved over to the computer, keying in some new commands. She returned to the machine and pushed the red button again. "It's just in a bad mood today," she explained with a laugh. "Now where were we?"

"You send drug screens out."

"Oh, yeah. They pick them up Monday morning and bring back the results the next Monday."

"Can you see if one for Pierce, uh, Shepheard, went out?"

"I probably shouldn't, Monika, but, what the heh." She headed toward a desk with a tall stack of interlocking plastic baskets crammed with files, mail and papers. She pulled a large envelope out of the top basket. "Confidential" was printed in big black letters on the front. She pulled a list out and scanned it, keeping the names hidden from me.

"Yep. Shepheard. Went out last Monday. Should be back next Monday." She slipped the list back in the envelope and closed the clasp securely. She held it to her chest, folding her arms around it. "That what you need?"

"What about the second blood? Did you run it?"

"I doubt it. And why would I? I don't need any more work."

"Come on, Mickey, just check it out, will you? It can't hurt."

"Yeah? Well, she's still dead."

✦ ✦ ✦ ✦

Down the hall from the lab was what was euphemistically called Environmental Services. We still called it housekeeping. A stout gray-haired woman dressed in a blue cleaning uniform with "Supervisor" stitched in red on her shirt pocket just above her ample bosom was seated at a metal desk in a cramped office. Clipboards with charts hung from hooks on the wall above the desk and several charts were stacked on top of it. The woman was eating a sandwich and reading a supermarket tabloid. She jumped when I knocked on the doorjamb.

"Sorry," I said. "I just want to ask a question."

"Yeah?" She took another bite of sandwich. Ketchup dripped out and plopped onto the desk top. It looked like drops of congealed blood on the gray surface.

"Your schedule. When did someone empty trash in ICU last Saturday?"

She looked at me with narrowed eyes. "You got a complaint, tell administration." She went back to her paper.

"No, no, no complaint," I said. "No problem. I just wondered what time they were around."

She sighed and reached up to pull a clipboard off the wall, stretching her heavy body over the desk. When

79

she sat down there was a fresh ketchup stain on the front of her uniform. She searched through several pages. "In the morning. Don't know what time." She dropped the clipboard back on the desk.

"Do you know what he got from room twelve?"

"Crap. That's what we always pick up. Body crap, paper crap, plastic crap. Everything's crap. We're the crap shooters." She hooted, shaking her plump bosom up and down.

"So you wouldn't know if the trash can from that room was empty or not," I asked after she stopped laughing.

She shoved her glasses up on her nose with the back of her hand. "Where you from? You think we write down the crap we pick up? Tons a day? You gotta be kidding. They don't pay us enough for that." She cackled again. "Come to think of it, they don't pay us enough period."

"Who picked it up?"

She signed heavily, gave me a long look and, when I met her stare, flipped through the pages of the chart in front of her. "Illias Tobias." She slammed the clipboard back onto its hook on the wall. "That's all I know." She was busy satisfying her enquiring mind as I mumbled a thank you and left.

✦ ✦ ✦ ✦

"You what? You actually made a complete stop?" BJ asked incredulously as her siren wound down. Red lights swirled on top of her patrol car, turning the rain into scarlet streaks of drizzle running down her face.

The sound of crunching metal still rang in my ears. Black Beauty had crumpled as her trunk peeled back like burned skin.

"I was reading a bumper sticker," I told BJ lamely as a second police car skidded to a stop inches from us.

"But no one was coming," she said, puzzled.

St. Louis was world renowned (so we'd always been told) for a large number of stop signs (more than most cities), and for local drivers who rolled through intersections ignoring them. Few people stopped completely.

BJ conferred briefly with her fellow officer, they both wrote in small notebooks and laughed. Several cars had stopped and neighborhood residents had come out for a look.

"What are you doing?" I asked BJ, anger causing my neck to hurt. BJ had told me to stay put, but now I struggled to get out. It seemed like too much effort, though, so I rested my head on the doorframe. The other officer moved off to interview the young man who had hit Beauty and me. A tow truck arrived and jockeyed into place in front of my car while BJ directed traffic around us. BJ came around and helped me out of the car, but I shook off her help. I slid awkwardly into the front seat of her patrol car, and we watched the tow truck pull Black Beauty out into the traffic, her back end smashed and her left back wheel dangling like a broken limb.

I wanted to cry.

"You all right?"

"Yeah." I rubbed my neck.

"Your neck hurt?"

"A little," I admitted.

"I think we better make a stop at the emergency room."

"I'm fine. Just shook up."

She gave me a long look and pulled out into traffic, turning her red lights and siren on. I knew arguing was futile so I closed my eyes and tried to relax. I felt sorry for the young kid who'd hit me.

We arrived at the emergency room entrance in a whirl of flashing lights (BJ had shut the siren off before we turned into the drive), bringing out several staff.

"I'm fine. I'm fine," I assured a nurse I knew slightly and a male tech whose bulging muscles spoke of hours at the gym. He flexed his biceps once and then slid his arms under me and lifted me effortlessly into the wheelchair they'd pulled out behind them.

"I don't need that! I can walk," I told them struggling to get up.

Mr. Muscles pushed me back down and wheeled the chair into the hospital as the doors swished open silently.

A clerk I didn't know asked if I had insurance. I started to answer but instead began to shake.

A woman moaned behind a curtain.

BJ put her arm around my shoulders. "She works here. She's a nurse. In ICU."

The clerk stopped popping her gum and looked over the counter. She shrugged, then glanced at BJ. "What'd you say her name was?"

"Monika Everhardt. She's head nurse up there." BJ spoke above my head to the clerk.

I tried to talk but couldn't seem to stop shaking.

Althea Lord, Jake's wife, came around the corner, exclaimed and said she'd be right back. She returned a moment later with a blanket.

"That should help the shakes," she said, patting my arm through the blanket.

Gritting my teeth to stop them from chattering, I nodded my thanks. Reassuring BJ that they'd take real good care of their prize nurse, she wheeled me expertly into an exam room.

A resident examined me, ordered X-rays and, after they came back negative, declared my injuries only soft tissue damage. He told me I'd feel worse in the morning. He wrote two scripts—an anti-inflammatory and Tylenol with codeine. Althea handed me a discharge sheet on the way out. It said I'd be off work three days.

I complained about my car all the way home. BJ kept saying I was more important than the car. I disagreed, reminding her unnecessarily that it had been my dad's, a comment calculated to gain her sympathy. Unreasonably, we were irritated with each other when BJ pulled up in front of my little house, and she jumped out to come around and help me.

"I don't need any help," I said turning to open the door. Pain stretched from my head down to my midback, pulling muscles into a bunch under my left arm. BJ reached under my arms and nearly lifted me from the car, struggling much more than the male tech had. I shook her off as soon as I could stand and tried to walk steadily to the front door. She pulled my keys out of my purse and opened the door onto Cat's flying leap. She reached for her gun in one swift movement.

"Don't shoot her!" I yelled grabbing Cat off BJ, forgetting the pain.

"That damn cat!" BJ chuckled as she snapped her holster shut. Then I laughed and soon we were giggling as if we were schoolgirls again.

"You're a good friend," I told her when we could catch our breath.

"You'd do it for me," she answered. "You'll be okay now?"

I nodded.

"You can use my jeep till we find out about Black Beauty."

"Thanks. I'll need to get to work tomorrow."

She frowned. "Didn't they say you'd be off awhile?"

I shrugged, causing another spasm to pull my midsection into a vise.

"Tomorrow," I said with conviction. "Early. I'm going to the funeral."

"Whose?"

"The girl who died."

"Okay," she said resignedly.

I nodded, more carefully this time.

"You never did tell me."

"Tell you what?"

"What that bumper sticker said. The one that made you stop dead."

"The devil offers sinful pleasures," I quoted.

"Is that all?"

"But always hides the price tag."

I could hear her guffaws all the way down the walk.

Chapter 9
Thursday, 22 March, 1030 Hours

The parking lot was crowded when I arrived at the Shepheards' church. The rain had stopped, but heavy clouds hung over the city reminding me of the smoky haze in my favorite corner tavern in our old neighborhood. Behind a black hearse stationed near the door stood the NRA-labeled truck explaining that "Guns don't kill people; people kill people." Mourners were greeting each other in hushed tones and lining up to sign the guest book inside.

"They don't know, really," said one woman.

"The Lord knows best," her companion pronounced.

Several others nodded agreement.

It was my turn to sign the book. I squinted at the lines, not the first time I'd had difficulty reading up close. I signed my name and added St. Teresa's Hospital in the address column.

After I was seated I noticed a woman across the aisle who looked familiar. I wondered if she or someone in her family had been a patient.

"Is this seat taken?" Tim asked.

"Saving it for you," I whispered as I slid over, groaning at a spasm in my back.

"I hate coming to these things." He glanced toward the casket that stood open at the front of the room. A large spray of red roses lay across the casket with a banner that read "Beloved daughter" and I wondered why it didn't say "wife and daughter." Flowers surrounded the casket, their sickening sweet smell reminding me of my terror at seeing my first dead body when my great-grandmother died and I was forced to kiss her clay-like cheek.

I shivered.

"Did you go up and see her?"

I shook my head. "I've seen enough dead bodies. Touched them. Cleaned them. Moved them."

"I agree. It seems like such a macabre ritual. Dressing up a body to make it look alive. Why do it?"

"For the people who knew her. To say goodbye."

Somewhere a clock chimed and a door behind us swished shut. There was a rustle at the front. The family was ushered in by a side door and took seats in an alcove at the front. Like everyone else, I strained to see. Mrs. Shepheard had an every-hair-in-place hairdo that spoke of a visit to the beauty shop. She was wearing a dark-blue long-sleeved dress with a white collar edged with crocheted lace that drooped on her overly slender frame. Her glasses were still held together with adhesive tape but it looked fresh today with no telltale ends to flop around as she looked about the room with jerky, bird-like movements. Mr. Shepheard, in an ill-fitting brown suit, held his wife's arm with more grip than seemed necessary. Charity, identical to her twin sleeping in the casket and nearly as pallid, held her mother's other arm. The young man I'd seen leaving the Shepheard's followed them.

Just then the door in back opened and a young man in an Army uniform, black beret in hand, strode to the front of the room, back straight, footsteps purposeful.

For a moment, I was elsewhere. *"How do I look?"* *Rick asked, standing military-straight, in a uniform he wasn't yet used to.* My husband had said that just before he'd shipped out to Vietnam.

The military man stood erect in front of the casket. His uniform hung loose on his large, gaunt frame. Light from a ceiling spotlight glimmered off his closely-shaven head, and the cheekbones in his long face stood out ridgelike underneath his tanned skin. A quiet shudder passed across his broad shoulders as he stared at his wife in the casket. He leaned in closer, and I thought he was going to kiss her. Someone coughed. Jack Pierce looked up as if he'd forgotten where he was, and then made his way to a seat in front with the family. Charity scooted over to make room for him and gave him a small smile. The others ignored him.

The service didn't last as long as I'd expected. Reverend Eden talked mostly about going home to God.

When it was over I followed the line to a room in the back of the church to greet the family. Tim left to return to the hospital. I stood behind the familiar-looking woman who had been sitting across the aisle from me. She was talking to a friend.

"It's what happens," she pronounced. "When God's laws are broken."

Her friend nodded.

"That's why we fight."

The picket line at the hospital! That's where I'd seen her. She'd screamed at the young nursing student.

I bit my lip. I wanted to argue with her, but I wasn't sure what I'd say. That I recognized her convictions but deployed her tactics? Or tell her that Hope hadn't really been pregnant so she hadn't had an abortion, and they could all go home and quit protesting at St. T's? I guess that wouldn't stop them, though, not as long as Jake Lord was there.

She moved away from the Shepheards. It was my turn.

Mrs. Shepheard looked at a spot above my head as she thanked me for coming and turned to the next person in line.

"Mrs. Shepheard—Faith—can I ask you a question? I hate to bother you at a time like this but I really need to know something."

"What is it?" she said with forced politeness, looking at her husband as if she was playing the part of a grieving mother.

"Hope's . . . ah . . . surgery. Do you know where she went?"

"Leave me alone! Quit asking those stupid questions! Get away from me!" The tape on her glasses had come loose, and she grabbed them as they slid down her nose. "Earl," she whined, turning a look of calculated helplessness on her husband.

Mr. Shepheard grabbed her arm, digging into the soft flesh of her muscleless upper arms, but her hands kept fluttering. She was staring at her newly manicured nails, bright with pink polish.

"For Godsakes, Faith, cut it out!" He turned to me. "Haven't you caused enough trouble?" he said loud enough for several people to turn and look. "We don't have anything to say to you." His face was flushed, and his eyes glistened.

I made my way out the crowded room trying to ignore the staring faces that told me people didn't think much of someone who'd upset a grieving family at their daughter's funeral.

Charity, looking wan, was standing in the hall talking to a young couple. The young man who had walked in with the family was gripping her arm. She hesitated, then introduced him to the couple as her husband, Bud. A flush spread up her pale face when he asked them if they were in the market for a new car. I turned away before I heard their answer.

Hope's husband, Jack, was standing by himself, looking lost in spite of his military bearing. I introduced myself and said how sorry I was about his wife. He looked startled, like he didn't know what I was talking about.

"I know what it's like," I said quietly. I looked off somewhere in the past, remembering. "I lost my husband. In Vietnam."

He lowered his head, swallowing unshed tears, then quickly regained his composure. "Thank you," he said softly, moving off awkwardly toward two other military-looking young men who waved him over. He glanced at Charity and her husband as he passed them.

Charity slipped out of her husband's grip and made her way through the crowd to my side.

"How are you doing?" I asked her.

"Okay, I guess." "It's just that. . . ." Her voice slid away softly. "Thank you for coming," she said, her voice sounding rote. "And for taking care of. . . ."

"That's okay. That's what we're there for."

Her eyes were a clear, light blue with a film of tears. She cleared her throat. "Can I talk to you?"

"Sure. What can I do for you?"

She looked around. "Not here."

Her husband was coming in from outside, flipping a cigarette butt into the air as the door swung open. He saw Charity and came toward us.

"Later," she said looking quickly at her husband. "Tonight. Eleven o'clock. At Shakes and Steaks on Chippewa." She walked away without waiting for an answer. She sidestepped around a group, but Bud caught up with her and grabbed her arm, shaking it. I didn't hear what he said, but Charity pushed him away and joined her mother, who was gesturing broadly to an older couple.

Making my way out, I passed Jack and Mr. Shepheard, who were talking intently. Jack's face was contorted with grief or anger, I couldn't tell which.

"But it's their fault!" Mr. Shepheard spit out.

"It won't bring her back," was Jack's reply. He wiped bony fingers across his eyes.

With a glance toward me, Mr. Shepheard said pointedly, "But they should pay."

Jack shook his head. "You can't buy a life. I won't do it." With that he headed out of the room while Mr. Shepheard stood fuming.

I made my way toward the front of the building and the parking lot, passing along a hallway lined with closed doors. One office had a small sign: *Reverend*

Joseph Eden, Pastor.   As I passed in front of the closed door, it opened.

"What can I do for you?" the tall minister asked me.   His tongue slid out of his mouth and across exceptionally full lips.

"Uh, I just came from the service.   For Hope Shepheard, uh, Pierce." I felt like I was back in Catholic grade school getting caught after one of the pranks BJ and I had pulled.

His mouth smiled but his eyes held mine longer than I wanted.   "Sad.   Yes.   You a relative?"   He frowned.   "Didn't I see you at the house?"

"A nurse.   From St. Teresa's." I turned to go.

"Oh." He stretched the word out as if it meant something else.   "Why don't you come in?" He opened the door wider revealing two offices, one behind the other.

His secretary looked up from a desk in the front office.   Blond teased-perfect hair matched her bandbox appearance.   "The burial," she reminded him.   "They're probably about ready."

A brief look of annoyance crossed his face.

"And your wife called," she added pointedly.

He nodded and turned back to me.   "Maybe you'll come by sometime." He reached out one hand as if to touch me on the arm but I guess my look put him off.   He drew back and gave me a knowing smile.   I shivered and pulled my raincoat tighter around me.

I got out of there fast.

Chapter 10
Thursday, 22 March, 1320 Hours

"Just in time," Berta told me. "Your arms are getting shorter, I'll bet." She chuckled.

I smiled ruefully. "I'm too young for this."

"Yep, you're about the right age." She chuckled again. "I get you all eventually."

Berta Gunther, distantly related to our pathologist Max, was the neighborhood optician. Never married, she'd known all of us since birth and could tell you everything that was going on in South St. Louis. And did.

After quizzing me on my family, she went in the back to search for another set of frames she said would be just right for my face.

I'd always enjoyed coming here with Aunt Octavia when she needed glasses or a talk with the good-natured gossip. Berta had remodeled her small house so that the living room was now a showroom complete with mirrored walls and glass shelves displaying a variety of frames. Carefully focused spotlights highlighted the various styles, shapes and colors. Tiffany lamps sat on low tables and the strains of classical music—Mozart now—was piped through hidden speakers.

"These really look good on you," Berta told me sliding lightweight wire frames over my ears and adjusting the stems.

I glanced in the desktop mirror. A stranger peered back. Not bad looking. Short, curly, black hair. Feathery lines around light blue eyes behind black metal frames.

"Are you sure I'll be able to see out of these? They look awfully small."

"That's the latest style. You won't have any trouble. I can fit your prescription in just fine. Even with the bifocals." A certificate on the wall said that Berta was a master optician.

"Um. I do look pretty serious. Maybe people will listen to me more with glasses. They tend to dismiss short people, you know."

She laughed as she removed the frames. "Everyone's always taken you seriously, Monika. Short or not."

"Really? Well, I have to work at it."

She made a few adjustments to the frames, wiped the lenses with a soft cloth and slid them back over my ears. "Speaking of work, that girl that died at St. T's? Shepheard?"

"I think I like these," I said, examining my face from various angles.

She studied my face, tilting her head from side to side. "You know what happened to her? The Shepheard girl?"

"Berta, I can't say anything about that." I took off the frames and handed them to her. "I'll take these."

Berta was making out a sales ticket when she tried again. "That father of hers."

"Mr. Shepheard?"

"Yeah. You notice the missus with broken glasses?"

"Yes."

"Well, she's come in here more than just a few times to order a new pair. Said she ran into a door."

"You think she didn't?"

"That's the third pair of glasses I've replaced because she ran into a door. How many doors do they have in that house?" she asked rhetorically. "I know what I'd do to anyone who hit me." I could imagine. A big woman, Berta had done much of the rehab work on her house herself.

"I need half today and the rest when you pick them up," she said handing me a bill. "In about a week."

I wrote the check, thanked her and left.

So Mr. Shepheard hit his wife. I felt like smacking him. I'd seen my share of women who turned around and went back to the bum after we'd patched them up.

✦ ✦ ✦ ✦

I'd taken the evening shift so I could go to Hope's funeral and see Berta, and we'd been busy from the moment I'd arrived until after dinner when most of the families had gone home. Only Mrs. Ritenour remained, sitting quietly beside her comatose husband.

I shut the door to my office and started on the paperwork on my desk. Paperwork now includes e-mail and voice mail as well as hard copies—real paper—many of them duplicates of messages on voice or e-mail. We were into networking in a big way so anyone with an idea put it on the network for all to see, which amounted to a lot of stuff every day that didn't apply to me. Like that day. I learned that I could sign up for Race for the Cure to raise money for breast cancer, attend a lecture on the enzymatic effects of grapefruit on cholesterol-lowering drugs and anti-hypertensive medications, or volunteer to help the Easter bunny distribute baskets on the pediatric floor next week. And those were just the first three choices of the day.

I answered the most pressing mail, tossed innocuous stuff into the wastebasket, skipped through most of the voice mail picking up only the gist of the message and answering if necessary, and deleted the rest of the e-mail messages unread. If it's really important, they'll write or call again, is my philosophy.

◆ ◆ ◆ ◆

I'd put off visiting Laura as long as I could. The psych unit was my least favorite place in the hospital. Its locked doors—heavy metal with only a small glass panel embedded with wire mesh—made it seem like a prison, which I guess it was to its patients. Hearing the lock snap shut behind me makes me want to run. I couldn't understand how my friend, Peggy, had wanted to transfer there from our unit where the fast-paced action gave you that adrenaline rush we'd all become addicted to.

Peggy was standing behind the nurse's station arguing with a young man dressed in unpressed khakis, a torn Cardinals sweatshirt, and house slippers with broken down backs.

"You've already had all the medicine you can have right now, Bernie. You can have something at bedtime but not now," Peggy explained with the calmness I'd seen her use to console patients and staff alike.

Bernie hung his head and mumbled something I couldn't hear.

"Now you go on in the dayroom and talk to Millie. She's been waiting all day to see you."

Bernie shuffled off, slippers flapping behind him.

"Monika." Peggy came around the counter and gave me a hug. "To what do I owe this pleasure?" She was dressed in comfortable-looking khaki pants and a pale yellow sweater. She had let her dark brown hair grow. It fell in soft waves, just brushing her shoulders.

"Looking good, Peggy. Psych agrees with you."

"I like it," she said, smiling. "And it's not so messy."

"You mean blood and guts and stuff?"

She laughed. "Yeah, but we actually do something. Not just talk to them. I like to clean them up and fix them!"

"You can't fix the whole world, Monika."

"I try."

Her smile faded. "I had to get away, Monika. I can't work like that, not enough help, people too sick. I was too afraid of what might happen."

"I'm afraid it did, Peggy. That's why I'm here.

"To see Laura?"

"Yes, how's she doing?"

Peggy shook her head. "She's not talking."

"Nothing?"

"Not yet. What really happened on Saturday?"

"Laura abandoned a patient, Peggy. A patient who bled to death!"

Peggy sucked in her breath. "She didn't do anything wrong, though, did she?" Peggy asked, worry creasing her smooth forehead. Peggy had befriended Laura when she came to work for us as a new grad a year before. "You don't think she gave the wrong medication? Or too much?"

I shook my head. "She just left."

"There was no indication of trouble before this, was there?"

"She's still making some mistakes, and she's too slow, but she's doing okay, I guess."

"But?"

"I don't know, Peggy, she just irritates me the way she's so hesitant. I want to tell her to just get on with it. Do *something*."

"But she cares."

"Yeah, I suppose."

"That's the problem."

"How?"

"Caring too much. That's when it hurts."

The phone rang. Peggy spent a few minutes reassuring someone that the patient was doing better and would be able to go home the next day. Apparently the family wasn't ready but Peggy explained that the medication had his symptoms under control. She hung up and turned back to me. "Poor Laura."

"Poor Laura? How about poor Hope? She's dead!"

"Well, yes, of course. Monika, you're so tough. You don't realize how traumatic it is for some of us to face death every day. That's one of the reasons I transferred to psych." She looked around. "They may be confused," she whispered, "but they're alive."

I laughed.

Peggy had worked in critical care for several years and was a compassionate, as well as competent, clinical nurse—a rare combination. I missed having her on my staff.

Peggy chuckled. "God, it's good to see you, Monika." She put her arm through mine companionably. "A normal person!"

I laughed and looked around as a disheveled woman who looked middle-aged but was probably younger shuffled by. "Do they ever get well?"

"Some do. Let's go see Laura. I think she's in her room. It might do her some good to see you."

She led the way down the hall past several double rooms plainly furnished with twin beds covered with colorful plaid spreads and watercolor landscape prints hanging on the walls. A couple of men dressed in street clothes were lying on their beds apparently sleeping. We passed a woman in a faded housedress, sneakers, and hose cut off at the ankle. She stared straight ahead, an unlit cigarette dangling from her lips. Peggy nodded to her but the woman ignored us.

"Laura?" Peggy asked as we entered an end room. A twin bed hugged one wall, a blanket stretched tight over its top, outlined with sharp, nurse-made corners.

Laura was sitting in a straight-back chair staring out the window at the fading daylight.

"Monika's here to see you, Laura."

She didn't move from her position, continuing to stare out.

Everything about Laura was pale—her face, her hair, her clothes—so that she seemed part of the background.

"Laura, turn around here," Peggy said more sharply.

"That's okay, Peggy. If she doesn't want to see me. That's okay."

Peggy walked over to Laura and put her hand gently on her shoulder. She spoke more softly. "Laura, Monika's here to see you. She wants to know how you are. Can you turn around and talk to her?"

Laura didn't move.

I felt helpless.

"Is she like that all the time?" I asked Peggy as we walked back down the hall.

"I'm afraid so. We haven't been able to do anything with her. So far."

"What's her diagnosis?"

Peggy hesitated.

"Come on, Peggy. She works for me. I need to know."

"We hope it's transient," she said finally. "First we thought it was just acute anxiety, maybe depression —situational, brought on by trauma. Then, when it didn't dissipate in a day or two. . . ."

"What about meds? Can't you give her something to bring her out of this?"

"Sure. A pill for every ill," she added sardonically.

Peggy was also a recovered addict—recovering, she frequently reminded me. She'd hinted that she'd rather not be around all the drugs that had fed her addiction and were so accessible in ICU. Psych had drugs, of course, antidepressants, lithium, tranquilizers, barbiturates. But few pain killers—Peggy's drugs of choice.

"You saw her. She's catatonic."

"So what's the diagnosis?"

"So far they're saying she has a brief psychotic disorder."

"Psychotic! She's not crazy!"

"Monika," she said with feigned patience. "We don't use the word 'crazy' in here. And brief psychotic disorder is just that—brief. No permanent damage is expected."

"Why does someone get this? I don't remember it from school."

"It's a new category. Well, it was introduced a few years ago. Caused by a traumatic event, usually. Sometimes drug-induced."

"Drugs? Laura?"

Peggy went on. "We don't think so. None of the signs—dilated pupils, shakiness—but we sent out a specimen, just in case."

"What's her prognosis? Will she get better?"

"She should."

"How long?"

Peggy shrugged. "A few days, weeks."

"Weeks?"

"We hope it's less than a month."

"What if it's longer?"

"There are several choices," she said. We had reached her office, and she motioned me inside.

"Choices? You can choose which one you want?"

She pulled a thick book off her shelf, flipped to a page she'd marked with a yellow Post-it note. "Schizophreniform disorder, delusional, psychotic disorder, lots of choices," she said closing the book.

"How long do those last?"

"Hard to tell. Several disorders, like Laura's—brief psychotic disorder—are time-limited diagnoses. If it goes longer than a month, then there are several others, and if more than six months, you can be pretty certain that it's schizophrenia."

"But she seemed to be fine, and she's been with us a year. You didn't notice anything while you were working with her last year, did you?"

Peggy shook her head. "No, and that's why I think it's going to be brief. I don't think, if I had to guess, that she has any underlying pathology."

"You mean schizo?"

She sighed. "Monika, the term is schizophrenia. I just explained that. It's a bonafide diagnosis with treatment indicators. I thought you were more enlightened."

"I'm sorry, Peggy." I paused. "What'll happen to her? Could she end up in an institution? Like State?" I asked, remembering the old psychiatric hospital from nursing school days where I'd learned more about psychiatric patients than I'd wanted to know. "The ones nobody wants."

"We hope not. And, Monika, it's not like that. It's just that there's no other place to put people who are that seriously ill. They can't take care of themselves. The ones who aren't there are out on the street—we call them 'homeless'," she said with emphasis.

I tried to picture neat, precise, clean Laura homeless, wandering the streets, sleeping in doorways, scavenging for food in dumpsters.

Peggy walked me to the door. A large key ring, loaded with assorted keys, dangled from a fabric-covered elastic band attached to Peggy's belt. She pulled a key away from her waist and unlocked the heavy door, but before opening it, she pulled a large red button out of her pocket and handed it to me with a smile. Blue letters— KU—were stamped on it.

"You wear that when you watch the game Saturday. It'll bring us luck," she added with a grin.

I gave her a thumbs-up and the door swung open. "Go Kansas!" she said as the door clicked shut behind me.

Not waiting for the elevator, I bounded up the stairs to the fourth floor.

✦ ✦ ✦ ✦

Max caught me coming through the door. "Let's talk," he said grabbing my elbow and heading me toward my office.

When we were seated with the door closed, he said, "I thought I was seeing double." He had taken off his thick-lensed glasses and his unfocused eyes were staring at something in his mind.

"The dead girl?" I suggested. "They're twins."

He nodded, wiping his glasses on the tail of his lab coat. "She came to see me. Wanted to know how her sister died."

"What'd you tell her?"

He hooked his glasses back behind his ears and studied me with magnified eyes. "Just what I told you. That her sister died from a hemorrhage."

"So, what's the problem?"

He pushed his glasses farther up on his nose. "I guess I should have called the medical examiner right away. I was in a hurry. Had that meeting to get ready for." It sounded like an apology.

"I'm sure you didn't do anything wrong, Max," I said as he stood and turned toward the door.

"I hope not," he said, his face grim.

◆ ◆ ◆ ◆

I left my shift a few minutes early to meet Hope's sister, and I'd just found a table by the window in the back when I saw her drive in and park a cherry-red Miata toward the back several spaces away from other cars.

"I'm sorry I'm late," she began. "It wasn't easy getting away." She glanced around as if expecting someone. She was wearing a gray sweatshirt over jeans, and she'd scrubbed her face free of makeup. With her blond hair pulled back in a ponytail, she looked like a teenage version of herself.

The waitress arrived with paper placemats, silverware rolled in a paper napkin and water. We both ordered coffee.

"Charity, what do you want from me? Why did you ask me to meet you here?" I asked when the waitress had left.

103

She took a sip of water. "Why'd my sister die? What happened to her?"

"Sometimes we just don't know," I said, noncommittal.

"There must have been something wrong, some reason she died."

"She hemorrhaged, Charity. We don't know why."

She shook her head. "That's not it. Something was wrong. She shouldn't have died."

"Look," I began. "We did all we could."

"I just want to know why she died. If it was anything . . . uh, genetic?"

"No, no, I'm sure it wasn't."

She looked skeptical.

"You're worried she had something that you might have, too?"

She dipped her head.

"There's no indication of that. No, I'm sure it was just one of those things that we don't know. You don't have to worry that the same thing will happen to you."

"How do you know that? Do you know why— for sure—she died? Do you?"

I looked away. Did I? Maybe Hope did have some weakness in the uterine wall or some reason her blood wouldn't clot.

"I don't want to do anything about it. I don't think we should sue you or anything." She gave me a little smile. "And my parents don't know I'm here." The smile faded. "And I don't want the money." She grimaced. "It's just. . . . I can't stand not knowing what happened—how she died."

She looked out the window and met my gaze in the reflection. "Please," she said softly, turning back to face me. "Don't you want to know what happened? In *your* hospital?"

I nodded slowly. "Yes, I do."

"Then help me. Try to find out what happened that morning. Monika . . . please."

I took a sip of coffee. I was already trying to find out what had happened. I wanted to prove that the hospital wasn't to blame.

"Help me," she whispered. "Please."

I nodded slowly. "Look, I don't know what I can do but I am trying—"

"Oh, thank you." She looked toward the ceiling and folded her hands as if in grateful prayer.

"Don't thank me yet. I'll just see what I can find out." And I knew if I found out we were to blame, I couldn't tell her.

"That's good enough for me."

She left, leaving her coffee untouched.

As her car peeled out of the parking lot I wondered if Charity knew about her sister's pregnancy. Or the abortion.

✦ ✦ ✦ ✦

"Which suit did they send?" BJ asked me later. BJ had worked the late shift too and was still dressed in her blue uniform complete with gun, handcuffs and nightstick. Her cap sat beside her beer on the bar.

We'd met at Hauptmann's, the corner tavern in our old neighborhood, which was nearly empty at this late hour. The odor of stale beer and cigarettes hung in the air.

105

Only a few men, who looked as if they'd just finished the evening shift at the brewery a few blocks away, straddled stools along the bar.

"Beer," I said to the bartender, climbing carefully onto the barstool. "Light, Busch." I pulled a five out of my pocket and put it on the bar.

Without a word, the bartender popped the top on a dripping bottle, plopped a well-used cork coaster in front of me, and put my beer on it. He took the five, rang up my beer and dropped four ones and a dime back on the bar. I left it there.

A few years ago I would have told him to place a bet with the change. But losing $500 on a Nebraska football game had cured me of gambling—almost. I missed the rush—laying money down, sliding it across the bar and holding my breath until the chips fell. After I wrote a bad check to cover my gambling debts BJ had bailed me out, but not before she'd made me promise to stop. So I fought the urge. So far. And stayed away from the casinos.

"Suit?"

"Yeah, which detective?"

"Harding. Seemed like a pretty nice guy." I smiled. "For a cop."

"Don's worked with him on several cases." BJ's husband, Don, was also a police officer who had been recently promoted to sergeant. "Harding's okay," she admitted. "For a cop," she added, tipping her beer toward me.

BJ had told me long ago that the "blues" (those in uniforms) and the "suits" (officers who wore street clothes—detectives mostly) didn't always get along even though the suits used to be blues. It had sounded like the same professional squabbles in nursing to me then; it still did.

"Say, how are you feeling?"

"Not bad. A little sore." I turned my head to the side and winced.

"Looks like it."

"I'm okay. But, BJ, there's more to the abortion death. So-called."

"Oh?"

"She wasn't really pregnant!"

"What? Why would she get an abortion if she wasn't pregnant?"

"I don't know. Must have thought she was, and then somebody pretended to do one."

"Why?"

"How do I know? If it was anything but an accredited facility, I'd say they'd do something like that for the money. But the clinic provides abortions for free. I didn't tell your detective, though."

"Didn't tell him what?"

"That she wasn't pregnant."

"Why not?"

"My boss told me not to."

"Told you not to talk to the police?"

"No, not exactly. I just thought I'd better not say anything he didn't ask."

"That's probably a good idea. Lots of perps get themselves in trouble by telling too much. But what difference would that make? She didn't have the abortion there."

"No, but our doctor. . . ."

"What about him?"

"He works at the clinic."

"What clinic?"

"Where they do abortions."

"Oh, so you're afraid he did it."

"I can't believe he would do an abortion if she didn't need it. So maybe something else was wrong with her. What I can't figure out is why he didn't say something when he admitted her. Or note it on her chart. They usually do if they know anything about the patient's history."

"Maybe he was just busy."

"But, BJ," I added. "He also pronounced her."

"Pronounced her?"

"Dead. Pronounced her dead!" The two men on adjoining stools glanced at us in the long mirror behind the bar.

BJ looked at the men and spoke softly. "I still don't understand. Why pretend to do an abortion on a woman who wasn't pregnant?"

I shook my head. "Doesn't make sense, does it? But, anyway, why are the police involved? Abortion's legal."

BJ shrugged. "Political. Just trying to cover their you-know-what."

"It's only one death."

"But isn't it dangerous to have an abortion."

"Yes, to a certain extent. Every surgical procedure is. Having a baby is dangerous."

"Is that so? I've never heard of someone dying from having a baby. Not in this day and age."

"Exactly. Few women die today from either."

She looked thoughtful. "Could be involuntary manslaughter."

"Woman slaughter," I corrected.

"Recklessly causing the death of another person, Missouri Criminal Code 565.024," she said, showing off.

"I went to the funeral." I said after a long swallow of beer. "Saw the husband—he's the Army ranger. And the sister—they were twins. I think the husband hits the wife."

"The husband of the dead girl?"

"No, the father. This guy is a real bigot. You should've heard what he called Jessie, my nurse who's black."

"The N word?"

I nodded, remembering the racial epithet.

"We hear it all the time. In the squad room, on the streets. How do you think we got the KKK signed on to clean up the highway?" BJ said, referring to the racist group who had won a court decision to adopt a stretch of highway around the city, but as soon as the signs went up, they'd promptly been torn down. Finally the state dropped them from the program because they failed to participate.

"You know they never even picked up the bags to clean up the highway and sure never picked up a piece of trash," BJ said about the KKK. "It was all political."

"At least most St. Louisans aren't racist."

"Some aren't," BJ said.

"Anyway, I went to Berta Gunther." I smiled at BJ in the mirror. "For glasses."

"You're getting glasses?" BJ laughed. "And me older than you! Ha!"

"Shut up," I said good-naturedly and poked her on the arm. "As I was saying. . . ."

"Yes," BJ encouraged with a smile.

"Berta says the mother's been in three times for repairs to her glasses after running into a door."

"Sure.   Same story I've heard.   Hundreds of times.   What about the ranger?   Those macho guys play pretty rough.   Don arrested one guy—came home on leave, found his wife in bed with someone else, took out his knife, and stabbed her a bunch of times."

"She die?"

"You kidding?   Of course she died.   Have you seen anybody with twenty stab wounds in her belly live?"

I shivered.

BJ took a drink of beer.

"I just think there's a lot more going on in this family than we know."

"I'm sure of it!"   BJ leaned back and looked at me with narrowed eyes.   "Families have tons of stuff going on—it's what soap operas are made of."   She laughed.   "That's why it's so hard to make headway on anything like this.   You don't know the family history and they won't tell you, or what they tell you is a lie— what they want you to think or what they want to think."   She shook her head.   "Psychiatrists spend their lives working on it.   We just see the results.   And do our best to put the bad guys—the ones who hurt people— away.   But we can't fix the world."

"Whew!"

"Sorry, Monika, I guess I got carried away."

"The sister, the dead girl's twin, asked me to help."

"Help?   How?"

"Find out what happened to her sister. Why she died."

"Why'd she ask you? You're not a detective."

"She's worried it was something they both inherited that could happen to her, too. They're twins. Identical."

"She doesn't know about the abortion?"

"I forgot to ask."

"You forgot? That's what everyone thinks caused it!" She spread her hands in the air. "See what I mean? That's the first thing a *real* detective would ask."

"She was so upset, I just forgot."

"I rest my case."

"Look, I'm no dummy."

"Of course you aren't, Monika. It's just dangerous when amateurs play detective. Even experienced ones can get into trouble. And they've had years of training." A strand of blond hair came loose as she shook her head. She tucked it back into her braid. "I just worry about you, that's all."

"I know you do, BJ. But I'm trained, too. I know how to talk to people, get them to tell me things. Personal stuff. It's part of my job."

She leaned back and looked at me. "You might be right. Lots of times the people involved know more and can find out more—like undercover cops—than official investigators who scare everybody off, including innocent witnesses who just might have the information we need."

"If I could just find out where she had the abortion—well, where somebody faked an abortion— maybe I could get the police and the family off our backs. Then they'd know it wasn't our fault. Well, not entirely, anyway."

"Just keep your cool, Monika, and watch your back."

Chapter 11
Friday, 23 March, 0722 Hours

"Ah knew it! Ah knew it! Ah knew it!" Ruby was shaking her head as she came through the swinging door to our unit.

"Knew what, Ruby?" I said distractedly. I was trying to find information about a drug a doctor had ordered that morning, a drug that wasn't listed in the PDR—our drug bible. We only had last year's edition, a result of the hospital's penny pinching.

"That bad would come when we got Doc-tor Jake. Now his woman's gone and got blown up."

"What?" I jumped up, causing a spasm in my back.

"Yep." She nodded knowingly.

"Althea?"

"Nah, not his wife. His woman. Takes care of the house."

"His housekeeper?" I carefully pulled myself upright.

Ruby nodded slowly.

"What happened? Tell me," I demanded.

"She picked up his mail and it blew up." Ruby's chins jiggled with the pronouncement.

"How is she?"

Several staff had gathered around to hear Ruby's latest news.

"They don't know yet. She's downstairs now. She may be up here or maybe. . . ." She shrugged, leaving us to guess the worst.

"Where's Lord?"

"I think he's down there."

"I'm going to ER," I said over my shoulder as I ran out the door, ignoring the pain stabbing my back.

✦ ✦ ✦ ✦

"It looks like she'll lose a couple of digits. She's in surgery now." Jake Lord ran his hand over his closely cropped hair. "God, I had no idea they'd go this far." He looked away. "What makes someone do something this horrible, Monika? Why would they hurt a poor innocent woman? Ruin her life?"

"What happened?"

He slumped against the wall; his white lab coat was splattered with blood. One small dot had landed on his lapel, looking cheerfully like a bright red button.

"Let's go sit down."

He followed me meekly to the row of connected plastic chairs that hugged the wall in the waiting room. Jake collapsed into a chair as if his legs couldn't hold him up any longer.

"She came in this morning at the usual time. She takes the bus. It stops at the corner of Mardel and Hampton and we live just a few houses west. If it's raining we pick her up at the stop but if the weather's not bad she just walks to our house. She yelled out 'hello' like she always does, dropped her purse and carryall bag—that's what she calls it—she carries her work clothes in it. Doesn't want to ride the bus in them." He smiled faintly, then went on. "She called out that we had a package. I was in the kitchen finishing breakfast, Althea was upstairs getting Elisa ready for school—we're driving her after last week." He stopped, gathering his thoughts and, it seemed, his emotions. "The next thing I heard was the explosion. She'd gone back outside and picked it up."

"What was it?"

"A package—well, not a package exactly—an overnight mail envelope. At least that's what they think it was. They're trying to piece it together." He looked up, pain constricting his face. "Addressed to me," he added softly.

"She just picked it up?"

He nodded, tried to speak, but couldn't.

"What'd the police say?"

"Police. Firetrucks. EMS. Postal inspectors. The mail," he explained. "But as soon as they realized who I was. . . ." He stopped and regained his composure. " . . . they called the FBI."

"The FBI?

"Terrorism, they said. That gives it to the Feds, they told me."

I shuddered.

"It was meant for me. To lose fingers." He looked down at his hands. "What if Elisa had picked it up? She would have, you know. When she left for school. Or Althea? One of them could have brought it in." His voice was soft but panic simmered just beneath the surface.

"Is she going to make it?"

"Without most of her right hand, yeah. If you call that 'making it.'" He sounded bitter. "She's going to leave me."

"Your housekeeper?"

He shook his head. "Althea. She's had a change of heart. She was the one who talked me into staying with it, but now she's given me an ultimatum. Her and Elisa, or the clinic." He looked up at me. "What can I do?"

I couldn't answer him; there was a knot stuck in my throat.

◆ ◆ ◆ ◆

Coming out of the ER, I ran into my boss. "Judy!"

She frowned.

"Judyth," I corrected myself. "What's happening? With the investigation?"

She looked around. "Let's get a cup of coffee," she said, nodding toward the cafeteria.

After we were seated, she said, "The police are trying to get her medical records."

"Can they?"

"If her executor agrees."

"I was afraid of that."

"Why do you say that?" Her eyes, through the tinted lenses, narrowed.

"The father threatened me the other day. He said something about how we'll 'pay.'"

116

"Oh, my God, now they're going to sue. I thought it was just the police!"

"I know. A Detective Harding was here a couple of days ago," I told her, trying to sound patient and calm.

"What? You should have called me. I would have—"

"Judyth," I said more sharply than I intended. "I didn't tell him anything. You told me not too."

"No, no." She wrapped long arms around her body and folded herself into them. "You can't trust them, Monika. They'll take what you say and twist it around. We'll all be fired." She began rocking, back and forth, slowly.

"Judyth, listen to me. I just told him what I know, which is darn little. I didn't do anything to implicate the hospital. I said I wasn't here. Here, drink your coffee," I said, shoving the mug closer to her.

She looked at it and unfolded her arms. She took a cautious sip and grimaced. "Cold." She pushed it away.

"I know this is tough on you, Judyth, a new job and then all this," I said, wishing I felt as sorry for her as I sounded.

She was looking out the window, her face still, her mouth tight.

"I'm trying to do everything you've said."

"This job is turning out to be more than I imagined," she said, barely moving her lips.

"I'm sure it is," I said, meaning it.

Two women brought their snacks to a table nearby. Judyth glanced around at the nearly-empty cafeteria and sat up straighter. "Is there anything else I should know about this death? Anything for us to worry about? I'd rather know now and be prepared."

"I was just wondering . . . about her meds."

"What about them?"

"I just thought maybe that'd tell us how she could sleep through a bleed like that."

"I don't understand, Monika. She died from the attempted abortion. She hemorrhaged and died. What would her meds have to do with it?" Her voice began to rise again. "She didn't get heparin or Coumadin did she? Or aspirin?" Heparin and Coumadin were blood thinners; any of the three would increase bleeding.

"Oh, no. But I checked her sleep meds, and she got a fair amount. But not too much," I added quickly. I wondered if Judyth knew a drug screen was being run on Hope's blood.

The PA system clicked on, paging her.

"What about Jake Lord?" I asked as she stood up.

"What about him?"

"They're giving him so much trouble. Can't you do something?"

"We are," she said, with a finality I didn't like.

✦ ✦ ✦ ✦

I was talking to the pharmacy when Jake Lord came through the doors. I jotted down the information the pharmacist gave me about the new hypertensive medication I'd been trying to find and hung up.

"How is she?" I asked.

"She'll survive." He ran a hand over his eyes.

"What happened with administration? I forgot to ask you."

He sighed. "I'm on warning. They didn't tell me I couldn't help out at the clinic, just that I needed to remember our image. He reached across the counter to the chart rack. "How's Mr. Ritenour? Anything new?"

I handed him the chart. "About the same. Have you talked to the wife?"

"I tried. She just keeps saying he'll be okay."

"That's what she told me, too." It took some people longer than others to accept the imminent death of a loved one. "Any more threats?"

"No, but Althea's taking Elisa to her mother's."

"She's leaving you?"

"No. At least not yet. But we can't stay at the house."

"How badly is it damaged?"

He shrugged. "We don't know yet. The insurance company's coming today. The front's all boarded up."

He asked about several other patients. The florist arrived with flowers we couldn't fit in a patient's crowded cubicle. I set them on top of the counter to wait until the patient moved to a regular floor. Lord finished charting and turned to go.

"Jake, about Hope Shepheard. Do you know where she got her abortion? Did she say anything when you admitted her?"

"Why?" He frowned.

"I thought if we knew maybe we could get these protesters off our backs."

"Humph! I doubt it. They're out for blood."

I winced.

"Mine." He made his way around desk and walked out.

Ruby handed me a pink message slip. She had scribbled, "Lab called. Second hemoglobin higher than first."

The second one should have been lower, or at least the same, if Hope had still been hemorrhaging. Maybe Ruby got the message reversed, but I knew she'd never admit it.

Mickey confirmed the blood test results when I reached her on the phone a few minutes later. We agreed the second test should have been lower if Hope had still been hemorrhaging, or at least it should not have been higher.

"Had she been transfused?" Mickey asked.

"No way. It'd be on the chart if she had been." I chewed on the end of my pen. "What about an error in the lab? You said some of them don't know what they're doing."

"No errors, Monika, not as long as I'm here."

I wasn't so sure.

✦ ✦ ✦ ✦

Max joined me and other weary day staff taking the elevator to the tunnel that led to the garage. We'd had three admits, and I'd sent one patient to telemetry who really should have stayed with us. I'd crossed my fingers, hoping that the staff there would monitor him carefully; I hadn't even had time to give them an update. In the garage, as Max turned toward his car in the section reserved for department chiefs, he glanced at me. "You okay?"

"Oh, sure. A patient dies who shouldn't have, a woman's raped in the garage, equipment's breaking down every time we look at it, and we're so short of staff, I'm terrified what else will happen next. I'm just dandy." I stomped in a puddle in the garage, splashing muddy water onto Max's gray flannel slacks. "Oh, Max, I'm sorry," I cried.

He looked at his dirty pants and shrugged. "They'll clean." He smiled graciously.

"Let me pay for it. The dry cleaning."

"Absolutely not. They need cleaning anyway." He put his arm around my shoulders. "It'll be all right."

"I just can't get that abortion death off my mind."

He frowned. "Me either. A bleed like that. . . ."

We had reached his car—a new model BMW. He popped the lock with the remote key.

"One thing puzzles me, though," he said, his hand resting on the door. "There weren't any defensive wounds."

"Defensive wounds?"

"On her arms or hands." He put his hands up in front of his face. "Here on the dorsal side of her arms or on her palms. If she was fighting someone off. . . ."

The automatic car lock snapped back down. We both jumped.

"Could she have done it to herself?" I asked Max. "Stuck something up inside, like a coat hanger or something?" I pulled my lab coat closer and hugged myself. "Could she have been trying to kill herself?"

He shook his head. "I don't think so. I've seen people do some pretty horrible things to their bodies. But they usually find easier ways to commit suicide.

121

And besides, a coat hanger wouldn't make a laceration that large." He climbed into his Beemer and rolled the window down. The engine purred quietly.

I leaned into his window. "How long would it take for her to bleed out? With an injury like that?"

"Not long. Less than twenty-four hours is my guess." He frowned up at me. "Why do you think I've been so worried about this?"

I stood up and stepped back. He backed out of his parking space and headed toward the exit as I just stood there, putting two and two together. "Then she was killed here," I said to his retreating taillights.

Chapter 12
Friday, 23 March 1820 hours

St. Augustine's Church was already crowded by the time Hannah and I arrived with the girls for our weekly Friday night fish fry during Lent. The line snaked out the door into the parking lot. I'd called planning to cancel, but the twins were looking forward to it, Hannah had said. I didn't have the heart to disappoint them.

Jumping up and down, one of the twins said, "Aunt Monny, how long will it be? I'm hungry."

"Gena, you're always hungry." I laughed.

"I'm Tina." A small foot stamped the ground. "People always get us mixed up," she complained to her mother.

When they were dressed alike, even I couldn't always tell them apart. Except Tina was the assertive one; Gena was more timid.

I asked Hannah how she knew which twin was which. She had the same answer every time.

"I just know, that's all."

"You're the only one who does. I'll bet they fool their teachers."

Tina—I think—giggled. "Just last week Gena took a make-up test for me. I was home sick."

"Does anyone know?" asked Hannah, surprised. "Lordy, I'll be called in to the principal's office and, believe me, Monika, it feels just like it did when we were in school if you get called in for your kid. You feel about three feet tall and guilty of something."

"Don't worry, Mom. No one knows," Gena— this time—answered. "And I got an A for her, too." She smiled proudly.

Hannah smiled back at her. "We will definitely have to talk about this at home."

The smell of frying fish spewed out through exhaust fans.

"Um, good." I grinned at the girls who were clinging to each of my hands. I looked at Hannah. She was as pale as Charity had been the day before. "You okay?"

She gave me a little smile. "Just not hungry, that's all."

"You look sick."

"Oh, you're just being a nurse. I'm fine." She turned away but not before I saw her gulp. "How's your garden planning going?" she asked, changing the subject. "Did you map out your yard on the graph paper I gave you?"

I had to admit I'd completely forgotten it. "It's been too wet, Hannah, to walk around the yard measuring."

"Don't wait too long. As soon as it dries up, we want to start planting." Hannah had the proverbial green thumb and was determined to prove that I had inherited it too. I had only lived in my little house since last fall so I hadn't had a chance to find out.

"What are you planting, Aunt Monny?" Gena asked.

"Can we help?" Tina chimed in.

"Of course you can help." I smiled and then looked at them seriously. "But it's hard work. I don't know if you're old enough yet."

"We are! We are!" they said in unison. "Please let us," begged Tina.

"Oh, all right. If you think you're big enough," I relented, with a wink at Hannah.

The line moved quickly after that and soon we were seated with freshly fried fish, macaroni and cheese, well-cooked green beans, slaw, and a soft roll in front of each of us. The girls and I dug in hungrily but Hannah picked at her food. She excused herself suddenly, returning later with beads of sweat dotting her forehead.

"You are sick, Hannah."

"It's just touch of the flu."

"Let's get out of here," I said starting to gather our plates.

"No, you finish your dinner." She smiled at the girls. "They waited all week for this. I'll just wait outside in the car. The fresh air will help."

Sure enough, she was better by the time we had cleaned our plates (I had, at least) and the girls and I had devoured huge slices of homemade cherry pie. I had wrapped another piece of pie in a napkin and told Hannah it was for her when she felt better.

"I gave up desserts for Lent," she said, but assured me someone at their house would enjoy it.

I dropped them off after an extra drive around the block in BJ's jeep. The girls had thought the open top a treat and had begged to stand up for another pass around the block but I cut it short. They were yelling for me to come back tomorrow for another drive as Hannah pulled them up the steps and into the house. I shifted into gear and started toward home, but instead drove around aimlessly, trying to get the worry out.

✦ ✦ ✦ ✦

BJ said she was watching a cop show on TV waiting for Don to get off work when I'd called her from Hauptmann's Tavern.

"You think what?" she said after joining me at the bar ten minutes later.

"I said I think she was killed there."

"Huh? Where?"

"At the hospital."

"What? How? In front of everyone?"

"Max said she would have bled out pretty quickly." I paused. "If so, it had to have happened there."

Her eyes narrowed. "What do you mean, if? Doesn't he know when she died?"

"We know the time of death, but it was a bad bleed. Laura noted she was fine at 10:15, and Tim found her dead about an hour later."

"And how long would it take? For her to die?"

"Not long, Max said. The bleeding was internal, mostly, so by the time someone noticed. . . ."

I swallowed and looked up. "I'm sort of creeped out, BJ. If it happened on the unit, who did it and how did they get in?"

"The staff?"

"Of course not! They're nurses!"

BJ smiled. "But not saints. You've heard about nurses killing their patients. And medical mistakes are costing lives, according to the news."

"Don't remind me. Ever since that report about medical errors came out, people have been badgering us. Doesn't matter if the doctor ordered the wrong dose or pharmacy made a mistake, it's the nurse who's blamed. 'Are you sure that's the right medicine, nurse?'" I mimicked.

"Okay, okay." BJ held up her hands. "You're all human."

"And besides, I know all my nurses. Hired most of them myself. No one there could have done it." I gave the counter a determined pat.

"What about that doctor of yours?" BJ asked.

"Jake?"

"Yeah, the one they're protesting."

"You heard about the bomb?"

"The Second got the call but we all heard about it."

BJ worked out of the Southside police station (one of three stations in the city) at the corner of Arsenal and Sublette. She was assigned to the first district, which covered the lower southeast corner of the city. It hugged the Mississippi River down to Chippewa Street, stretched west to Kingshighway, then south until Kingshighway stopped at Gravois, continuing south on Gravois to the lower city limits. Her district included the south city area known as Dutchtown, where we both had grown up and, just south of it, Holly Hills, where I lived now. St. Teresa's Hospital was at the western edge of the district.

"Bloody mess." She shook her head. "How is she? They bring her to St. T's?"

I nodded. "She'll lose at least two fingers. On her right hand. And part of a third. The rest will be mangled but they don't how bad yet."

"Christ! What those creeps won't do!" She signaled the bartender who slung a dingy towel over his shoulder and popped the top on a Busch Light, placing it on the stained cardboard coaster in front of BJ.

Next to me someone slid a few bills across the bar and the bartender palmed them, and I felt the old rush. For me nothing could top the thrill of having a hundred dollars riding on the point spread of a football game or watching the fights on TV above the bar, keeping my fingers crossed that the right guy goes down in the seventh. I thought about playing the now-silent 25-holer in back. The bartender would have rolls of nickels to sell.

"Don't even think about it, Monika," BJ said.

The bartender set a beer in front of me.

I took a long swallow to clear my throat and my thoughts. I straightened up on the stool. My back was still sore, but the sharp pain had faded.

The TV was on. A cop car was chasing a red convertible, tires squealing. A black Lincoln ran into a UPS delivery truck and blocked the cops. The red convertible made a clean getaway.

"A nurse I used to work with is there now."

"Where?"

"The clinic. Where they do the abortions."

"Is your doctor the only one there who does them?"

"Nah. I think a number of doctors volunteer, but they keep it real quiet."

"With good reason," BJ added.

"I might go see her."

"Would she tell you anything?"

"She might. We worked together a while. Hey, did I tell you about that preacher?" I asked BJ.

"No, why?"

"He just seemed too creepy to me. And too friendly."

"Uh oh."

"It's just that feeling you get. You know. My antenna was up."

"What's his name?"

I told her his name along with the name of the church: Light of Salvation Fellowship.

"What denomination's that?"

"Their own, I think."

"Want me to check him out?"

"Would you?"

"I'm not supposed to."

"But you could?"

"I could. Mules."

"Mules?"

"Missouri Uniform Law Enforcement System," she said, sounding like an automated answering machine. "Tells you if they've been arrested anywhere in the U.S. of A.," she added. "Or if there's a warrant out for them. Say, we might have a lead on that rape in the hospital garage. Don says they got a tip. I just hope we catch him before he does it again." She grinned. "I'd like to get my hands on him."

"Good. Now back to checking on the reverend. Will you?"

She blew on the top of her beer bottle, making a whistling sound. "Other cops do it. I guess I could," she said, putting the bottle down. "But how could anyone just come in and cut her up without her screaming?"

The bartender looked up from polishing glasses, and then just as quickly glanced away.

"I can't figure it out. Max said she didn't put up a fight."

"How'd he know that?"

I pointed to the inside of my arms. "No defensive wounds."

"Maybe he—or she—pretended to be a doctor or a nurse. Said just enough to reassure her."

"You mean they told her to lie still while they stabbed her, for God's sake?"

"Who's allowed in there?" BJ asked.

"Anyone who works in ICU. Or anyone else from the hospital. Or someone who happened to wander in. It could be anyone. A patient, family member, or a person off the street."

"Don't you have any restrictions on visitors?"

"Sure, officially. But you can't keep people out when a family member is so sick. And the hospital can't afford to lose their goodwill. We're only running about sixty-five percent full. A lot of days we lose money. So we don't question visitors unless they bother someone or make a lot of noise. It's not the best situation for getting our work done but it usually cheers up the patients. Sometimes that's the best medicine."

"How would they get in?"

"They could come in through the main doors or they could get into a patient's room through the corridor."

"How could they do that?"

"Each room has a door to the corridor that parallels the outside wall. Families can come and go through that door and not get in our way, or see other patients."

"How do they get to the corridor?"

"They go through a door by the elevator. There's a sign. 'Family and staff only.'"

"What's to keep anyone from going through the door? Don't they have to have a pass? Or is there a guard?"

"Are you kidding? I just lost three staff to our 'right-sizing' plan. The hospital wouldn't waste money to staff a door!"

"So you're telling me that anyone could have just walked in or come right through your unit if they looked like they belonged? Wasn't anyone checking on her? To see if she was bleeding?"

"Of course. We'd been monitoring the bleeding. Checking her pads—"

"Pads?"

"Perineal pads. We check them for blood—how much, consistency, color, and so forth and count them to see how much blood she's losing, or if it's stopped."

She looked puzzled. "How do you do that?"

"Say you were bleeding from the vagina."

"Ugh."

"Just say you were. And you're lying in a hospital bed. I come in, ask you how you're doing, tell you I'm going to check you."

"And then?"

"I'd turn back the sheet, pull up your gown, check your abdomen to see if I could feel the uterus, take the pad off, and check under your hips to see if any blood had pooled there. That's it, more or less depending on what I found."

"So someone could pretend to be checking her and—"

"—plunge something up in her," I said.

"Wouldn't he have gotten blood all over him?"

"Probably. But, again, a nurse or doctor with a blood on them wouldn't be that strange."

"You know what this means, don't you? If it happened at the hospital?"

I nodded. "We're talking murder."

"Yeah, we are."

Chapter 13
Saturday, 24 March, 0845 Hours

"I've been thinking," BJ said after she took a sip of coffee. "About the girl's death."

I cut BJ a large slice of Liederhofer's coffeecake.

She took a bite. "Could she just have started bleeding again without anyone doing anything? Doesn't that happen?"

"Sure. But not at all likely in this situation. She was a healthy young woman."

"You said this guy operated on her when she didn't need it. Couldn't it have been from that?"

"It's the timing. She'd had the "abortion" before she came in Friday morning, and she had already stopped bleeding that night. The night before she died from bleeding to death."

"But you kept her."

"Yeah, we wanted to make sure it wouldn't start again. She was going home that morning."

"Maybe he—or she—didn't mean to do it."

"Who?"

"Say Hope—that was her name, right? Say Hope had the abortion—or what she thought was an abortion—and was getting better. Then someone comes and examines her, like you said, and breaks something loose inside."

"Like a clot?"

"Yeah. You said she bled inside for awhile. Maybe whoever it was didn't know he'd hurt her until she died and then he was afraid to say anything."

"That puts the blame on the hospital."

"At least it wouldn't be murder," BJ said.

"You'd think if someone wanted to murder her, they could have done it somewhere else where there wouldn't have been so many people around."

"Who'd want to kill her anyway?" she asked me.

"Maybe some guy thought he got her pregnant and didn't know she got rid of it, or maybe he thought she'd tell."

"What's there to tell? You said she never was pregnant in the first place."

"BJ, we must be missing something else. She died in the hospital. She was badly cut up on her insides; it had nothing to do with an abortion. Was it a senseless act of random violence, or did someone mean to kill her? And if so, why?"

"She didn't even live here, you said. Wasn't she living somewhere in Georgia with her husband?"

"It could have been connected to something that happened a long time ago. And whoever did it must have done it on the spur of the moment. Hope came to the hospital unexpectedly and had been there just over twenty-four hours when she died. But why would anyone want to kill her?" I played with the crumbs of coffeecake on my plate.

"Money, lust, revenge. Those are the usual motives. In that order."

"She didn't have any money."

"It's usually someone close."

"Her parents?"

"How about the sister? Maybe she was jealous of her or hated her for some reason. Sibling rivalry."

"No, the sister's asked me to help find out what happened. She wouldn't do that if she did it." I poured BJ more coffee and warmed mine, adding cream and sugar and stirring slowly. A few coffee grains floated in the cream-laden liquid.

"So she was cut again. Wouldn't she scream bloody murder? Oh, it's too gross to think about."

I shook my head. "She must have been doped up. It's the only way she'd have slept through it."

"I thought you said you checked her pills and they were okay."

"What we gave her would have made her groggy, but it wouldn't have knocked her out so much that she'd sleep through an attack like that. But maybe she took something herself. Brought it with her. You have no idea how many people bring meds to the hospital. All kinds of vitamins, herbs, junk they think will cure them."

BJ wet her finger with her tongue and blotted up the remaining crumbs on her plate.

I motioned to the coffeecake, but BJ shook her head.

"If you really think it's murder, Monika, you have to tell that detective who gave you his card. Harding. They've got the know-how and the clout to find these things out."

"Would they listen to me?"

BJ shrugged. "I don't know."

"But if she was killed by someone, we need to find out, right away. Otherwise we—the hospital—will be blamed."

"Leave it to the cops, Monika. Call Harding." She pushed her plate back and glanced at her watch.

"You in a hurry?"

"I just have to run some errands. Why?"

"How'd you like to go look at cars with me?" I asked.

"Is Black Beauty wrecked beyond repair?"

"I haven't heard the prognosis yet, but I've been thinking about something smaller. Better gas mileage. That old car drinks it up. Don't you think I'd look cool riding around town in a little Mazda Miata?"

"Yeah, it's more your size, too. I always thought you looked snooty in that Caddy with your nose in the air."

I laughed. "That's 'cause I can't see over the steering wheel."

"Really, Monika, you need a car with a shoulder belt and air bag. That's why you got jerked around the other night. A lap belt isn't enough. You need one across your chest." She bent her elbow to simulate a shoulder belt and patted her chest. "Here's where you need protection."

I burst into tears.

"What'd I say? What's wrong?" BJ asked. "I know that car means a lot to you. I'm sorry."

"That's not it." I pulled a tissue out of my jeans pocket and blew my nose. "No, it's something else."

"What?"

"A boy. . . ."

BJ waited.

". . . touched me," I finished, letting out a breath.

"Touched you? Where?"

"In the park."

"No, I mean where on your body?"

I sighed and pointed to my left breast, reluctant to touch it.

She frowned. "How? He attacked you?"

"No, I was out walking, and he was riding his bike and grabbed my boob as he went by."

"God-damn him."

"It's all right, BJ. I wasn't hurt. It's just that I feel so . . . I don't know . . . dirty, somehow. I know it doesn't make sense."

"Monika, you didn't do anything. That's what it does to you. Believe me, I've handled plenty of rape cases. They all say the same thing. They're embarrassed. Ashamed. Just like you. He doesn't have to hold a gun to a woman's head to make it rape. All she has to do is say 'no.'"

"But I wasn't raped. I wasn't even hurt."

"It's still molestation. 'Inappropriate touching,' we call it. Do you know who he is? I could put the fear of God into him."

"No, I didn't recognize him. But I'd sure know him if I saw him again. I'd like to kill him myself!"

"That's the spirit. Most victims don't get mad at the perp; they're mad at themselves even though they didn't do anything." She shook her head. "You just stay angry at him. It's good for you."

"But he got away with it."

She grimaced.

"So far," I added.

BJ looked like she wanted to say more but finished her coffee instead. She stood up. "Ready?" she asked. "To look at cars?"

She asked me which dealer. I told her. "The brother-in-law works there. Hope's."

"How do you know that?" she said, slinging her jacket over her shoulder.

"He was trying to hustle some people at the funeral. And he had a dealer's tag on his Miata."

"Do you think he'll give you a deal on a car? After his wife's sister died at the hospital? Your logic escapes me."

"What I think," I said, "is that maybe he'll have some information that could help me figure this thing out."

"Monika." She looked down at me. "If she was killed at St. T's, you need to tell someone in administration. Stay out of this. Let the hospital and Harding handle it."

"Will you say something to him, BJ?"

"What, and give them one more reason to talk about how female officers—and not even a detective—go off half-cocked speculating about something that might not even be a crime?" She shrugged into her jacket. "Not me, kiddo."

"Look, I'm going," I said standing up. "I'm going to look at a car and just talk to the guy. It wasn't his wife who was killed, but he may know something. We can just talk to him."

"Okay, okay." She pulled out her car keys. "I better go along and keep an eye on you."

I put our dishes in the sink, gathered up my keys and wallet, grabbed my jeans jacket, and gave Cat one last petting.

Outside the sun was shining for the first time in a week.

BJ mimed a pointer. "Okay, Sherlock. Lead on."

✦ ✦ ✦ ✦

The spotlessly clean showroom housed a sparkling collection of the latest-model Mazdas and one very sporty-looking Miata.

"What can I do for you girls?" Hope's brother-in-law asked. A tan sport coat covered a white silk shirt, tightly fitted. His red tie featured billiard balls. He patted the eight-ball in the center.

"I've been thinking about a Miata," I said, glancing toward the one a few feet away.

"You've come to right place," he said, moving toward the car. "You drive a stick?"

"Huh?"

"Stick shift." He pulled open the door and pointed to the stubby gearshift protruding from between the seats. "That's the way to really feel it." He smiled. "Gets your engine going, know what I mean? More pickup this year –155 horses under there." He patted the hood. "Never could tell, could you? Low to the ground, you can really move in one of these babies."

I walked around the car watching the light sparkle on the car's cherry-red finish. The convertible top was folded into the back.

"You're just the right size for this one," he said.

I bent down to look at the dash and inhaled the new car smell. "I thought black," I said, raising back up. "With a tan interior,"

"I like a lady who knows her mind," he said, winking at BJ.

She rolled her eyes.

"There's your car right out there," he said, pointing to a coal-black Miata poised outside the window. "Let's go for a spin. Show you what I mean." Before I could answer, he said, "I'll get the keys." He headed toward a rack near the door, his black cowboy boots sporting the ace of spades and queen of hearts and promising more than I was sure he could deliver.

I swung the tiny car out of the lot and onto the outer road of the highway and by the time we'd reached the on-ramp to the interstate, I had that baby under control.

"Got something to trade?"

I looked up sharply. "For what?"

"For this sweetheart." He patted the tan leather dash.

"I don't know if my car can be repaired and. . . ." I resisted the urge to pass an eighteen-wheeler.

"What do you have? Now?" he asked.

"A '69 Caddy convertible, black, and it's perfect. Well, it was until this week when I got hit."

"A '69! My god, I haven't seen one of those since I don't know when. A Coupe de Ville?"

When I nodded, he said, "That's a classic. How many miles? You buy it off somebody in town?"

"Just over a hundred fifty thousand," I told him, accelerating smoothly around a battered minivan. "It was my dad's. He bought it new."

"You'd be much better off in this little cookie," he said, shifting into his salesman mode. "Much more your size." He gave me a sidelong glance. "Don't I know you? Been in before?"

I shook my head.

"Where'd you go to school?" He voiced the question St. Louisans ask first when they meet.

"St. Agatha's," I said, naming an all-girls Catholic high school on the Southside and placing my religion, education and social status.

He shook his head. "I could swear we've met. I'm good with faces. Have to be in my job," he bragged, nicotine-stained fingers drumming nervously on his scrunched-up knees as he continued to stare at me.

I began to feel uncomfortable. What was I doing in a strange car with an even stranger man? I turned off the interstate at the next exit and headed back toward the dealership.

"I'm a nurse," I admitted. "At St. Teresa's."

"Yeah. Some hospital." He smacked his hand down on his thigh. I let up off the gas and the car jerked. I depressed the clutch before the engine died, but the driver behind me laid on his horn and swerved around me.

I smiled an apology to Bud.

"You don't like St. T's?" I asked, innocent-like.

"My wife's sister died there last week. Hope Pierce."

I felt his eyes on me. I negotiated a sharp turn, downshifting at just the right time.

"You work there?"

"Uh uh," I answered, turning into a residential neighborhood. I slowed down gently to stop at the

corner. "But I wasn't there when she died. Were you?"
I asked.

"Nah, had to work," he answered. "I could swear we've met."

"I came to the funeral."

"Why?" he asked sharply.

"I'm the head nurse and I usually try to. For the family's sake. Her parents, I mean."

"Oh, yeah." He was drumming his fingers on his knees again. "But they're not going to get anything from it."

"Get anything?"

"Yeah, the old man, her dad, wants to stick it to the hospital." He coughed a laugh. "He doesn't even want any money; he just wants to get back at the hospital."

"I think that's natural when someone dies. It's easy to blame the hospital." I shifted into first gear and let the clutch out smoothly.

"Jack's going to get plenty, though."

"Plenty of what?"

"Money," he said. "Dollars. A hundred-thousand dollars. I'd call that plenty."

"A hundred-thousand?" I asked almost forgetting to depress the clutch as I slowed for the next stop sign.

"Insurance," he said. "Through the Army. Lucky bastard."

Lucky?

"You know where your sister-in-law went for her, uh, surgery?"

"Why?" he asked sharply, turning toward me. "You trying to pass the blame?" His arm slid along the back of the seat.

"Just curious."

The Mazda showroom was just ahead.

"How about it? You want to drive this baby home?" he asked as I pulled into the lot and reluctantly turned off the softly purring engine.

"I don't know if my car can be repaired yet."

"I'll make you a really good deal. See as how you took care of the family." He grinned.

"I met your wife. I met Charity."

He pulled his arm back and regarded me coolly.

"She came to the hospital for some jewelry of her sister's. And at the funeral."

"Oh, yeah. She's pretty broke up."

"I'm sure she is."

"She has a car just like this," he said as I handed him the keys.

"Good thing she has you," I said, smiling sweetly. "Especially now."

"She's staying at her folks." He didn't look pleased.

"They probably need her."

"She'll be back," he said, pocketing the keys. "Soon."

✦ ✦ ✦ ✦

"I learned one thing," I told BJ later at Hauptmann's. We were having a burger and coffee waiting for the NCAA semi-finals to start. Kansas and Iowa State were warming up on the floor but the sound on the TV was turned down. Most of the shots swished through the net. I didn't tell BJ if I'd bet on the game. Or not. And she didn't ask. "The husband gets a hundred thousand. Life insurance on Hope."

"Didn't I tell you? Money!"

"But he was off in the woods somewhere. Army training."

"What about the car?"

"He gave me his phone number." I threw a crumpled business card on the bar. "At home," I added with emphasis.

"He wants to keep in touch," BJ said with a smile. "He knew what you wanted."

"Well, not him!"

"The car, though."

"What makes you think I want it?"

"I saw that look. Love." She stretched out the word into two syllables.

I sighed. "I was enamored of that car."

"But not its salesman?"

I snorted.

"I found out some things, too." BJ had stayed behind in the showroom while I test-drove the Miata.

The sound went up on the TV and the first whistle of the game blew. Kansas got the tip but Iowa State stole it, ran down the court and sunk the first basket less than one minute into the game.

"Go Kansas," I screamed, pounding the bar.

"Fuck Kansas," a guy in the back yelled. His buddies laughed.

"What's the deal with Kansas? You didn't go there." Her eyes narrowed. "You don't have a bet on, do you?"

"My friend, Peggy, went there." I pulled the KU button Peggy had given me out of my jeans jacket.

"Wanted me to wear this for good luck." I clipped the button on my lapel.

Kansas tied it up. Iowa State called time out.

"What'd you find out?"

"He's their top salesman."

A shout from the back accompanied an Iowa State three-pointer. KU had the ball but not for long as an Iowa State player stole it but missed the shot. Then it was KU's turn to miss. I squirmed in my seat as KU called time out.

"All right!" I yelled to the TV screen after Kansas made a three-pointer.

"Fuck Kansas," came the shout in the back like a broken record.

Kansas stole the ball and sunk another basket.

The bartender filled our coffee cups again. Kansas sank another three-pointer; they were on a roll.

"Did you hear me?" BJ asked. "I said he's their—"

"I heard you. Their top salesman. He didn't try to pressure me, though."

Iowa State had the ball, then Kansas. KU turned it over. Iowa State missed several shots; a Kansas player was fouled and made his free throws. Kansas called time out.

I let out my breath.

"Not after I told him I'd met his wife. He thinks the father wants to sue us."

Iowa State sunk two more free throws.

"But the only thing he was worried about was his brother-in-law getting the money. Said the father didn't care about the money, just wanted to get back at us."

"Everybody cares about money. He probably wants a piece of the action."

"You find out anything about the preacher?"

"Monika, you only asked me last night. I haven't even been in to the station yet."

"Okay, okay."

"While I'm at it, why don't I check out all of them?" BJ reached behind her to her bomber jacket and pulled a small notebook out of the pocket. "Give me some names," she said, clicking her pen in place. "The sister? And the husband? I'll check out the dead girl too."

"And the father. Earl Shepheard. Remember the wife's glasses. We think he's been pushing her around. What else could he be capable of?"

She nodded. "Shepheard. Like 'I heard it through the grapevine?'"

"Yes. You know them?"

"No, but there's a Shepheard's Gunshop. It's where we go to get guns of our own. He likes cops so he cuts us a deal. It could be the same Shepheard."

"That would explain all the guns around the house."

"I'll check to see if we've had any domestic violence calls from there although that doesn't always tell you much. Most abused wives don't call, and some of them call just for spite."

"You mean they call and there wasn't any abuse?"

"Yeah, just an argument—usually screaming, maybe pushing, and it could go both ways, her pushing him, he pushing back."

"He's a lot bigger. She's too skinny to hurt him."

"That's why we take them all seriously. And hope the woman doesn't back down. How about your staff?" Her pen was still poised over her notebook.

"I told you. It wasn't them." I set my coffee cup down hard.

"Humor me, Monika, just give me their names."

I rattled off a list: Tim O'Connell; Jessie Longacre; Laura Corcoran; and, Serena McAlney. "Those are our regulars; others fill in from other units but they're not very good. Don't know ICU and don't want to. Oh, and we've got two new nurses just started this week, but they were still in orientation."

"So they weren't working there then?"

I shook my head.

"Couldn't they be there, though, without arousing suspicion?"

"I guess. Seems pretty unlikely, though."

"Not if they intended to attack a patient. Just a thought." BJ closed her notepad and started to put it in her pocket. She stopped. "What's your doctor's name? The one from the clinic."

"Jake?"

She opened her notepad. "His last name?"

"It's not him."

"Just let me check him out, Monika. While I'm at it."

I sighed. "Okay. Lord, Jake Lord. You better add the chief nurse, too."

"Oh? Was she there?"

"I don't know but there was some trouble at her last hospital. According to our ward clerk."

"What?"

I shrugged. "I don't know. Just that she was fired."

"How do you know that?"

"Why would she leave a high-powered job in a big medical center in Chicago to come to a small, troubled hospital in South St. Louis?"

"Okay. Her name?" she asked, clicking her pen back open.

I told her.

She slid her notepad into her jacket pocket and looked back at me. "What is it?"

"Just thinking about the Shepheards. I wonder who would know what goes on there?"

"Neighbors, usually. That's who we use. Especially the older ones who have lived there a long time. They know everything. And usually are delighted to tell. They like the attention."

"I could try that."

"Guess it wouldn't hurt. I don't suppose you'd get into trouble talking to neighbors. Not in our old neighborhood." She smiled. "Just be careful."

After BJ had gone I had another cup of coffee and watched Kansas finish off Iowa State. The Iowa State fan in the back was gone. I thought about the Shepheard family. Someone must know where she went for the abortion.

I dropped a three-dollar tip on the bar and checked the phone book on the way out. I got the address I wanted, and it only took fifteen minutes to get there.

Chapter 14
Saturday, 24 March 1640 Hours

A stuffed deer stared at me with glassy eyes, his antler-studded head guarding the door. Someone had tossed a Cardinal baseball cap over one of his antlers. Guns sat upright in padlocked cabinets. Some were mounted on the wall above the cabinets. Several, with bayonets attached, looked old. A small "for sale" sign was propped in the window.

Mr. Shepheard was behind the counter showing several handguns to an older man with a young woman. The woman held a petite handgun delicately by the thumb and forefinger of her left hand, flashing a huge diamond conspicuously. The man put his hand over hers showing her how to hold it.

"Bring out that catalog from Glock," Mr. Shepheard yelled over his shoulder toward the brown canvas curtain that hung haphazardly over an opening to the back.

Shuffling sounds indicated a search going on behind the curtain.

"Hurry up," Mr. Shepheard snapped.

"I can't find it," a female voice called.

Mr. Shepheard scowled, then turned and flung the curtain aside as he strode into the back.

"We use it all the time," he yelled at the unseen assistant.

"I can't know everything," she snapped back.

I heard books spilling on the floor and a large three-ring binder slid under the curtains. Charity came through the curtain grabbing the notebook just as it came to rest behind the counter.

"That's it. You order from it all the time. What's the matter with you?" Mr. Shepheard's face was red all the way to his gray crew cut.

Charity slammed the heavy notebook on the counter, rattling the glass doors of the open case. The guns inside vibrated. "For what you're paying me, you find it!" she said, turning around. The back door slammed shut.

"We'll come back later," the older customer told Mr. Shepheard as he steered his partner toward the door.

Mr. Shepheard locked the cabinet with a key attached to his waist with elastic. It snapped back against his leg, jangling change in his pocket as he looked up.

"It's you," he said, making it an accusation.

The phone rang in the back and he disappeared through the curtain.

I took a breath and looked around at the antique guns on the wall. Rows of bullets stood at attention on wall-mounted shelves with rust-stained swords suspended above them. I turned back toward the counter. Mr. Shepheard was standing behind his case of guns, staring at me, expressionless.

"Could I talk to you?" I smiled my best smile.

"What now?" He leaned on the glass case separating us. A pair of handguns were pointing at each other under the glass.

"I know this is a bad time. . . ."

A muscle jumped on the side of his still face.

". . . but I wonder if you know anyone who'd want to hurt your daughter."

The door opened behind me. I jumped.

"I'll be right with you," he told the two men who'd entered. One of them nodded as they moved toward the wall with the antique guns. Mr. Shepheard looked at me, his eyes narrowed.

"You know where she went? Which clinic?" I kept my voice steady.

"It's your fault, missy, you and that damn n _ _ _ _ r doctor! He's the devil himself, killing babies! She may have sinned, but she wouldn't have had no abortion. Not my daughter, no sirree. She'd never kill her baby no matter what she'd done." He raised his arms threateningly.

I stepped back.

"Butchers! Killers!" He brought his fists down on the top of the glass, shattering it. Ignoring the cuts starting to ooze blood, he stared at me, black marble eyes under bushy brows. "Now you get outta here!"

I did, as fast as I could. The two customers were right behind me.

✦ ✦ ✦ ✦

I could hear the phone ringing as I tried to unlock the front door. I dropped my keys and as I got down on my knees to fish them out of the shrubbery beside the front steps, tears of frustration welled up. As I opened the door the ringing stopped.

"Damn," I told Cat as she bounded into my arms.

The phone rang again, and I grabbed it.

Breathing.

Disgusted, I was ready to hang up when I heard a hiccup.

"Monika," my cousin's voice sputtered, deteriorating into a sob.

My heart jumped. "What is it? The girls? Roger? Who?"

"No, no, no. They're all okay."

I tried to slow the roar in my ears. "Damn, Hannah, you scared me to death. What is it, then? Oh my God, something's wrong with you."

"I'm okay." Her voice didn't convince me.

"You don't sound it."

"Just a minute." I heard her blowing her nose. She came back on the line. "I'm pregnant."

"What?"

"I said, I'm pregnant."

"But you're on the pill."

"I missed one," she said, her voice a whisper.

"Are you sure?"

"I just did the test."

I pulled Cat onto my lap as I sat down.

"It's definite," she added.

"Oh, Hannah. Want me to come over? Have you told Roger?"

"No, he thinks every kid is great." Her voice held a tinge of sarcasm. "He doesn't have to carry them."

She'd had uterine bleeding during her last pregnancy with the girls—her second set of twins were her fourth and fifth children—spending the last two months of her pregnancy in bed. That's when she'd said she was taking the pill, church or no church.

"He'd be so happy I'd want to kill him." She laughed, sounding like nothing was funny.

I heard voices in the background. "'They're home," Hannah whispered. "I'll talk to you later." The phone clicked in my ear.

I knew that Hannah wouldn't consider an abortion any more than she'd consider killing one of her children. She had made that clear. But I also knew she wished she wasn't pregnant. Maybe now she could understand—just a bit—how some women felt—frightened, angry, overwhelmed.

.

Chapter 15
Sunday, 25 March, 0635 Hours

I awoke to Cat walking on my head and meowing for her food and attention—probably in that order—but I tossed her on the floor, checked the time and remembered I didn't have to go to work. The rain was back, falling gently. It could have lulled me back to sleep but Cat resumed her march around my head. Finally I gave up.

After quieting her with Purina Cat Chow and fresh water, I donned a warm-up suit—it would keep some of the rain off—and pulled the jacket hood over my head and grabbed my oldest sneakers.

By the time I reached the park the rain was just a drizzle. A few trees were sprouting buds, promising canopies of shade for a summer that seemed a long way off. I thought about the garden Hannah had promised to help me plan and plant. I hoped she'd feel better about the pregnancy by the time we were knee deep in topsoil and seedlings.

The sidewalk around the park emerges on one side to run parallel with the street for a block before winding back into the park. As I neared the corner, I noticed a field of small white sticks sprinkling the lawn of a church opposite the park. Coming closer I saw they were small crosses lined up like rows of dead soldiers, making the lawn look like a miniature Arlington Cemetery. Puzzled, I crossed the street to read the sign erected prominently near the church entrance. "Each cross stands for a baby killed in St. Louis," it read, "Stop abortion now." I hurried along the walk and back into the park.

Just as a sprinkling of rain began again, a bicycle approached in the distance. I recognized the rider, and my arms rose automatically to defend my chest. This time he was riding in the street, peddling easily, one hand on the handlebars, the other hanging loose at his side. Anger crept up my neck and grabbed my jaws, grinding my teeth. I kept walking, watching, but not looking directly at him. Just as the sidewalk wound again toward the street and he came nearer, a woman I'd often seen walking her little dog came toward me. Today her pace was slow and there was no dog attached to the leash she pulled behind her.

"Oh, your dog!" The words popped out.

She looked down at the leash as if seeing that her dog wasn't there for the first time.

The boy was coming closer.

"I'm so sorry," I told her as the boy's eyes swept over me. He rode on by us, his blond hair damp, blue eyes innocent.

The woman looked up, tears filling her cataract-clouded eyes. Her hand reached out and claw-like fingers gripped my arm. "I'm not getting another one; I'm too old," she said. "You can't take back what's happened," she added philosophically, letting go of my arm.

Cat was sitting in the front window waiting for me when I returned. I gathered her up in my arms. "It's going to be a good day," I told her as she squirmed to free herself from my damp embrace. "After all."

✦ ✦ ✦ ✦

I parked BJ's jeep down the street from the Shepheards' house and walked past the few houses to their next door neighbor's. I doubted anyone in the Shepheard household would notice me but just in case I'd picked a time when I thought the Shepheards would be at church.

The rain had stopped but water dripped from the overhanging trees that lined the sidewalk. Thunder rumbled in the distance. I stepped around puddles that gathered in cracks on the uneven sidewalk. With any luck, I'd talk to the neighbors and be out before it rained again.

The door had an old-fashioned peephole—a square, eye-level opening behind thin wrought iron bars and a small, inward-opening hatch. The hatch sprung open. A wrinkle-wrapped eye peeked out.

"Yes?" said a soft voice.

"Uh, I know the Shepheards and they're not home. . . ."

Rain splashed around me. Shivering, I moved closer to the door under the meager overhang.

"You better come in, dear, before you get soaked." The door swung open and a small woman, managing a cane with one hand and holding the door open with the other, smiled me inside.

"I was looking for the Shepheards next door," I told her, introducing myself.

"Nellie Krickshaw," she said, wispy white hair bobbing. "They should be home soon if you want to wait."

She motioned me into her tiny living room and toward a Victorian style sofa. The house smelled musty with a faint scent of lavender. She said she was just getting ready to have some tea and, when I accepted her offer to have some she disappeared into the kitchen where a teakettle had begun to whistle.

I sat down cautiously on the antique sofa and looked around at a room crowded with knick knacks. China figurines of cats, dogs and elaborately dressed women, tasseled lamp shades, and old photos in curlicue frames covered the surface of every table. A curio cabinet in the corner was jammed full of Hummel figures; a key protruded from an insubstantial lock in its glass door.

Cups and saucers clattered in the kitchen and soon she came in rolling an old-fashioned tea cart, steadying herself on the handle. She waved off my offer to help and arranged herself opposite me in a chintz-covered chair, its flowers worn off in spots. Arranging the tea things with some ceremony, she poured tea through a strainer into nearly translucent china cups decorated in a variety of floral patterns. I felt like I had been transported to a nineteenth-century English manor house.

"One lump or two?" she asked, waving silver tongs toward the cup in her hand.

"Uh, one."

157

"Those poor folks. Tragedy." She shook her head as she handed me the cup and a threadbare white cloth napkin edged in torn crochet.

"Now," she began, sitting back with a cup on her lap. "How do you know the Shepheards?"

"I knew Hope." That was true. "And I just wanted to pay my respects," I said, accepting a still-warm chocolate cookie on a delicate china plate.

"Nice girls," she said, sipping her tea.

Tree branches scraped against the window as the rain picked up.

"You've known them a long time." I made it sound like a question.

"Their whole lives." She settled back in the chair, adjusting a fluffy pillow behind her. "And I never could tell them apart. To this day." She smiled crookedly. "They were always trading places. I used to peek out the window to see if I could figure out which one it was, then I'd open the door and call out the name. They were so good, though, that they'd answer to either name. They even had a double wedding and I wondered if they ended up that night with the right husband!"

"Do you know how her sister's doing?" I said, accepting another cookie.

Her face seemed to sag. "She's back home, you know." She laid her cup on the cart with a rattle.

"To live?"

"For now, but. . . ." She propped herself up on her cane. ". . . he's going to win her back," she said.

"He is?"

"Oh, you should see. The flowers. Every day the Letties' truck over there with another bunch."

158

"He's quite a salesman, I heard."

"That he is, Miss Everhardt. That he is." She frowned.

"Something wrong?"

She wiggled a little in her seat. "They just have some different ideas, though."

"Different?"

"He's into all that military stuff, owning a gunshop and all."

"Oh, the father."

She leaned forward. "And then there's the water."

"Water?"

"He thinks fluoride in the water is a government plot." She sat back. "To poison us," she added, her voice carrying an edge of satisfaction.

I looked at my watch and saw that twenty minutes had passed, according to Minnie's arms. "Oh, dear, I'd better be going." I stood hurriedly dropping my napkin. As I bent over to retrieve it, I spilled the remaining tea from my cup. After profuse apologies and mopping up with the now tea-stained napkin, I started for the door.

"But they should be back any minute," she said glancing at the mess I'd left on the tea tray.

"I just remembered. I have to see my cat."

I left her looking puzzled as I ran out the door.

The red Miata pulled up to the curb just as I reached the sidewalk. Charity looked surprised to see me. "Do you know something?" she asked, unfolding herself out of the car. She pulled a plastic grocery back out of the back seat and shoved the door shut with her hip. "About my sister?" she whispered, as if anyone could hear. Raindrops pinged lightly on the car hood.

I shook my head. How could I tell her what Max had said, that he thought her sister had been injured after she came to the hospital. That would only fuel her father's resolve to sue the hospital. I had to figure out who had killed Hope before I could tell her sister anything.

She looked up at her parent's house and frowned.

"Let's take a drive," I said, motioning toward the jeep.

She looked hesitant, then with another quick glance at the house, she tossed the grocery bag back in her car and swung her leather bag over her shoulder. We took off in BJ's jeep.

"Tell me about your family," I began as I steered the jeep onto Itaska. The rain was coming down steadier now, and the jeep's plastic windows rattled in the wind.

She sighed. "Not much to tell. Dad you saw at the store yesterday. Sorry about that." She stopped. "I shouldn't have lost my temper."

"You seemed pretty mad."

"Well, I know better now."

"Oh?"

"He's always right, you know. About everything. And he's having a hard time. Gets angry instead of crying."

I glanced over. She seemed to be trying to keep herself under control.

She took a breath. "Mom's. . . ." Charity dipped her head in embarrassment. "Oh, so holier-than-thou, and so put-upon. Acts like she's Miss Virtue. Always worried what the neighbors think." Her voice sounded bitter, betrayed. "Anything doesn't go her way, wham! She blows up!" She looked over at me. "I'm sorry, you don't need to know all this. My family's just kinda screwy, that's all."

The windshield wipers swatted rhythmically while I waited for her to go on.

"Sis and I . . . well, we had our problems. Like most sisters. Always trying to win, do the best in school, get the most attention, not that there was much to go around. And Jack and Bud hate each other." When I didn't say anything, she went on. "It's an old fight. They got into it at school a lot, and then a girl they both knew got pregnant and tried to get rid of it and. . . ." She shivered.

I waited.

"Anyway, she died, and Jack and his friends blamed Bud."

"Why?"

"Bud had bragged that he'd knocked her up. Jack and his friends beat him up. Bud ended up in the hospital. Lost his spleen. He hates their guts."

"Kinda tough on you and your sister."

"Not really. We don't see much of each other now, living so far apart."

I stopped at a red light. "Tell me what you know about her abortion."

"I don't know anything. She didn't tell me anything."

"She must have told someone. Look your sister thought she was pregnant and apparently didn't want it—"

"No! Something happened to her at the hospital—your hospital." Blond hair fell forward as she jerked her head emphatically.

"Charity, she went somewhere to have an abortion. She told me."

She bit her lip. "I know she said she had an abortion, but when I saw her the bleeding had stopped."

"You saw her? When was that?"

"The night before."

"You were there?"

"Yeah. I stopped by to see her. The bleeding had completely stopped. She said you wanted her to stay overnight just to be sure. But she was fine then."

A horn honked behind us; the light had turned green. I turned back down the street where her parents lived and pulled up behind the Miata. The rain had let up to a slow drizzle. I let the jeep idle.

Charity stared at her car. She began softly. "Someone did something to hurt her." Her shoulders were hunched forward, protecting her from imaginary blows. Her voice rose as she continued. "And it happened there. In your hospital." She looked around wildly.

I took her cold hands in mine and looked her in the eye. "Charity, I'm trying to find out what happened." I spoke slowly, holding her attention. "Give me time, will you? I'm doing my best." I gave her a small smile.

She nodded as if she didn't believe me.

"Anyone mad at her? Enough to hurt her?"

Her head fell forward, blond hair covering her face.

"How about her husband? Jack?"

She pushed her hair off her face as she looked up. "He didn't do it. I know he didn't."

I admired her faith in her brother-in-law, and I hoped she was right.

"I met your husband."

She turned to me as if she had just realized I was there.

"Bud. I was looking at a new car."

"He's not my husband," she said, glancing up at her parents' house. She struggled with the door handle.

"He's not?" I asked as the door swung open.

"Not for long." She slammed the door, ran up the steps to her parents' house and slid quickly inside.

She had forgotten her groceries, I realized, as a curtain fluttered in the window next door.

✦ ✦ ✦ ✦

Cat greeted me at home with loud meows. I tossed my raincoat on the sofa and gathered her up in my arms, her soft fur comforting me. Carrying her under my arm like a sack of flour—for once she didn't object—I went into my tiny bedroom and plopped down on the bed. She snuggled under my arm as I kicked off my shoes and sank into the comfort of Aunt Octavia's quilt. "It's been a tough day," I told Cat rolling over on my side to pet her. She stood up, turned around a few times and then folded her legs under her as she settled in a cat-perfect position. I heard her soft purring as I drifted off to sleep.

✦ ✦ ✦ ✦

I heard the alarm and pounded on the top of my clock, but I couldn't get it to stop. Finally I woke up enough to realize it was the phone.

"Monika, this Tim."

"Uh uh," I said sleepily.

"It's your cousin."

I sat upright. "Hannah? What's wrong? Is she all right?"

"She's been admitted. Hemorrhaging." Tim's voice was calm, steady, like I try to sound when I'm giving family members bad news.

"How is she?" I nearly screamed into the phone.

"She's asking for you," was his reply.

"I'll be right there."

I barely remember driving to the hospital.

Chapter 16
Sunday, 25 March, 1854 Hours

Hannah was sleeping when I got to ICU. Her auburn hair lay in damp tendrils around her smooth face, belying her nearly forty years, and her pale face reminded me of Hope's. Roger, sitting by her bed, looked up as I came in.

"Why didn't she tell me?" he asked as we stepped out.

"How is she?"

"She lost it. Our baby." He shook his head. "I wish she'd told me."

"There's nothing you could have done."

"It's just that when I found her in the bathroom. Blood everywhere. I thought she was dead." He stopped and took a breath. "But she had just fainted. From losing so much blood, they told me."

Jake Lord came out of another patient's room. "How's she doing?" he asked nodding toward Hannah's room.

"I don't know yet. I just got here."

"She needs a D and C."

"A what?" Roger asked.

165

"Dilatation and curettage," I told him. "It's to clean out the uterus."

"Why?"

"It's routine," I said, my voice level. I wasn't about to tell him that they needed to make sure all the fetal products had been expelled.

"Okay, if you say so, Monika."

His faith in me made me feel a tiny bit duplicitous.

"Does she know about the surgery?" I asked Lord.

He nodded. "A resident told her. She signed the consents."

"When are you going to do it?" Roger asked.

Lord checked his watch. "As soon as the OR calls. We're just waiting on the anesthesiologist on call. They should be coming for her shortly. We've given her something to relax her."

"Take good care of her," Roger added, concern etching his tired face.

Jake Lord smiled. "Of course," he said turning to go. "She's my favorite nurse's cousin."

"Will you go in with her?" Roger asked me.

I shook my head. "No. They don't like extra people around in surgery, especially not relatives. I'll stay with you. By the way, where are the kids?"

"The boys are home with Gena and Tina. I told them I'd call when I knew something."

"Did they know about the pregnancy?"

He shook his head. "She didn't tell anyone. Including me," he added wryly.

After Hannah had been wheeled out for surgery, I turned to Roger. "Let's go get coffee. And maybe something to eat. I'm hungry," I added, glancing at the clock. "It's after seven."

"Maybe coffee. I don't feel much like eating."

"You need to, Roger. Hannah's going to need you and you'll need to keep up your strength."

He nodded as if he didn't believe me.

✦ ✦ ✦ ✦

Roger was dozing in the chair when Jake Lord finally came into the surgery waiting room a little before ten. She had been in the operating room longer than I had expected, but I'd kept calm to keep from worrying Roger. I knew sometimes things got more complicated than anyone anticipated. Jake's scrubs were blood-splattered and his surgical mask dangled around his neck.

"She's fine," he said, startling Roger awake. "Some complications, though. The uterus bled some, and we had to do a repair."

They'd nicked the uterus!

"How bad?" I asked.

"Just a small tear." He said evenly, looking at me.

I stared back. Cut, he meant.

"We got her all cleaned out. She should be fine in a few days." He pulled his glasses off and rubbed his eyes.

"She still has her uterus?" I asked him, annoyance in my voice.

"She can have more kids, if she wants."

"Thank you, doctor." Roger reached out to shake Lord's hand, pumping it with gratitude.

"Yeah, thanks," I said, not entirely grateful. I knew it was difficult to do a D and C on a woman who'd had several pregnancies. The uterus was often a spongy mess and difficult to clean out without damaging it, but still, this was Hannah.

I followed Roger into the recovery room. Hannah moaned softly when Roger called her name.

"You're fine," he told her. "It's all over."

"Can I go home?" she mumbled.

I smiled. "Not yet. But soon. You just sleep now."

She already was.

We tiptoed out.

"She'll sleep all night. You go on home. I'll stay. I have to be back at seven anyway."

"I should get home to the kids. You'll keep an eye on her, won't you?"

"I'll be sleeping right next to her bed."

I accompanied the gurney upstairs, my hand resting on Hannah's blanket in the elevator. As she slept, an IV bag dripped fluids into her depleted body. I fussed, probably too much, when the attendant—a young man with a dirty ponytail—jostled her through the doors. Hannah moaned softly. Tim came around the counter, grabbing the corner of the gurney as the attendant asked where he wanted Hannah. Tim nodded toward the back wall. "Number twelve."

"No! Not there!"

"Why not?" Tim asked.

Hannah groaned.

The attendant looked at his watch. "I gotta get back."

"Don't we have anything else?" I asked Tim.

"Nope, no empty rooms." He started on ahead, pulling Hannah into the room that Hope had died in.

I helped Tim transfer Hannah to her bed, cleaned her up, shot another dose of morphine into her IV, and went out to chart what I'd done. I had changed the pad she'd soaked just since leaving the recovery room: amount—heavy, color—bright red, consistency—clot-filled. It reminded me about Hope's pads. We had never figured out why nothing had been charted about them that morning.

A shout came from room eight. "Call a code," yelled Tim. "Sorenson's coded."

I ran out to the desk to call the operator. Tim shooed Mrs. Sorenson out, and a nurse pulled from telemetry to our floor led her down to the family waiting room outside the unit. I told her to stay with Mrs. Sorenson.

As I came into the room Jessie slapped defibrillator pads and paddles on Mr. Sorenson's chest.

"Stand clear," Jessie yelled as Tim pushed the discharge buttons for the charge.

Nothing.

No shock.

"God-damned machine!" Tim shouted as Jessie tried again.

Zilch.

"Start CPR," I shouted, motioning to two nurses who had joined us.

"Get another crash cart," Tim yelled to an assistant coming through the door. "No charge," he added to her puzzled look. "Stat!"

She scurried out while two nurses started CPR. The assistant came through the door dragging the cart. I helped her shove it close to the bed. Tim grabbed the paddles and slapped them on Mr. Sorenson as Jessie jumped out of the way.

Mr. Sorenson's body bounced as the charge held, but a straight line continued on the monitor.

Tim continued shocking him, alternated with drugs I added to the IV as the resident ordered them. Cyanosis was coloring Mr. Sorenson's face, arms and legs bluish-purple, and streaks of purple and blue mottled his chest. The paddles had left faint burn marks.

The respiratory therapist came through the curtain. "Blood gas report," she said. "His pH is 6.9— completely incompatible with life." She had come in shortly after the code was called and drawn arterial blood for analysis done just down the hall in the stat lab.

"Stop CPR. Stop drugs," the resident ordered as he moved to the bedside. He checked Mr. Sorenson's pulse, listened to his chest, and put his ear next to his mouth. He shook his head.

"We're calling the code," he said.

Jessie responded. "You're calling the code." She glanced toward the clock, her one good eye focused on the time. "I have the time as 2130 hours," she said, her other eye looked away, unseeing.

✦ ✦ ✦ ✦

Two hours after he had coded, when we had cleaned him up and sent him to the morgue to await pickup by the funeral home, I called his doctor. Telling Tim to wake me if he needed me, I stretched out in the recliner in the corner of Hannah's room. As I drifted off to sleep something was niggling at my mind. I'd forgotten something, I thought. It skittered through my head just at the edge of sleep.

Hannah was calling for me but her voice was a long way off. I looked out over the water, but I couldn't see her. Her voice was getting weaker as if she were moving farther away. I tried to reach out toward her, but I couldn't raise my arms. They were too heavy. I struggled to pull my arms up but, no matter how hard I tried, I couldn't get them above the water. Water splashed in my face as I struggled. I pushed myself up out of the water and saw Hannah. And another. There were two of them about five years old—and they both were screaming for me to help. I tried to yell, for them to hold on, I was coming but I couldn't get any sound to come out of my mouth.

"Monika."

I opened my eyes.

"Monika." Hannah's voice sounded far away.

It was the sort of dream I'd had since childhood, a dream reminding me of the helplessness I'd felt around my mother's disability. I always struggled in the dream to help her but no matter what I did, it was never enough. I shook my head, trying to shake off the fear. And the past.

"Monika?" Her voice was weak.

"Hannah? You okay?" I glanced over at her lying in the bed.

"You were talking in your sleep," she said slowly, sounding a little drunk. She started to turn over and groaned.

"Here, let me help you," I said, struggling awkwardly to free myself from the blanket that was caught in the fold of the recliner. Finally I tore it and broke loose.

She moaned as I rolled her over on her side, holding a pillow firmly against her abdomen. I straightened the sheet and blanket, tucking both around her. "You're a good nurse," she added with a little smile.

"I should be. I get enough practice."

"You were talking. Were you dreaming?"

"My old dream. Only this time you were drowning, too."

She was already asleep as I crawled back in my makeshift bed.

The clatter of the breakfast cart woke me again later. It was time to start the day.

Chapter 17
Monday, 26 March, 0630 Hours

In the restroom I splashed cold water on my face, then dried it with stiff paper towels. After two cups of coffee and as many donuts from the hospital cafeteria, I felt almost human.

Serena was emptying the washbasin in the bathroom, telling Hannah she still had to change the bed. Hannah gave me a wan smile and looked away. "I didn't mean to do it."

"What?"

"Lose the baby. Just because I didn't want it. . . ." Her voice drifted off.

"You didn't do anything to cause this," I told her. "It just happens. We don't know why."

She didn't answer.

"Did you?"

"No, no, of course not. I could never do that. I know that's not how it works—I can't make myself miscarry."

"If that was the case, there wouldn't be abortions. People would just wish them away." I laughed and Hannah responded with a smile. "Besides, you're not that powerful," I said, leaning awkwardly over the bed to hug her.

"I'm glad you were here."

"Nowhere else to be. I work here, remember?"

She laughed, then winced as her abdomen complained.

I asked Serena about the pad she'd just changed, and she showed it to me. Only tiny clots were scattered among the bright red blood staining the soft white cotton. The bleeding was slowing. Good.

I slapped the palm of my hand to my forehead. "Pad!" I said.

"Huh?" asked Serena.

"Something wrong?" Hannah asked.

I shook my head. "Not with you, just something I remembered. I gotta go."

That was it! Hope's pads. That was what I wanted to ask Tim last night.

"Tim," I said, catching him heading into the med room. "Do you remember, did Hope have a pad on? When you found her? You remembered there were no pads in the trash. Think back. Was Hope wearing a pad when you found her?"

"Pad?" He frowned. "No, I know she wasn't. And she should have! Even if the bleeding had slowed down or stopped, we'd have left one on just in case. Here, ask Illias," he said as the man came out of the next room. Illias towered over the cleaning cart, long arms protruding from the too-short sleeves of his navy-blue uniform. He was holding two plastic trash bags—a red one for contaminated waste and a clear one for everything else. He dropped the bags in the two marked containers on his cart. I asked him if he'd remembered the woman in the next room, the one who'd died.

"Lots of them die. Can't remember them all." Dreadlocks tumbled forward as he shook his head.

"A week ago Saturday, St. Patrick's Day, bled to death."

"Oh, yeah," he said as he picked up a can of antiseptic spray and a rag hanging on the side of the cart.

"Do you remember what was in her trash?"

"Oh sure." He waved the can of cleaner toward the cart. "I remember it." His sarcasm was barely concealed. "I hardly have time for a break. How do you think I can remember what trash I pick up? A week ago at that!" He slammed his hand down on the frame of the cart dislodging a paperback book.

I reached down to pick it up and bumped heads with Illias. He tucked the book between rolls of toilet paper stacked on the cart's shelf.

"Did you see anything unusual? That you can remember?" I asked rubbing my forehead where we'd hit.

"Nooo. Well, wait. A doctor tried to toss a bloody towel in my clean bag. I remember I yelled at him to use the dirty one." He pointed with the can of cleaning spray toward the red bag.

"Did he?"

"Nah, he just walks out with it." He shook his head. "I remember because . . . ," he paused, looking toward what had been Hope's room.

"What?"

"He wasn't wearing no gloves."

"No gloves?"

"Nope."

Tim and I looked at each other. "Student," we said simultaneously. "Or first-year resident," Tim added.

"You sure it was a doctor?" I asked Illias.

"Looked like one."

"A man?"

"Yeah, with a white coat. Listen, I got too much to do to be talkin.' I got the fifth floor now too, you know." He waved the rag in my direction and disappeared into the next room.

"You going to give some blood, Monika? For your cousin?"

"I didn't even think of it," I said. "With all the confusion."

The hospital had a drive on to encourage relatives to give blood in case their family member needed it and if they didn't, the donation helped replenish the blood bank supply.

"Let's go see our patient this morning," Jake told me, grabbing Hannah's chart from the rack.

He pulled a chair up to Hannah's bed. "Mrs. Schumann, you've had a spontaneous abortion—"

Hannah winced as she sat up. "Abortion? No! Never! I'd never have an abortion." She sounded close to panic.

Jake patted her arm. "Mrs. Schumann, a *spontaneous* abortion is a miscarriage. Sorry about the medical jargon. I know you didn't have a surgical abortion. But the result is the same—you're no longer pregnant."

She lay back on the pillow but kept her eyes on his face.

"We did the D and C," he went on, flipping through the chart. "And we had to repair a small spot on your uterus. But everything's fine and you should have a full recovery. And there's no reason you can't get pregnant again. If that's what you want."

"You're that doctor," she said slowly, her eyes narrowed.

"Pardon me?"

"Butcher!" Her jaw tightened. "Get out of here! Get away from me! Monika, get him away from me. Help me!" she cried, reaching toward Roger who was coming through the door.

"I'll get the resident," Jake said over his shoulder as he left the room.

"Did he operate on me?" Hannah asked through tight jaws. "That killer?"

"He's good, one of our best surgeons."

"I want to go home." Hannah clung to the sheet pulled up to her chin, fingers clamped tightly.

"You just had surgery. You need to stay until tomorrow at least."

"Please, honey," Roger said.

"Okay," she said, leaning back wearily on the pillow. "Just keep that murderer away from me."

"He probably saved your life, Hannah. But it's your right to have another doctor." I left her with Roger and met Jake coming out of Mr. Zalensky's room.

"Sorry about my cousin."

"I'm getting used to it, Monika," he said turning toward another room. "I guess I do stand out in a crowd."

That must be the way he handles harassment, I thought. Just shrugs it off.

Ruby hung up the phone. "I hear something else broke." She waved the incident report Jessie had filled out on the broken defibrillator in my direction. "And he died."

"Mr. Sorenson."

"I told you that would happen. If they don't fix stuff, people die."

"I don't think that made the difference. We got him hooked up to another one right away. He probably wasn't going to make it no matter what we did."

She picked up a stack of lab reports. "Just like in Chi-cago," she said with a backwards glance.

Before he left, I asked Jake about his housekeeper. She had gone home, he told me, minus most of her right hand. It was splattered all over the front of his house, he added grimly.

Chapter 18
Monday, 26 March, 0755 Hours

An e-mail message told me to come to Judyth's office STAT. In medical language that meant immediately. She wasn't in but her secretary brought me some coffee and told me she expected Ms. Lancelot would return any minute. I looked around her office wondering, as I had several times since Judyth had arrived at St. Teresa's, what kind of person she was. Oriental artwork seemed to be the motif. A tall vase sat on the floor with several large rectangular-shaped prints hanging above it. No family photos graced her desk or the credenza behind it. Neat stacks of papers and files sat on the desk next to a book on managed care.

The phone rang in the adjoining office. The secretary answered it and then left. I glanced over at the files. The top one had a red-striped label along its tab. Shepheard had been crossed out, and Pierce written in. I looked toward the outer office; the secretary was still gone. I slid the file off the pile and into my lap, flipping it open. A letter from an attorney was on top. I skimmed it, closed the file and, as I started to put it back on the stack, I noticed the next file folder. "Corcoran,

Laura" was typed on a blue-edged label. I read the top page.

I had just slipped the files back in place as the secretary returned, followed by Judyth. "I needed to talk to you about several things," she began, dropping a black, envelope-style briefcase on her desk beside the stack of files. "The budget for one."

She arranged herself in the tall black leather chair and removed her rain-splattered glasses, wiped them with a tissue, and put them back. The tinted lenses made her eyes look like large brown orbs. She leaned forward. "How's it coming?"

"What?"

"Your budget for the last quarter of this year. I told you I needed it by the end of the month." She flipped open her planner. "That was a week ago; today's the 26th."

I sighed. "We'll meet your goals this year if we don't have to pay Laura's salary."

"But how about next year? What have you got for me?" she asked.

"Do you plan to cut our census? There'll be a lot more deaths if we don't have the staff to take care of them." I tried to keep my tone even, but some anguish must have come through.

"Monika, we're on the same side here. If we don't get expenses down, the whole place is going under." She leaned forward. "We can't compete with the big systems. They'd like to swallow us up or shut us down. And they don't care which." She looked me in the eye with something that seemed to be concern etching her smooth face. "I need your help."

"All right. I'll try to do something, figure something out. Maybe I could use the newer nurses more. They're cheaper." And less experienced, and slower, and it was riskier.

"Doesn't cutting Laura's salary do it?"

"Isn't she coming back? You can't fire someone because they're sick. Mental illness is covered under ADA." The Americans with Disabilities Act.

"I know that, Monika, but she abandoned a patient who then died. If we keep her and something goes wrong later, then we're liable."

I changed the subject. "What about the investigation? Anything new to report?"

She sighed. "They're still trying to get her medical records." She tapped red-tipped fingernails on the file in front of her.

"Who is?"

"Police, city prosecutor's office. That's who ordered it," she went on.

"Didn't you say the family had to okay it?"

"Either that or they need a court order, and they need to show probable cause to get that."

"Can they? Show probable cause?"

"Legal doesn't think so. She says they just need the family to agree."

"The whole family?"

"No, just her executor."

"Who's that?"

"I understand she didn't have a will so it's her next of kin. In this case, her husband."

"Will he? Agree to release her records?"

"That's the problem. It seems the family's having a dispute. The husband keeps saying no, and the father wants them released."

"But if the husband says no—"

"Apparently the father says they were separated, and he has the say. He's talked to an attorney."

I almost said I knew about the letter but caught myself in time. Reading the files on her desk wouldn't enhance my reputation with Judyth. "What for?" I asked instead.

"Wrongful death action, according to legal."

"Don't we have insurance to cover that?"

"Yes, but the publicity would kill us—sorry—bad choice of words. Could be the final straw."

"So how does it help the family if the police get the records?"

"It helps to prove their case," she said, smoothing the file folder protectively. "But that's not the worst. The records could also show criminal negligence."

"How's that? We didn't do anything wrong?"

"Your nurse did."

"But she didn't kill the woman. She may have left her—"

"Abandoned, Monika, she abandoned the patient."

I kept quiet.

"Well, so far the files are safe here." She turned to the credenza behind her, unlocked the center compartment, slid the files inside, and relocked the cabinet. She turned back to me. "Just tell the police what you know about her the day you saw her. Just what you saw. Don't speculate about anything," she added with emphasis.

"I thought you didn't want me talking to the police."

"We decided, on advice of counsel, that you should talk to them. We can't give the impression of a cover-up." Judyth looked up as her secretary signaled from the doorway. "They'll be calling all of you down to security," she said standing.

"My staff?"

"Just tell them to answer honestly. They should just say what they observed." She looked at me through the tinted lenses. "Nothing more."

✦ ✦ ✦ ✦

I made it back to the unit just in time for the ten o'clock staff meeting I'd called to talk about the budget cuts. Now I'd need to tell them about the interrogation they'd each have to undergo.

We met in the conference room, also called the report room, break room, lunch room, and sometime the cry room—if we'd had an especially tough loss. The room was small with a narrow table in the center and a few chairs scattered around. A small refrigerator held lunches and a few sodas. A microwave sat on top of the refrigerator. A lot of quick meals—sometimes only bites—were grabbed in there.

Most of the staff were already seated around the table when I arrived. "You know the problem?" I asked them, dropping the pile of budget sheets on the table.

A few nods.

"Another cut," Tim announced bluntly.

"That's about it. We need to cut a little from this year's budget—it ends June
30—"

"Is Laura coming back?" Serena interrupted.

"I don't know yet. If she doesn't, we can meet this year's shortfall. It's next year I want to talk to you about. Another ten percent cut. That's one-half of one person's time all year. They don't care how we do it— by attrition, layoffs or unpaid days."

Unpaid days were the days we told staff to stay home even though they were scheduled to work, and they weren't paid. That was one strategy to cut the budget, but it usually was used only when floors had a lot of unfilled beds. It wasn't a very good strategy for planning because you couldn't count on enough unpaid days to make up a large cut, certainly not a ten-percent cut.

One of the new nurses asked why they were cutting the nursing budget when patients were in the hospital for nursing care.

"Good question," Tim said.

"There's no way to figure it," Jessie explained. "Patients don't pay for 'nursing care'—it's included in the room charge—so administration doesn't think they're collecting anything for the expense of nursing salaries."

"It looks like nursing costs money but doesn't make any," Serena said.

"You could say that," Tim said.

"Hasn't that changed with managed care?" a student nurse with a spiral notebook open on her lap asked. "Hospitals aren't reimbursed after they give the care like they used to. They just get a certain amount for 'covered lives.'"

"Exactly," Tim answered. "So hospitals are incentivized to keep costs as low as possible. And competition from the big hospital systems, who can give bigger discounts to subscribers, forces places like St. Teresa's to cut costs everywhere they can and the easiest is to cut the nursing budget."

"Isn't that dangerous?" asked the student. "If there aren't enough nurses?"

"You bet it is!" snapped Tim.

Serena turned to me. "Isn't she a nurse? Our new chief? Doesn't she understand?"

Tim snorted. "If so, it's been a long time ago."

"I think she's struggling—" I began.

"You on her side now, Monika?" Tim said. "You been corrupted into administration? I thought I knew you better." He scooted back his chair.

"Settle down, Tim. I'm as upset as the rest of you. Judyth's doing the best she can. If we don't cut somewhere . . . I don't know, maybe we'll have to close."

"She said that?" Tim asked.

"No, I'm just thinking aloud." I tapped the stack of computer-printed pages. "Let's think about this. We could reduce everyone's hours a little," I offered.

"It just isn't fair!" Serena declared.

"Life isn't fair," Tim told her grimly.

Everyone was silent.

Serena's face brightened. "Maybe they'd let us take a smaller cut."

Tim and Jessie looked doubtful.

"They can't do that, Serena. They'd have all the others units complaining. I'll think about it and if any of you have an idea, let me know. Thanks for your help," I told them as I stood.

Jessie stayed behind after the others left. "I could cut back," she offered, squinting her functioning eye. "I'd like more time with my new grandchild." Her round, smooth face broke into a broad smile.

"I'd hate to lose you even part of the time but I'll think about it."

She nodded. "I just wanted to offer."

I thanked her, thinking as I often did how lucky I was to have such a good staff.

"They want you," Ruby told me when I came out of the conference room. "In securitee," she added stretching out the last syllable.

"Later. I haven't even checked on the patients," I said, picking up the day's roster. Two new admits had come in during the night, both critical, and I'd been busy with everything but our patients.

"They said as soon as you git here," Ruby added with a sniff. "I told you. You don't go, that's your problem." She waddled off taking her large drink cup, a *People* magazine and her red sweater that usually hung on the back of her chair.

I sighed. I might as well get it over with.

✦ ✦ ✦ ✦

The security department was located on the basement level near the entrance to the garage. The receptionist buzzed me in and told me to go on in the first office on the left. Detective Harding was sitting at the desk.

He looked up as I plopped down in the chair facing the desk. The desk was metal with a laminated top stamped with imitation mahogany. The laminate was chipped off on one corner, exposing a jagged edge of pressed board underneath. The only decoration in the windowless room was a wall calendar open to February. February 14th was outlined in a heart. A gray metal wastebasket lined with a clear plastic bag held the remnants of a McDonald's breakfast, its sausage odor lingering.

"I have a few more questions," Harding began, looking at his notes.

His jacket—the same navy-blue blazer from the week before—hung on the chair behind him.

"Tell me what happened the day before Mrs. Pierce's death." He rolled his shirt sleeves up as he talked.

I sighed. "I already told you everything I know last week."

He rummaged through the papers on the desk until he found what he was looking for. He handed me the list of staff he'd made the week before. "What can you tell me about them?"

"What do you want to know about my staff? Everyone did everything they could for Hope."

"Just trying to finish my report."

I sighed. "O'Connell, Timothy, RN," I read from the list. "Tim's a good nurse, experienced. Been here several years."

"Did he know the dead girl before she came into the hospital?"

"Not that I know. He was in charge of the unit that day so he'd seen her, but she'd just come in the day before."

"O'Connell. He have a drug history?"

"What do you mean? There's nothing wrong with Tim. He's a top-notch nurse!"

Harding shuffled through a stack of papers on the desk, pulling one out. "Yes. A report from your boss." He glanced up at me. "Says there's been some problems with narcotics on his shift."

"That's nothing. He's just busy. We all are." I leaned forward. "You might as well accuse me of stealing drugs as accuse Tim!"

"Oh?" When I kept my mouth shut, he went on. "Tell me about the others. How about the one with the bad eye?"

"Jessie Longacre. She has strabismus—cross-eyed."

"Can she see okay?"

I nodded. "But after a while, the bad eye—the one she can't control—loses some sight from misuse, but the good eye makes up for it."

"Does it bother the patients?"

"It's a bit disconcerting at first, but she's so good, I think they forget it."

"What more can you tell me about her?"

"She's been here for years, ten at least on my unit, but at St. T's for her whole career—twenty-five or thirty years. And I know one thing."

"What's that?"

"If I were sick, I'd want Jessie to be my nurse."

He took a sip of coffee.

I nodded. "And something else."

"Yes?"

"In all the time she's worked for me, she's never missed a day of work."

188

"Really? Hasn't she ever wanted to advance? Take your job, maybe?"

"No, she told me long ago that she came into nursing to take care of people and that's where she'd stay—at the bedside."

"Because she's a minority?"

"What would that have to do with it?"

He shrugged. "I don't see any people of color in your higher ups. And this is South St. Louis." He smiled. "No offense. The others," he said nodding toward the list in my hand. "What about the one with the earrings."

"She's a student and works for us, too."

"She was there that day, wasn't she?" He consulted his notes. "And assigned to Mrs. Pierce, right?"

"Laura was Hope's—Mrs. Pierce's—primary nurse. Serena was her assistant."

"Laura's the one in the hospital."

I nodded.

"Tell me about her."

"A new grad, still learning."

"Does she know what she's doing?"

"She just graduated in December, but she's finished orientation and passed her boards. She knows what to do." A little exaggeration.

"What's wrong with her?"

"You'll have to ask them in psych. I don't know much about that." I knew he couldn't have access to Laura's medical record, and I wasn't going to make it worse for her.

"She just walked out on the girl, didn't she? Left her to die?"

I leaned forward. "She's just a kid. Besides it wouldn't have made any difference. The woman was dead by then. It wasn't Laura's fault. Someone killed her and it wasn't my staff!"

"I didn't say anyone *killed* her. She died unexpectedly, and it's our job to investigate suspicious deaths. That's all," he added in an effort to placate me.

I took a breath and gathered my courage. "Well, *I* think someone got in here and attacked her."

He gave me a narrowed-eye look. "Why do you say that, Ms. Everhardt?"

I raised my chin. "Because no one here did anything wrong. And because she shouldn't have died like that. Just start bleeding again."

"Doesn't that happen sometimes?"

"Yesss."

"What makes you think this was different?"

"She was young and healthy."

He continued to stare at me.

I shifted uneasily in my seat. "We had the bleeding under control the night before." I sounded defensive.

"Umm. Sounds to me like you're trying to shift blame away from the hospital."

"Whoever did this is to blame. And he's still out there."

"Or in here," he said.

"Why don't you quit picking on my staff and get out there and find out who did it?"

"Look," he said, scribbling on his pad, "You're just a nurse. Leave those sorts of decisions to us." He didn't look up.

I gritted my teeth.

He stared at the notes he'd been taking on a yellow legal pad. "What about Dr. Lord?"

"What about him?" I tapped my foot on the chair rung.

"He works at the clinic where they do abortions, doesn't he?"

"He works here; he volunteers there."

"Umm."

"And he's had his problems. "And then. . . ." My voice caught in my throat.

He looked up, interested.

I swallowed. "The bomb at his house."

"I heard about that. Who do you think did it?"

"Those crazies! They won't stop at anything! And that poor woman with half her hand gone. It could have been his hand. Or any of ours."

"You don't know anyone specifically who might have a grudge against the doctor?"

I shook my head. "He's a good doctor, really cares about his patients, no, I can't imagine . . . I'm sure it's about the clinic."

"Did he know Mrs. Pierce?"

I hesitated. Had Lord done Hope's abortion? He hadn't answered when I'd asked him if he knew where she'd had the abortion, but he didn't say he knew her when she was admitted. Or don't doctors even look at a patient's face when they clean out the uterus? "You'll have to ask him," I answered.

"Why would someone start bleeding after an abortion?"

"For many reasons. If they were on blood thinners, if there was some pre-existing condition."

"Did Mrs. Pierce have anything like that?"

"Not that we knew."

"One more thing, Ms. Everhardt," he said as I got up. "Did you find out if they did a drug screen?"

"Look, I can only tell you what I know, and I've told you everything. I have to get back." I turned and knocked over my chair, righting it quickly, annoyed that I'd allowed my emotions to show.

✦ ✦ ✦ ✦

I had just checked the OR schedule when the door swung open and a male surgical tech in blue scrubs came through pulling a gurney with a fresh surgical patient, with two IVs hanging, chest tube, catheter, and who knew what else beneath her blankets. Ruby, who had neglected to tell me a new patient was arriving, was laughing at something the young tech said.

I spent the next hour settling the patient, who'd had surgery for lung cancer, and monitoring her early post-op recovery. She was awake intermittently, but we had kept her pain under control. She was fairly cooperative when I roused her to cough. Her prognosis was "guardedly optimistic" Jake had told the worried family. Jessie returned from a quality assurance meeting and took over her care.

Tim was standing at the counter when I came out of the room.

"Got a minute?" I asked him. "To catch up?"

He nodded and followed me into my office. I closed the door.

"What's up?" he asked.

"It's Hope," I said, hesitating. "Max told me she would have bled out pretty fast after she was injured. Tim, if that's so, then she was attacked here."

He frowned. "This is hard to believe. You mean you think someone just walked in and assaulted her? While we were all here?"

"That's what I want to ask you. Did you see anyone who shouldn't have been here?"

He thought. "I was in with a fresh MI most of the time. I don't remember anyone in particular. A couple of residents were in and out and I really didn't look at them. They all look alike—dark pants, white coats and tired faces."

"Men?"

He shook his head. "Both. Maybe. I don't know. It's been too long, and I was too busy to notice. And why? Why would anyone want to kill her?"

"That's what I'm trying to find out."

"Monika," he said, leaning forward. "Did you tell the police? Do they have any leads?"

"I tried, Tim. They wouldn't listen to me."

The phone rang. It was Ruby asking for Tim.

"Gotta go," he said after he hung up. "I think you're off base on this one, Monika. She had complications and died. We all did the best we could."

Before I had a chance to say anything more, he was gone.

✦ ✦ ✦ ✦

Hannah was recovering as expected; her bleeding had nearly stopped before I left work. If she'd been anyone else, she'd have been on a regular floor but Jake knew I wanted her nearby. Judyth would probably be after us, though; ICU doubled the room cost.

At home, I fingered the slip of paper with the phone number I used to know by heart as I cuddled Cat on the sofa. I was still undecided. Kansas was the favorite but they'd had problems before losing at the end to less accomplished teams. They'd beat Iowa State on Saturday, but Kentucky would be a different story. And anything could happen in the tournament.

I jumped when the phone rang.

"You ready? Tonight's the big night," BJ said.

I felt a flush of guilt.

"You there, Kansas?" She laughed. I could hear bar sounds in the background.

"Just let me take a shower. I spent the night at the hospital."

"Working overtime?"

"No, I'll tell you when I get there."

◆ ◆ ◆ ◆

Thirty minutes later I was sitting across from BJ at Hauptmann's best table—facing the TV. Our burgers were ordered, and we both had cold beers—Bud Light— in front of us. The game was more than an hour away. BJ tossed down a handful of peanuts after asking me about my day. I told her about Hannah. The burgers arrived, just like we liked them—topped with grilled onions in a juice-soaked bun. Fries on the side. BJ asked if I'd seen the boy from the park.

"I have a plan," I said.

"Uh oh."

"Nothing illegal. Just a little payback."

"Be careful, Monika. Adolescent boys can be strong. And fearless. They'll strike back and you could get hurt. By the way, how are you feeling?"

"Just a little stiff. And Black Beauty's recovering too."

"So you won't be seeing cowboy with the winning hand—or should I say feet." She laughed, choked on her beer and spit out a mouthful.

I grabbed a too-small cocktail napkin and tried to wipe up BJ's mess, but I knocked my beer over, hitting hers and spilling beer spilled onto the floor. Fortunately it missed us both. The bartender came over, picked up our two empty beer bottles and swiped at the table with a tattered cloth. We ordered coffee, black for BJ, cream and sugar for me.

I told BJ about my visit to the Shepheards' neighbors, my ride with Charity and the interview with Harding.

"He thinks my idea that she was murdered is just an attempt to shift the blame away from the hospital."

"I'm not surprised." She looked at me. "You have to admit, it is pretty far-fetched. Murder in the ICU."

"But not impossible."

"No, but isn't that even more damaging? That someone could get in and kill a patient?"

"I'm not worried about whether or not this is damaging the hospital at this point. I just want to know the truth. Our pathologist says he thinks she was hurt shortly before she bled to death." I stirred my coffee. "But I even told that to Tim and he didn't believe me either."

"Tim?"

195

"A nurse on my unit. I'll have to find out something else to make the police believe me."

"Monika." She leaned forward. "You should stay out of this. If it is murder we're talking about," she paused and took my hand, "it's dangerous work. Leave it to the professionals." Her voice was a mixture of concern and exasperation.

I pulled my hand away. "Yeah, yeah. I'm just a nurse. Harding already told me that." I squirted ketchup back and forth across my French fries. "So what have you found out?"

"Your nurse. The one that found the vic." BJ stabbed a French fry with her fork and waved it in my direction.

"Vic?"

"Victim. The person who finds them is often the killer."

"Laura?"

"Yeah. Isn't her last name Corcoran?"

"Yes," I answered, stretching out the word.

"This wasn't her first time."

"Her first time what?"

"She found her sister. Killed herself. Slit her wrists, and this Laura found her when she got home from school."

"Oh, how awful. I didn't know that. Poor thing."

"You don't sound like you mean it."

"I do feel sorry for her. Always have. It's just I don't like her. She's so . . . I don't know . . . timid. She won't say or do anything for herself. I just want to shake her. How do you know about it?"

"I knew the guys who worked on it. They wondered for a while whether it was a suicide."

"But it was?"

She nodded.

"Why did she kill herself? Do you know?"

"Over some guy, supposedly. He dumped her."

I pushed the ketchup-soaked French fries around on my plate. They didn't look so good any longer. "BJ," I began. "What about the family? Learn anything about them?"

"You're not going to leave it alone, are you?"

"I doubt it."

"Okay. We have some calls on the record from the Shepheard house. Three, to be exact."

"See, I told you. What happened? Did he hit her?"

"We're not sure."

"BJ, what are you talking about? Tell me! Did he or didn't he?"

"The guys who caught the calls thought it was all an act."

"What do you mean—an act?"

"We see it sometimes. People exaggerating, acting like something's a big deal. You know, real dramatic." BJ swung her arms wide to make-believe applause.

"I still don't understand," I said.

"They said it was her. She's the one went after him."

"What? She's just a skinny thing, and he's a big tough guy. Are you sure you got it right?"

"She made the call and blamed him but never followed through."

"What would make the guys think she hit him if she was the one who called?"

BJ shrugged.

"You said the cops buy their guns from him. Maybe they just didn't want to arrest him."

"Could be." She didn't sound convinced. "He is listed with the Feds, though."

"What list? What'd he do?"

"It's just the FBI. They act like they're so smart and the rest of us in law enforcement are just peons. And they take all the credit. No matter who gets the collar, they get the credit."

"What about Shepheard? What kind of list?"

"Some right-wing militia group. It's nothing. Just guys who like to run around the woods and raving about their right to bear arms."

"Has Shepheard done anything illegal?"

"Nothing that they know about. The Feds just like to keep their eye on those guys. Remember Ruby Ridge? Waco?"

"He's got a temper, I can tell you that."

"Who? Shepheard? How do you know?"

I told her about going to his gunshop. "I thought he was going to shoot me."

"Why'd you go there?" she asked, clearly disapproving. "What did you think you could find out?"

"I thought he might know who'd want to hurt his daughter, or where she went for the abortion. What about the others? You find out anything about them?"

"Your staff's all clear."

"I told you. What about our chief? Lancelot?"

"Her, too. What makes you think she did anything? Didn't you say she was new in town?"

"Don't count this as gospel, but Ruby's been hinting around that they had too many unexplained deaths at her former hospital."

She raised her eyebrows.

"It's nothing, BJ. Mortality rates are really hard to figure. You have people come in who wait too long or don't take care of themselves or are in poor health to begin with, and your rates go way up. And it's nothing to do with the hospital. Or the chief nurse."

"Okay, that preacher—Eden. I heard there was a complaint on him. It's only hearsay."

"Oh? What for?"

"Seems some lady at that church decided he was doing a little too much 'ministering' to her daughter."

"A child?"

"Teenager. About 15, I think. Underage, for sure."

"Still a child. What's the charge?"

"Nothing now."

"What? He can't get by with that!"

"He can if they drop the charge. The girl refused to say anything. Without her cooperation, it's only hearsay."

"Maybe she's scared."

"Maybe the mother's making it up. Maybe she's nuts. Or maybe she wanted ol' Reverend for herself, and he said no. Any number of reasons, but without the girl, the prosecutor's got nothing."

"Umm."

"What?"

"Maybe he molested Hope, and she threatened to tell."

BJ shrugged.

"I've got more news. I was busy."

"Who else?"

"I talked to the sister again. She says her husband—well, they're separated and she's living with her parents—when he was in high school, supposedly, he got a girl pregnant and she killed herself."

"I heard about that," BJ said. "Stuck a coat hanger up inside herself and bled to death."

"Ugh."

BJ mopped up ketchup with her last French fry. All this talk about blood hadn't dampened her appetite.

BJ went to the bar to get us each a beer. The place was filling up in anticipation of the big game. Two young guys—military by their haircuts—were sitting at the bar joking and punching each other. BJ stood next to them. I squeezed through the crowd and the cigarette smoke to her side.

"You girls want to join us?" asked the taller man, winking at his friend.

They were Hope's husband's buddies from the funeral.

"Where're you guys from?" I asked friendly-like.

"Georgia," the tall spokesman said proudly. "Savannah. Ever been there? Garden spot of the South."

"No, but I know a guy there. A ranger."

"Oh, yeah? We're rangers, too. How about that, she knows a ranger," he said, punching his friend on the arm. "Who is it?" he asked me.

"Well, I don't remember his name, I only met him once. Oh, I know, Jack Pierce."

"I'll be damned! Oh, pardon me, ma'am. Ma'ams," he corrected, looking at BJ.

She had on her cop face so he looked back at me quickly. "We joined up together. I've known him since school."

"Small world," I commented, taking my beer from BJ and leaning back against the bar. BJ poked me, but when I stayed put she shrugged and went back to our table.

"Sad about his wife," I said, taking a swallow of beer and trying to look casual.

"Yeah." He shook his head. "Bad."

"He was in training, I heard."

"Nah, he was bein' re-cycled." He emphasized the first syllable.

"Recycled?"

"Flunked. Had to repeat."

I frowned. "Then he wasn't out in the woods?"

He laughed. "Ranger school is lots of places. The woods, mountains, swamps. We train for everything," he boasted. As I told BJ later, I could see his chest swell out right in front of me. "But he flunked the swamp. They're flunking more of them ever since the guys died down there a while back."

"So where was he? When his wife died?"

"Hey, d'you see him in the parade?" Spokesman asked his buddy.

"Nah, he wasn't there," was the answer.

"Parade?" I asked.

"Yeah. It's a big deal in Savannah. You don't hear of it much 'cause of New York and Boston but

Savannah's known all over the South for its St. Paddy's Day parade."

"Tied with Dublin for third place," his buddy added without looking up.

"I heard that," I said, remembering an article in the paper complaining about St. Louis being snubbed by the rankers of the top ten list of St. Patrick's Day parades.

"You'll hafta come down sometime." He smiled at me, very friendly.

"But you say Jack Pierce wasn't there? For the parade? Even though he was back from training?" I asked him.

He looked beyond me to the door. "Speakin' of the devil." Spokesman waved his friend over. "How're doin' buddy?"

"Hungry," Jack said, grabbing a handful of peanuts from a dish on the bar.

Spokesman turned to me. "They don't get anything to eat but what they can find out in the woods or wherever. I lost thirty pounds when I went," he added.

"What're you doin?" Jack asked his friends.

"Tellin' lies and talkin' trash," said Spokesman.

All three laughed.

"An' war stories," the friend added.

"Roger that," said Spokesman with a mock salute.

More laughter.

Jack swung easily onto a barstool, leaned his muscular arms on the bar as Spokesman handed him a beer. "We're just talkin' to this pretty lady," he said turning to me. "Says she knows you."

Jack looked surprised when he saw me but quickly assumed a non-committal face. "How you doing?" he asked politely, tipping his beer in my direction.

The place got quiet; the players were forming up for the tip-off.

"I better get back to my friend."

They didn't hear me; the game had started.

An hour and a half later Kansas was down more than twenty points. They'd missed twice as many shots as they'd made. Shooting only thirty percent, the announcer told us.

"Cheer up, Monika. There's always next year. At least you didn't lose money." When I didn't answer, BJ added, "Did you?" Her eyes narrowed to slits.

"Hey, cut it out. I was thinking about him." I nodded toward the bar where the two rangers were laughing louder now as Jack sat quietly watching them.

"Him?" she asked.

"The husband. Of the girl who died. He flunked training, according to his friends."

"Uh uh."

"It can't be him," I told her. "He's too broken up by her death."

"He doesn't look so broken up tonight."

"He can be with friends, can't he?" I said, unaccountably defending him.

"You've just got a soft spot for a guy in uniform. Especially Army uniforms." BJ looked over at him. "A ranger, you say?"

"Yeah."

"Then he knows how to kill," BJ said, turning back to me. "With his bare hands."

203

I winced.

"Where'd you say he was when his wife was killed?"

"On the Army post. In Georgia."

"You sure?"

"They called him there after she died. What about the rest of the family? They're all nuts."

BJ threw back her head and laughed. "If being nuts was a felony we'd have to build a lot more jails!"

Several people got up to leave since the game was all but over. After a group of men passed through the door, a woman came in. It was Charity.

She glanced around the room, her look landing on her brother-in-law, and made her way around the tables to Jack. Neither of them looked at us.

I poked BJ. "That's her," I whispered.

BJ turned to look. "The twin?"

I nodded.

"Pretty," BJ observed.

Charity slipped off her jacket. It was the camouflage one I'd seen her wearing the week before. The gold cross sparkled in the folds of a pink turtleneck sweater.

Jack moved off the stool so Charity could sit down.

Charity said something I couldn't hear to Jack. The bartender was telling the men they'd had enough to drink but they didn't seem to agree. Jack's right hand slid around Charity's back as he leaned over her to say something to his friends. The two men half slid, half fell off their stools, dropping arms around each other as Jack took Charity's arm and the four of them made their way out of the bar, the two rangers chanting "Rangers lead the way" as they each tried to get through the door first. Finally Jack pushed open the door and they stumbled through it. Charity followed.

"That one married?"

I nodded.

"So where's her husband?"

"Beats me."

Chapter 19
Tuesday, 27 March, 1035 Hours

"Bomb."

My heart dropped into my gut.

"What? What'd you say?" I asked, trying to think of what we're supposed to ask. And remember.

The voice was quiet, intense. "Thirty minutes." Click.

"Wait. Where? Where is it?" I asked a dial tone.

I checked my watch: 10:36.

I punched the number for security and waited, watching the clock as the second hand swept slowly around once. The line went dead. I let out a howl and dropped the receiver. I took a breath and tried again. This time the operator answered and I gave her the report, keeping my voice calm even though blood was pounding in my head.

Serena laughed at something Hannah said.

Hannah!

I slammed the phone down and banged my hip on the corner of the desk trying to get to Hannah. The phone rang again, but this time Ruby grabbed it as she flopped into her chair and listened. I stood still and took a few breaths, trying to slow my pounding heart. Finally Ruby said something about a pharmacy order.

I was heading toward Hannah's room when Jerry Wagner, chief of security, burst through the swinging doors. Two other officers were on his heels.

"You took the call?" Jerry asked me. He turned to his officers. "I told you we need more staff."

I wanted to scream: We're all going to die!

"Do we have caller ID on these phones?" one of the other officers asked Jerry. He spoke fast.

"Not up here. Just in administration," Jerry told him.

"Which phone?" the officer asked.

I showed him the main line into ICU and explained that it's accessed through the hospital operator or directly by anyone who knows the number.

"Who has that?" he asked glancing at the clock

Seven minutes had passed.

The doors opened again, and BJ came through. A male officer—older, heavier and looking tired—followed her. BJ looked alert, professional and just a tiny bit excited. "Radios off," she ordered Jerry and his staff. "Now!" she barked, when one of them didn't move fast enough. "Static," she said turning to me. "Can set it off."

I dropped the day's roster onto the desk. They all jumped.

"First," BJ said, "keep calm."

"I'm Sergeant Greeley," the older officer said. "Tell me about the call."

I swallowed my fear and told him. He asked a few questions about the caller's voice—did I recognize it? No.

"Any sounds in the background? Bells, clanging, banging, traffic, train?"

"Nothing. But it was muffled, like he had something over the mouthpiece."

"He?"

"Yeah."

"Old? Young? Accent?"

"Adult, not old, no accent. But it was muffled."

"Like with cloth?"

"No." I closed my eyes to remember. "More like his hands were cupped around the receiver."

He turned to BJ. "Evacuate everyone." He waved an arm toward the rooms. "And the floors above and below this one," he said, turning to another officer, who sprinted out the door.

"These people can't be moved," I said, my voice rising. "Their equipment, they're hooked up to the wall. . . ."

BJ moved closer to me.

"Everyone you can," Greeley said. "All visitors. Any who can walk. Any staff you can spare. We need the most experienced ones to stay. Check for anything unusual," He continued. "You know this place the best, what's out of place.   A package, briefcase, box, envelope even. Anything that doesn't belong."

"Lord's house. The bomb!"

"What?"

"One of our doctors. A bomb went off at his house."

He looked at BJ. "Get the dogs," he ordered BJ, then turned to us. "If you find anything, don't touch it. Just get one of us. Understood?"

The phone rang, jarring us all. Jerry answered and told us 4 West had been the only call. So it was meant for us.

I split up the staff, directing them to different areas, and they moved off quickly, action staving off panic. Visitors emerged from rooms looking frightened but moving out without hesitation, except for Mrs. Ritenour, who insisted on staying with her husband.

"He stays; I stay," she said with a determined shake of her gray sausage curls.

Sirens screamed in the distance.

I headed toward Hannah's room.

She had heard the commotion and asked what was happening.

"A threatening phone call. That's all," I told her. "We need to move you." I opened her closet and grabbed her robe and slippers.

Hannah tried to sit up but moaned as she fell back on the pillow. "Hot in here." She tossed the sheet off. A foul-smelling odor escaped.

I felt her forehead. Uh oh. Fever. Infection. I laid my hand cautiously on her abdomen. She jumped.

"You have to get up, Hannah. You have to get out of here!" I slid my arm under her shoulders and pulled her to a sitting position.

She screamed.

I let my arm drop.

"Can't, Monika," she whispered through dry, cracked lips.

She looked small lying still, her face cramped in pain.

"Don't make me." Sweat stood out on her upper lip.

"I'll be right back," I told her.

More city police and most of St. Teresa's security force had descended onto the unit. Maintenance was there too, gawking for the most part. BJ shooed them out the door. The police had stopped the elevators and were moving visitors and all non-essential personnel down the stairs. The rest of the staff were moving in and out of rooms, quietly intent. I held my breath praying that no one would code; I hoped She was listening.

"Where's Lord?" I asked Ruby.

"We all be dead!" she wailed.

"Stop that, Ruby!" I grabbed her fleshy arm. "We've got patients here and I need Lord *now*! He's got to order a culture and antibiotics for Hannah. Get him!"

"Okay, okay," she said, picking up the phone.

I heard the page as he came through the doors.

"What's going on?" he asked me, looking around.

"A bomb scare."

He sagged against the counter, looking as if he'd been punched in the gut.

"It's my cousin."

"She's the bomber?"

"No, no," I said impatiently. "She's got a fever."

"We'll need a culture. Get the resident. She won't let me near her," he said.

I sent the resident in to do the cultures, ordering antibiotics stat on the way. I debated about dragging Hannah out of the bed and down the stairs. Without elevators, neither a gurney nor a wheelchair would help.

"Perimeter secure," BJ told her sergeant after a call to a colleague from our desk phone. "We've got people around the building," she said to me.

"That oxygen in there?" Sergeant Greeley asked, waving toward Mr. Ritenour's open curtain.

I nodded.

"Dangerous," he said.

"Keeping him alive," I told them.

"Let's hope." He shrugged and moved off to follow Tim into the med room.

"The flowers!" I yelled.

BJ grabbed my arm. "What flowers?"

"There." I waved toward the counter at the nurses' station.

BJ and Greeley exchanged a look. "When did they arrive?"

I tried to think. Jake was here. We were getting ready to make rounds. "Last week. A few days ago. I don't know, BJ, I can't think!"

She put her arm around me. "It's okay, Monika. It wasn't this morning, was it?"

"No, I'm sure of that."

"Friday," Ruby interjected. "That's when they git here. For Mr. Sorenson. 'Fore he died. They been here ever since."

"Then that's not it. Let's check outside," she said, guiding me through the doors. The door to the stairs opened, and a police officer with sandy hair came in leading a dog with a coat to match. The dog, unaccountably named Spot, and his handler were from the county bomb squad. We followed them back into the unit. The dog plodded along, nose neither up in the air nor sniffing the ground as he wove in and out of each patient's room, past the linen closet, into and around the med room, then circled the table in the center of the conference room. He and his handler moved out into the hall where they walked in and backed out of my small office and made a round in the storage closet.

"Are you sure he knows what he's doing?" I asked BJ. "He's not smelling anything."

BJ checked her watch. "Eighteen minutes gone," she told Greeley.

She looked at my face. "The dog knows what he's doing. You'll know if he smells something. If he does nothing, there's nothing there. Believe me."

Twenty minutes later, eight minutes after the half hour had passed, Spot finished his rounds of the rest of the fourth floor and sat at his handler's feet looking for all the world like a bomb was the last thing on his mind. I hoped it was. The handler nodded to Greeley who, in turn, nodded to BJ. Chain of command, of course.

BJ turned to me. "You're clear. Tell everyone to go back to work. They have nothing to worry about," she added smiling. Her casual demeanor annoyed me somehow. I should have been glad to hear her assurance, but her words made me unsure. And afraid.

She gave me a wave as she, Greeley, Spot and his handler, and most of the other officers stepped on the now-running elevator. She was laughing at something one of them said as the doors slid shut.

I took a breath and turned back toward the unit.

✦ ✦ ✦ ✦

"There is no bomb," I told the staff as everyone was getting settled in the conference room. Serena took a swig of Coke, dribbling some down the front of her scrubs.

"This is just to cause us trouble. That's what most of them are. They don't have to make or place a bomb, just call," I added.

"Scared the bejesus outta me," said Ruby with a hollow-sounding laugh.

"Why here?" Jessie asked, her bad eye quivering.

I slumped down in my seat as it hit me. Jake Lord. They'd missed him last week. Maybe they wanted to make a bigger statement.

"Honey, you the bomb queen," Ruby said to me.

"The bomb queen?" Serena asked.

"Not my idea of royalty," I said.

"You the one knows all about them," Ruby pointed out.

"I took the class, yes, and learned just enough to be scared shitless," I told them all.

"What's going to happen?" asked one young nurse, new to our floor. "What about our patients?" Fear tinged her voice.

"Some people," Ruby said shaking her head. "Scare us all to death."

"That's the idea," Jessie said.

"What if there was a bomb?" Tim asked for all of them.

"We goin' to die," Ruby wailed, rocking back and forth.

"Ruby, stop that! We're not going to die. The police didn't find anything. Neither did the dog. And he knows his business. It's only a threat." I looked around at their tense faces. "Let's get back to work," I said, making it sound more like an order than I intended.

I came out of the conference room to see Jake Lord standing calmly at the counter of the nurses' station. "Everything okay?"

"No thanks to you!"

"Me?"

I ran my hand through my hair and sat down. "I'm sorry, Jake, it's not your fault. God knows you've had enough trouble. It's just . . . I wondered if they were after you."

He shrugged. "Only administration's after me," he said dispassionately.

"Something new?"

"I'm not sure. I think they're going to cut back on residents."

"Why?"

"Cost. Why else? That's all that matters these days. How's your cousin doing?"

"She's been sleeping. Missed most of the excitement."

"How's her I and O?"

If her input from drinks or IV fluids were approximately the same as her output, measured by her urine, then the kidneys were functioning adequately.

"Okay. So far."

After he left, I went in to check on Hannah. "How are you?" I asked, pushing damp strands of auburn curls off her sweaty face.

"I don't feel so good." She smiled apologetically.

"You're going to be fine," I told her, grabbing a cloth and heading for the bathroom. "Just give those antibiotics twenty-four hours." I rinsed the cloth in cool water and came back to Hannah's side. "Then we won't be able to keep you down."

She closed her eyes as I wiped her face. I checked her IV and the catheter running from her body to the bag. Clear urine dripped soundlessly into the container. She was snoring softly as I slipped out of the room.

The sooner she was out of the hospital, the better I'd feel.

Chapter 20
Tuesday, 27 March, 1322 Hours

Peggy caught up with me in the cafeteria line. It was after one o'clock, and traffic in the cafeteria had dwindled. "You're late today," she said, ladling chili into a bowl. I had stayed after the police had left to be certain everyone—patients, staff and visitors—had calmed down and the unit was running smoothly again.

"You heard what happened to us?" I picked up a grilled cheese sandwich that looked like it had been sitting on the serving tray since long before lunchtime. "We had a bomb threat this morning."

"No!"

"There was no bomb. But it scared the hell out of all of us."

"I heard the sirens, but I thought it was an accident." She picked up a dish of custard and added it to her tray. "Why? Do they know?"

"Just one more hassle. On top of all the others."

"What do you mean?"

"Broken equipment. No money to fix it or buy new. The phone didn't work this morning when I tried to call security."

216

She sat her tray down on the counter. "My god, that could be dangerous. What happened?"

"I must have dialed wrong. It worked then."

"I bet it was about Lord."

"About his work at the clinic?"

"A life's a life. No matter what." She grabbed a carton of milk from the refrigerated case.

I put my hand on her arm. "But you wouldn't hurt anyone. Or scare them to death."

She shook my hand off and turned toward the cashier. "Of course not. I have enough to do to stay with my program."

"How's that going for you?" I asked her as we waited to pay.

"Good. And I've found a recovery group for doctors and nurses. I can talk about taking patients' drugs, and no one looks appalled. Did you know one man at an AA meeting told me he didn't want 'no junkie who stole somebody's pain shot' at his meeting?"

The cashier looked at Peggy, her eyes following us as we made our way to a deserted table by the window. Red and yellow tulips bloomed in a large bed on the hill rising toward the administrative wing of the hospital.

"How's your sister? I heard she'd been admitted."

"Oh, you mean my cousin."

"What's wrong with her?"

"Miscarriage. Spontaneous abortion."

Peggy winced.

"He nicked the uterus and—"

"Who?"

"Lord. He did the surgery. Now she's got an infection."

"She'll be okay, though, won't she?"

"Yeah. He started her on antibiotics right away. Of course it happened right in the middle of everything this morning." I pulled my sandwich apart and ate a bite. The cheese tasted like warm rubber.

"How's Laura doing?" I swallowed a bite of sandwich, the cheese sticking to my teeth.

"She's better." Peggy crumbled crackers into her chili. "Crying a lot. But that's good. She still has spells where she just sits and stares, but she's coming out of it." Peggy dusted the cracker crumbs off her hands and wiped them carefully on her napkin.

I looked around at the nearly-empty cafeteria and lowered my voice. "This isn't the first time, is it?"

Peggy looked up.

"That she's been in. She's had another episode, hasn't she?"

"Where'd you hear that?" Peggy paused with her spoon over her bowl. When I didn't answer, she nodded knowingly. "Ruby?"

"Is it true?"

Peggy took a small bite of chili, tested it on her tongue and chewed slowly. She opened her milk carton and poured it into the glass and took a drink. She patted her mouth with a napkin and seemed to make up her mind. "Yes," she said slowly. "A long time ago. She was about 12 or 13, I think." She stopped and looked around. "She found her sister. She'd killed herself," Peggy said, her voice a whisper.

"How awful! What happened to Laura?"

"She got like this, according to the file. Wouldn't speak. Just stared."

"How long did it last? That time?"

"Not long. About a week, I think. She's been okay from then on."

"Till now. Peggy, you don't think she's faking, do you?"

"Malingering? Nah, I don't think so."

"But she could be?"

"I suppose."

"You like her, Peggy."

"Yeah, and that makes it hard."

"To be objective or to take care of her?"

"Both," she said, taking another napkin from a stack in front of her. She dabbed at the corner of her mouth.

"It'd get her out of trouble."

"Yeah, everyone feels sorry for her now."

"She abandoned a patient. She'd have to act crazy—"

"Monika!"

"Act like this," I corrected, "to stay out of trouble with the law and the nursing board."

"And administration." She nodded toward the window and the CEO's office opposite.

"It seems to me," I said, standing to return my tray to conveyor belt, "it wouldn't be worth it."

+ + + +

I checked Hannah one last time before leaving for the day and reassured her the antibiotics would soon kick in. Jake said he expected an uneventful recovery, but I was

219

glad Roger would be spending the night with her. He promised to call me immediately if anything happened.

The elevator stopped on the lower level between the lobby and the basement tunnel to the garage. I glanced down the hall as two cleaning women used mops to push heavy-duty wheeled buckets onto the elevator. As the elevator doors began to shut, I reached a hand between them and stumbled over the buckets, escaping just as the doors closed behind me.

"An' I told him that he could just do his own dirty clothes from now on," proclaimed a loud female voice as I reached the open window of the lab. A chubby young woman was perched on a lab stool cradling the phone receiver under her chin.

I tapped on the window.

She looked up, annoyance coloring her face. "What you want?"

"No, not you," she said into the phone.

"Mickey. Is she here?" I looked through the window into the room but the young woman whose name badge said she was Kiki was the only occupant. The machines continued humming without interruption.

"Nah." She turned back to the phone.

I reached through the window and twisted the handle on the door, releasing the lock. I pushed the door open with my other hand and slid inside to face a scowling Kiki.

"You can't come in here. I'll call security." She dropped the receiver with a thud on the counter and slid awkwardly off the stool to face me. We were the same height.

"I work here," I told her, wiggling the ID badge hanging from my lab coat lapel. "I want to know where Mickey is."

A grin crossed her face. "Gone."

"Gone? Where?"

"Don't know. She's just gone. For good," she added maliciously.

"What happened?"

A shrug.

I felt defeated and angry. Mickey had been here forever; she was a permanent fixture in the lab. I turned to go. Mickey's favorite bumper sticker was still pasted to the concrete block wall above the door. "When?" I asked.

"Don't know. I just know when I came in, they told me."

✦ ✦ ✦ ✦

Mickey answered on the first ring. She sounded tired.

"What happened, Mickey? I just stopped by the lab and they told me you were gone."

"Fired." Her voice sounded resigned.

"They can't fire you! You run that lab!"

"Calm down, Monika. Of course they can."

"But why?"

"The reason for everything these days: money."

"Money? What'd they think, you stole it?"

"No, I just cost them too much."

"They told you that?"

"Of course not. They just made up an excuse about late reports on tests."

"Was it true?"

221

"Yes, it was. We can't do twice the tests in half the time. They said I was too 'particular' about details."

"Quality, you mean."

She didn't answer.

"What are you going to do?"

"Don't worry about me, Monika. I've already got another job. Start next Monday at Memorial. They've been after me for years."

"But, Mickey, St. Teresa's home. Memorial is big, too big."

"I know people there, Monika. I'll be all right."

I knew she would, and Memorial would be lucky to have her.

"What'd you want anyway?" she asked.

"I almost forgot. Did you get that report back on the twin? Her drug screen?"

"I didn't see it. It may have come in, but I just cleaned out my stuff and left. What do you mean— twin?"

"Oh, she was a twin."

"Identical?"

"They looked like it."

"Umm."

"What's that mean?"

"Just thinking."

"What?"

"Their blood would be the same."

"Same what?"

"Type."

"Not that it matters.

"Well, I'm out of it now," she added, a small crack in her voice.

"I'll miss you, Mickey."

She was quiet.

"You left one thing, though."

"What's that?"

"Your bumper sticker: 'Lab techs do it with precision.'"

She laughed. "That's all right, Monika, maybe that'll remind them."

We hung up, promising to keep in touch.

The phone rang immediately.

"Mickey?" I asked into the receiver.

"Your boyfriend?" asked a vaguely familiar male voice.

"Who is this?" I asked.

"Hold on there. I'm sittin' here holdin' the keys to the sweetest little Miata. And it has your name on it." Bud laughed.

"No, I'm not interested."

"Get you back and forth to the hospital." He laughed again. "You need something reliable, you know. Hey, I heard you been having trouble there at St. T's."

The pit of my stomach seemed to drop. "No, just a call. There wasn't any bomb."

"Oh. That's good. But how about this car? You'd look pretty cute toolin' around in this baby."

"No."

"It's just your size."

"Look, I'm just not interested. I'm not buying a new car. I'm getting my old one back Friday."

"Okay. Okay. But you know where I am if you want it." His tone implied he was offering more than a car.

I hung up.

Chapter 21
Wednesday, 28 March, 1145 Hours

"Don't do it! Don't do it! Don't kill your baby!" The heavy-set woman towered over me as she leaned down, her face inches from mine. "Don't go in there! Don't kill your baby!" she screamed again, ignoring a drop of spittle that ran down her chin.

Only a few protesters were standing around the clinic entrance when I'd arrived and they looked mostly cold and wet. I had thought I'd get in without a hassle.

Someone behind the woman handed her a package wrapped in white butcher paper. "Look at this," she said, her voice a menacing whisper. "This is what your baby looks like." She opened the paper. Among the blood lay a tiny carcass.

"That's a pig fetus!" I said.

A dark flush spread up her doughy face. "You'll be sorry! You'll go to hell! For murder!" she screamed, looking around at her followers. Several nodded agreement.

A policewoman, her face blank, opened the clinic door as I scooted inside. A receptionist directed me to an office down the hall, looking for all the world like this was an everyday occurrence. After giving me a quick hug, Jocelyn asked if I'd had any trouble getting in.

"Hah! I nearly smacked that woman!"

"She didn't touch you, did she?"

"Nah, just came right up into my face and screamed."

"We're trying to charge one of them with assault but so far they stop just short of it."

"I started to tell her I wasn't pregnant but realized it wouldn't do any good."

"No, it wouldn't. She'd just think you were lying."

"She showed me that pig."

Jocelyn shook her head as if shaking off the threat. Her eyes—slightly narrowed—appraised my small form. "You're not here for yourself, are you?"

"Just some information."

"Coffee?" she asked motioning me toward a chair in her crowded office in the clinic. Jocelyn had worked on our unit until the walls closed in and she'd gone to the health department, running their family planning clinics and then, realizing she could do more, she'd gone back to school, finished a master's degree and been certified as a women's health nurse practitioner. She was one of the few paid staff in the clinic where Jake Lord volunteered.

"No, thanks. I'm on my lunch hour. Just talk."

"Shoot."

I winced.

"You know Jake Lord's on our staff."

She nodded.

"But he also helps you out here."

Another nod. She tapped a pencil on the file folder on her desk in front of her.

"The woman who died, Hope Pierce, did she get her abortion here?"

"Monika, if I knew, I couldn't tell you."

"Jocelyn, I'm not going to tell anyone. I can keep patient confidentiality. I'm just trying to find out what happened. It's my neck when something like this happens."

She played with the pencil in her hand, tapping it on the file in front of her. "I can tell you this."

"Yes?"

"No one named Pierce has been in here."

"Oh, how about Shepheard?"

"I don't know. I just checked her name when I read it in the paper. Why? Wasn't Pierce her real name?"

"Yes, it is. Or was. She used her maiden name when she was admitted to St. T's. Maybe she used it here."

"Anyway, I can't tell you."

"She's dead, Jocelyn. Why not?"

"Because the press is after us. Because of a lawsuit. And the police have been here. Wanted our records." She snorted. "I told them to get a fucking court order!" She slammed the pencil down on the file in front of her, breaking the point. "The God-damned archdiocese. Oh, sorry, Monika. I forgot you're Catholic. Correct that—the blank-blank archdiocese." She gave me a little smile.

"That's okay. I understand about patient privacy. What I really want to know is: was she pregnant?"

"If she had an abortion, I'd say so!"

"The post showed she wasn't."

"What? How could she have an abortion if she wasn't pregnant?"

"That's why I'm here."

She looked around, taking her time to think. "I guess it's possible. If the woman thinks she's pregnant, goes to someone who's just doing it for the money and they just scrape out the uterus anyway. Not that they'd get anything, but the woman wouldn't know that. Then they'd tell her she wasn't pregnant. . . ." She smiled. "Well, that'd be the truth. But that wouldn't happen here." She picked up her broken pencil, looking at it as if she couldn't figure out what had happened to it.

"Didn't someone die after having an abortion here? A few years ago?"

"She was allergic to anesthesia—malignant hyperthermia very rare, genetic. Few people even know they have it. They lack the enzyme to metabolize the anesthetic and they literally burn up. She'd have died if she'd had an appendectomy and been given an anesthetic. It had nothing to do with the procedure."

"Just one more question."

Annoyance flitted across her face.

"Why would someone start hemorrhaging again if she'd stopped bleeding following an abortion?"

"Could be she'd been taking an anticoagulant but usually it's because they didn't get all the birth products out. The placenta's implanted in the wall of the uterus and it starts to bleed later."

"Could that have happened here?"

She shook her head no as she stood up. I didn't know if that meant they wouldn't have done anything like that or she wouldn't tell but her expression was clear—I wasn't going to learn anything more from her, friendship notwithstanding.

We walked down the narrow hall to the waiting room. It was empty. Clinic hours were over for the day, Jocelyn told me. Jocelyn glanced through the wire mesh embedded in the waiting room windows. The policewoman stood by the door, her arms folded across her chest, guarding us.

"I don't know how you do it, Jocelyn. Every day."

"I believe in helping women who don't have anywhere else to go. You know, Monika, most of what we do here is not abortion. We do basic health care for women. Pap smears, breast exams, pelvics. Family planning. If that works, they don't need abortions."

"I didn't know."

"Most people don't. They don't understand that if we don't take care of these women, they get no care. And, believe me, there'd be a lot more pregnancies. Most of them have no insurance, no money, some are not even Medicaid-eligible. They'd have nothing!" Jocelyn leaned close to me, red splotches dotting her freckled cheeks.

"Then I'm glad you're here."

She unlocked the door to let me out. "So am I," she said with a firm shake of her head.

The demonstrators were gone. Thank God.

✦ ✦ ✦ ✦

Ruby called me to the phone as I came through the door. Laura was being discharged, Peggy told me, but I could see her if I came right up.

Serena, standing by the nurses' station, stopped me. "How's Laura? Is she going to be okay?" She picked at a loose cuticle on her thumb.

"Peggy says she's talking. I'm heading up there now."

"I thought it was my fault."

"Your fault?" I frowned. "How could Laura be your fault?"

She shrugged.

"How, Serena?"

She put a finger in her mouth and tugged at the errant cuticle.

"What makes you think that?"

She looked around as if she wanted to escape.

"You better come in here and tell me." I motioned her into my office and closed the door. When we were seated, I leaned forward and spoke gently. "Serena, if you know something, you must tell me. It's very important."

She seemed to make up her mind, and the words spilled out in a rush. "It's the drugs. I thought I killed her."

With effort I kept the anxiety out of my voice. "What about the drugs, Serena?"

"I gave them."

"I know. You told me. You gave her Ambien."

"Both of them."

"Both?"

"Yeah, the Ambien . . ." she hesitated. ". . . and the Amytal."

I shook my head. "No, you couldn't."

"I know but—"

"You didn't give the Amytal. Laura did. She charted it."

Serena shook her head slowly. "I knew I wasn't supposed to but Laura was busy and I know what I'm doing with drugs—I've been checked off on them at school—so I just gave it. Laura had already checked it out. I forgot to tell Laura that night and then we worked a second shift and were so busy and . . . ." A sob rose in her throat. "I'm sorry. I didn't mean to kill her." Serena laid her head down on her arms; her body shook with silent sobs.

"You didn't, Serena. Laura probably assumed you gave Hope the Amytal and charted it for you."

She raised her head. Mascara-encircled eyes reminded me of a raccoon. I handed her a tissue.

"You think so?"

I nodded, hoping I was right.

✦ ✦ ✦ ✦

Laura was sitting on the edge of her perfectly-made bed. Her white-blond hair was pulled back at the nape of her neck in a blue ribbon and the skin stretched over her cheek bones looked translucent in the light. She was dressed in jeans with an untucked T-shirt hanging on her slim frame. A suitcase sat flat on the floor at her feet with a vase of flowers teetering precariously on top of it.

"How are you?" I asked, sitting down on the edge of her bed. My feet dangled above the floor.

"Okay, I guess," she said, her words coming slowly as if the sound was alien to her. She hung her head. "I'm sorry," she said softly. "About Hope."

I patted her shoulder. "It wouldn't have made any difference."

"I should've been there."

"Yes, you should have." I shifted uncomfortably on the edge of the bed. "Listen, Laura, I don't want to upset you, but I need to ask you some questions about what happened."

She seemed to shrink down into herself.

"Do you remember anything unusual that morning? Anyone strange around?"

She scrunched up her face, her eyes folding inside.

"Laura. Please answer me," I said as gently but forcefully as I could.

"That's what she wanted, too."

"Who?"

"Ms. Lancelot. She said it was my fault." Laura seemed to sink into the mattress. "She wanted me to sign something that said it was all my fault."

"Did you sign it?"

She opened her face, but her eyes were looking a long way off. "I couldn't sign anything. I don't remember, Monika. All I see when I close my eyes is blood. Everywhere. And Sylvia."

"Sylvia?"

She looked startled. "Did I say Sylvia? I meant Hope."

"Was Sylvia your sister?" I asked softly.

She nodded, tears glistening in her eyes. "I guess you know then. About Sylvia." She looked around the

231

room. "I thought I was over it, but seeing Hope, the blood . . . I guess I just lost it." She choked back a sob. "I wish I could stay here, but this is all the insurance will pay for."

I sat there wishing she could tell me more.

"Monika," she said, looking at a spot above my head, "what do you think the police want?"

"They've been here?"

"They couldn't get in, but Peggy says I'll have to talk to them when I get out." She scrunched up her face. "Are they going to sue me? The family? One of the nurses here said she heard they were going to."

"I don't know, Laura, but we're insured."

"I'm not!"

"Sure you are, you're an employee."

"But I don't have any of my own. I'm trying to pay off school so I didn't get any yet."

"You're covered when you're at work. Don't worry about it now. Just get well."

"When can I come back to work?"

"I'm not quite sure." I hoped she could take the truth about what I'd seen in the file in Judyth's office. "Lancelot's sent a report to the board."

The Missouri State Board of Nursing accredits nursing schools, grants licenses to graduates who pass the licensing exam and revokes the license when a nurse is judged incompetent or dangerous. Or on drugs. Laura was drug-free when she was admitted; I'd found that out from her file in Judyth's office.

"What will happen? Will I lose my license?"

"I don't know, Laura," I told her. "Abandoning a patient is cause for discipline. At work and your license."

She slumped forward, her eyes closed.

"It takes the Board long time to investigate, and they don't have many people to do that. It'll be several months at least until you hear something."

"I knew I wouldn't make it. I knew I couldn't be a nurse." She choked back a sob.

"Don't give up now, Laura. You can have a lawyer. They can't just toss out your license. They have to prove you did something wrong. And they might just put you on probation for awhile." I felt as if I were arguing with her, which was often they way I felt when talking with Laura.

"I just wanted to do the right thing, and she'd had so much trouble sleeping—"

"Serena told me."

She looked up, a question on her face.

"The Ambien and Amytal," I explained. "Serena said she gave them."

"Serena didn't give them. I did."

"Both of them?"

"No, she gave the Ambien and I gave the Amytal."

I tried to keep the shock off my face. *Two* doses of Amytal?

"You wasted one."

"No, I thought I'd pulled it, but when I went back in, it wasn't there so I took another dose out of the cabinet."

Tim had said he assumed that Laura had accidentally wasted the dose she'd signed out but hadn't had time to get it cosigned. Instead, Serena, knowing Laura intended to give Hope the Amytal, had done so. Then Laura, unable to find the original dose, took out another, and gave it to Hope. They'd both given Hope the potent narcotic, and when all the drugs kicked in together, she'd been so drugged, anything could have been done to her and she wouldn't have known.

Laura was looking at her hands like she was seeing them for the first time.

"It didn't matter," I said, as much for myself as for her.

✦ ✦ ✦ ✦

"How is she?" Serena asked as I came through the doors a few minutes later.

"Much better."

"Is everything okay?" she asked, deliberately vague because Ruby was listening.

"Everything's fine," I said evenly, grabbing a chart from the rack. "Just fine."

Chapter 22
Wednesday, 28 March, 1723 Hours

Tim offered to drop me off after work at the body shop where Black Beauty waited to be discharged from the car hospital. Tim had a bright red Nissan Xterra—brand new—that he was showing off, rounding the corner at Hampton and Gravois so sharply that I had to grab the handgrip to keep from being tossed around.

Tim laughed. "Hold on, Monika, I'll give you a ride you'll remember."

"I remember some of these SUVs roll over."

"Not mine," he said, but he took the next corner a little slower.

"Do you still think someone got into the unit and killed the Shepheard woman?" he asked as we settled behind a large van stopped at a red light.

"Her real name was Pierce, but, yes, I do think someone came in from the outside and attacked her. But there are some things I can't figure out."

"Such as?"

The light turned green and we pulled away.

"Well, the two bloods. The count on the one drawn in the ER was low, not low enough yet to

235

transfuse, but the ER doc had ordered another one to type and cross-match after she got to ICU in case she needed a transfusion. They hadn't drawn enough in the ER. So the reason there were two bloods is solved, but here's the kicker, Tim."

"Yeah?"

"The count on the second was within normal limits. It was higher than the first!"

"How could that be? A mistake in the lab?"

"Mickey said not."

"It sure wouldn't go up if she'd been bleeding. There's a slight chance it would stay about the same, but it couldn't possibly be higher."

I chewed my lip.

"Something else?" Tim asked as he turned down the street toward the body shop.

I hesitated. Should I tell Tim that Hope got two doses of Amytal, rendering her nearly unconscious and unable to even know she was being attacked, much less fight anyone off or call for help? "Everything, I guess. Just everything."

Tim slid smoothly into the body shop parking lot and kept the engine running as I gathered my things. He put a hand on my arm. "Take it easy, Monika. It's all going to work out eventually. These aren't your problems. Or mine."

I nodded my thanks and scooted down off the seat to get out.

Tim was smiling as he peeled out of the lot.

Black Beauty looked like her old self, only better. Her coat had been shined and her trunk looked like new. Now all that was left was to pay the bill. I already knew it was a big one because I couldn't get insurance on the car itself—it was too old and too expensive to repair, my insurance agent told me—and the kid who hit me was without insurance. Beauty was worth it, though. I patted her hood and noticed another old black Cadillac, not a convertible, a few cars down, its right rear fender dented. I peeked inside. It looked pretty good for an old car, only a few tears on the upholstery. You could almost mistake it for mine. I gave it a pat, too, hoping its owner loved it as much as I did mine.

As I opened the door to the shop, it hit me. I stood still, waiting as the pieces tumbled into place. I knew what had happened. I didn't know why or how, just what. Hurriedly I paid the bill and dashed home, barely savoring Black Beauty's return.

✦ ✦ ✦ ✦

My heart was pounding as I let the phone ring. Please, God, let her answer, I entreated.

"Hello."

Thank you, God, I told Her.

"This is Monika Everhardt."

"Do you know something?" she said, her words coming quickly.

"Meet me at Uncle Bob's," I said hanging up.

✦ ✦ ✦ ✦

She arrived at the all-night pancake house ten minutes later.

"Who are you?" I asked.

She was pouring a cup of coffee from the pot the waitress had left on the table. She sat it down carefully and looked at me. "What do you mean?"

I reached across the table and put my hand over the two of hers. "You were the one admitted to the hospital, weren't you?"

She looked straight at me.

"You traded places—I don't know how or when—and now she's dead."

Her eyes filled with tears.

"You asked me to help . . . Hope."

Her face collapsed like a balloon leaking air. "No matter what, I loved her. I didn't know anything like this would happen." Her voice cracked.

I patted her hand. "It wasn't your fault, Hope. You couldn't have done anything."

"I just wanted to see Jack." She bit her lip and looked away.

"Jack?"

"My husband." A tear hung on one eyelash waiting to fall. She shook her head and the tear ran down her cheek dragging a ribbon of mascara with it.

"Where was he? Your husband?"

She swallowed and looked up, eyes clearer now. "He failed a part of ranger school and they gave him a three-day pass. I'd just done the pregnancy test. I didn't know what to do. I thought I was being punished."

"Punished? Didn't you want kids?"

"I was only eight weeks." She pulled a tissue out of her purse and dabbed at her eyes.

"You can get an abortion at eight weeks."

She folded her tissue into a neat square and looked at me pointedly. "Jack had been gone three months."

"Oh."

"I just did it, that's all. I didn't stop to think about it. It was all over in an hour."

"Until you started bleeding."

She looked chagrined.

"So who's the—"

She shook her head. "It doesn't matter."

"Of course it does!"

"It wasn't like that. I don't know. Reverend Eden said I 'tempt' men."

"Listen, Hope, that's not true. That's a hoax perpetrated on women since Adam met Eve." I squinted at her. "Was it him? Eden?"

She shook her head. "Look, it's over. I'm not going to tell you or anyone else. It's never going to happen again, believe me." She took a sip of coffee. "I was mad at her—Charity—I'd just found out about the shop—Dad was going to give her a third of the money when he sold it, and none to me. She always was his favorite and she had left Bud and Jack was gone and I had one too many margaritas and . . . I regretted it immediately. And. . . ."

"Yes?"

"It was only one time."

"That's all it takes."

"I found out."

"Did you tell anyone? Your sister? Your parents?"

"I never told Charity, or my parents, or anyone what happened that night. But when I went into the hospital my dad suspected the worst. He told me I was a sinner, and that it was al my fault. And then he told the preacher."

"Was that when I saw them in your room telling you to confess?"

She winced. "Yes."

"So they knew about the abortion?"

She looked startled. "They didn't even know I was pregnant!"

"Then what did they think caused your bleeding?"

"Monika," she said with mock patience, "bleeding from you-know-where means I'm a sinner. It was a sign from God, according to Reverend Eden, of my sin."

"And you believed it?'

"Well, I did have sex with someone not my husband," she said, staring out into the nearly empty restaurant.

"So you traded places with your sister and then you left," I said, jerking her back to the present.

She looked down for a moment and then went on. "I took the bus, and it took forever. I didn't get there till late Sunday night and then I couldn't find anyone who knew where Jack was. Finally, the next morning I found out."

"About your sister."

"No, just that someone had died. They said he'd gone home because of a death in the family. They didn't know who."

"You must have been scared."

"No, not really. I was just tired. Dead tired."

"Weren't you worried who had died?"

"I thought it was his grandfather. He's been sick for a long time."

"Then what'd you do?"

"I got back on the bus to come home."

"And when you got here, you found out."

She nodded, tears threatening again. "I never thought something like this would happen."

I waited while she got herself under control. "You've been pretending to be your sister since then?" I said when she looked up.

"It hasn't been easy. But Charity and Bud were separated. We were both staying at home. We were so much alike. Wore the same kind of clothes. . . ." She swallowed. "We even use the same makeup. Mary Kay that Mom sells." She stopped again. "The only hard part's been Jack."

"Does he know?"

"He does now. He couldn't figure out what was going on. He thought it was me but didn't know why I'd pretend to be Charity. He thought he was imagining it because he just wanted me alive."

"You didn't tell anyone else?"

She shook her head.

"Why not, Hope? Why didn't you tell everyone? The police, especially."

She spoke so softly, I could barely hear her. "I was afraid," she said. "Afraid that whoever did that to Charity was really after me."

I took a moment to gather my thoughts. Hope might be right to be afraid if her sister had been murdered.

"What about your parents?" I asked. "Surely they can tell you apart."

241

"Mom knew right away, but she likes to pull one over on Dad. And I was always her favorite, if you can call it that. She liked it when I caused trouble so she could play the long-suffering mother." Hope tossed her head back in dismissal. "And, she could go on being the grieving mother, regardless of who died."

"Your dad doesn't know?"

"No. Charity worked at the shop with Dad, and you saw what happened there. I don't know where anything is or how to do stuff that Charity did." She looked up. "I found out why he was giving her part of the shop—he was paying her less than minimum wage. I wish I'd known," she added softly.

"Your dad can't tell you apart?"

"I caught him looking at me funny a couple of times. I think he's not sure."

"Don't you think you should tell him? Doesn't it look like you're trying to get Charity's third of the store?"

"I guess, but I'm afraid of him because he's so angry at everything right now. Especially at the hospital." She looked straight at me. "He's talked to a lawyer, Monika. He just wants to get even; he doesn't care about the money, but he doesn't want Bud to get anything. The day Charity, uh . . . died, he told Bud that he wasn't going to help him out any more."

"Help him? How?"

"Gambling debts, Bud's a gambler," she added with disgust.

I shifted uneasily in my seat.

She looked around and excused herself to use the restroom.

I puzzled over what she'd told me. When she returned I asked her, "How'd you get your sister to trade places with you? Not many people want to spend the night in ICU."

"She suggested it. She wanted to get away from Bud. He was pestering her to get her to come back." Hope shivered. "After he found out about the money."

"The money?"

"The money she would get from the sale of the shop. But Charity says he'd just gamble it away. He makes plenty selling cars but it all goes to the boats. Right down the river," she added with a laugh, referring to the gambling boat anchored on the Mississippi.

"So what happened when she came in to see you?"

"She had come to the hospital to give blood. For me." Hope's voice caught and she swallowed. "She thought I might need it." She took a breath and went on. "She said she wished she was safe in a hospital . . ." Hope gulped, ". . . bed like I was. We thought of it at the same time." She smiled. "We did that a lot."

"Weren't you feeling weak? You'd lost a lot of blood."

"Yeah, I was. I had to sit down a while after we changed clothes."

"What did you do about your IV? When we found your sister she had one running?"

Hope smiled. "I just yanked it out. It ran all over the floor."

"I saw that in the chart. Laura started another one, but she didn't know it wasn't on you." I took a sip of coffee. "That's why she had another stick."

"Huh?"

243

"Your sister had a stick in her other arm. From giving blood earlier," I explained. "Otherwise when Laura came in to start the IV, she would have noticed that she hadn't had an IV before."

"Only thing was we didn't know what to do about that band." She circled her wrist with her thumb and forefinger. "The one they put on at the hospital."

"ID bracelet."

"We couldn't figure out how to get it on Charity after I'd cut it off me. I didn't want to look like an escaped patient."

"You threw it away."

She nodded. "Then I just got on the bus and went to sleep, even without the pills."

"Pills?"

"The ones that doctor gave me."

"What doctor?"

"The one who did it. Got rid of it," she added softly.

"What'd he give you?" I asked, worry tickling at the back of my mind.

"Tylenol something. I had dropped them in my Coke—I never could swallow pills—and had just had a few sips when Charity came in."

"Tylenol number three?"

"Yeah, that's it. For pain, he said."

Tylenol with codeine. Controlled substance, schedule II opioid. In lay language: narcotic. If Charity had taken it, it would have depressed her breathing. In some patients it can bring on euphoria, which would have kept her awake. No wonder she complained twice that she couldn't sleep.

244

"That didn't kill her, did it? Please tell me it didn't!" she said louder.

"No, no." I shook my head emphatically. "What was in the Coke definitely did not kill her."

She slumped in her seat. "Then what? Tell me!"

"I really don't know," I said. "You're going to have to tell your family about your trading places with your sister. And the police."

She didn't answer me.

"You have to, Hope, or I will. It all has to come out. You have to go to the police." I reached in my pocket for Detective Harding's card. "Here's the name of the detective you should talk to." I wrote it down on a napkin and gave it to her.

"Okay," she said slowly.

"Where's your husband? Jack."

"He's staying with his mom and dad, but he's due back in Georgia next Monday, the day after Easter. He goes back to ranger school. He has to do the part he failed over again."

"Tell me one thing," I said. "Who did your abortion?"

She pulled her purse toward her and slid out of the booth. "Some doctor who doesn't have a license anymore," she said, tossing her bag over her shoulder.

"You didn't go to the clinic?"

She looked at me like I was stupid. "Dad's there whenever it's open. He wouldn't have let me in."

✦ ✦ ✦ ✦

I woke up BJ.

"We need to talk."

"Uh? What time is it?" BJ asked, her voice full of sleep.

"Eleven. Time to get up."

"The morning?" she mumbled.

"Uncle Bob's. Now. It's important."

✦ ✦ ✦ ✦

Twenty minutes later she was seated where Hope had been, and I had called for more coffee.

"I know how they did it. She was drugged."

"A druggie?"

"No, it was an accident. Well, actually, two accidents." I told her about all the medications Charity had consumed.

"The drugs killed her? I thought you said she bled to death." BJ rubbed her eyes, still red with sleep.

"The drugs didn't kill her. She just slept through it. She couldn't have woke up if she'd tried."

BJ shook her head. "How'd this happen?"

"They traded places, BJ. In the hospital."

"What? Traded places! Why?"

"The one sister—the one who died—was trying to get away from her husband. They were separated, but he was after her to come back. I guess she thought the hospital was as safe a place as any." I took a breath and went on. "And the other one, the one who had had an abortion, she wanted to go see her husband in Georgia who had a pass from the Army."

"Good grief!"

I poured us both more coffee while she thought it over.

246

BJ traced her finger on the table. "Why didn't the twin who is alive explain what happened? About switching. Was she afraid she'd be blamed for her sister's death?"

"She said she was afraid. She couldn't figure out why her sister died. Why she would suddenly start bleeding badly enough to bleed to death. There wasn't anything wrong with her sister. That's why she thought maybe it was something genetic. Something maybe she had too. That's why she asked me to try to find out. Then I think she got afraid someone had wanted to hurt her and killed her twin by mistake. That's why she hasn't told anybody."

"She could be in danger, then."

"If her sister was murdered, which we're assuming at this point."

"She tell you who the guy was?"

"She wouldn't say."

"Could it be him?" BJ asked. "But what reason would he have if she'd already had the abortion?"

"She says it's over and she won't tell anyone who."

"Doesn't anyone know about them trading places? Her family, surely?"

"They will. She's going home to tell them."

"Is she calling the department? Harding needs to know."

"I gave her his number."

"Harding needs to know right away. He'll need to talk to her. Find out who might want to hurt her. He'll get her to tell him who got her pregnant," she said with a small smile. "I better call him." She looked at her watch. "Well, first thing in the morning. How are you doing? No more bombs?"

"You saw the news?"

"No. We kept it away from them. For once. We didn't want any copycats to start threatening our hospitals."

"Then how'd he know?" I asked out loud.

"Know what? Who?"

"Bud. The salesman. He said he heard about it."

"He said he knew about the bomb threat?"

"No," I said, thinking. "I guess not. He just said he heard we had some trouble."

"That's true. You've had plenty of other things in the news." BJ's beeper sounded. "I gotta go," she said looking at the message.

"I thought you were off tonight."

"On call. Now, you go home and get some rest. And leave the detecting to us," she added as we went out the door.

Chapter 23
Thursday, 29 March, 0735 Hours

I'm hardly ever late for work, but that morning I couldn't seem to get moving. I'd had another dream in which I was drowning. This time I was trying to reach Hope. She kept swimming away from me, looking back and laughing. Cat woke me up, and I'd hugged her in relief until she'd squirmed out of my arms leaving cat hair clinging to my nightshirt and my mouth.

Harding and his partner were waiting for me, Ruby told me, in the conference room. "Just a few questions," Harding told me as I joined them at the table. "What's this about the twins trading places here." It sounded like an accusation.

"We didn't have anything to do with it," I answered defensively.

Harding asked what Hope had told me. I explained how I had figured out that they must have traded places and told him that Hope had explained why and how.

"You've been a big help, Ms. Everhardt," he said. "We'll need to see your staff again."

249

I nodded, feeling too tired to respond. Later I realized I hadn't told him about the triple dose of drugs.

After they left, I pulled Tim aside. I told him about the twins trading places.

"So that's why," he said, settling himself in a chair by the counter.

"Why what?"

"The tattoo."

"Huh?"

"You saw it. The butterfly on her breast."

"Yes?"

"I didn't remember seeing it on Hope when she was admitted."

"Why didn't you tell me?"

"I thought I had just missed it."

"We might have figured this out sooner."

"So what would that help? She'd still be dead."

"Maybe not, but you're to blame, too."

"Me?"

I told him about the double dose of Amytal. "You signed that it was wasted, remember?"

"That didn't kill her though."

"It helped. She also got some codeine."

"Not from me she didn't!"

"No." I explained about the mix-up.

"Whew! That would have knocked her out. Wouldn't that show up in a tox report?"

I slapped my forehead. "I forgot about that. Damn! Mickey said a drug screen went out Monday—last week—and would be back this Monday. Then she was fired. I'll try to find out from Max." I reached for the phone.

"Monika, why?" Tim asked.

"Why? So we can know for sure. If she was drugged that deeply, anything could have happened to her."

"But it's so obvious that she was drugged twice, probably three times. Maybe you're right, maybe someone did get to her here."

"But who?" I whispered as a young family pushed aside the curtain to the room across from us.

"Or how?"

"Or why?"

"Maybe some nut just got in while we were busy. She just happened to be in the wrong place," Tim said.

Ruby yelled through a curtain, "We need help over here."

"I better go," Tim said, standing. "Tell me if you learn anything else."

Could Tim be right? Could it just have been a random killing? There'd have to be some reason why a person, even if he was intent on murder, would come up to the fourth floor, make his way into intensive care where lots of people are working and milling about, to find a victim.

I put in a call to Max, who was in a meeting. I left a message that it was important and for him to call me right away.

I grabbed Jessie and told her about the twins.

"It wasn't the one we admitted? Then why'd she die?" Her black skin seemed to pale. "Oh, my God, it couldn't be."

"Couldn't be what? Do you know something, Jessie?"

"No, it's just I can't believe it. How could someone get in?" She looked around absently. "I guess they could just walk in."

"Did you see anyone that morning? Anyone who shouldn't have been here?"

"Just as I got here the MI coded twice. Mrs. Lattimore was going bad. And every bed was filled. We were barely keeping them alive, much less able to look around to see who's coming and going." She shook her head, loosening a lock of smooth gray hair from behind her ear. She pushed the errant strand back into place. "I don't remember, Monika, that morning's just a blur."

I sighed.

She stood. "Are we okay, now? Are we safe?"

"I hope so, Jessie, I hope so."

✦ ✦ ✦ ✦

Serena had classes in the morning but I knew she'd be in after lunch so I would have to wait until then to talk to her. It was unlikely she had noticed anyone who shouldn't have been there or she would have said something by now. I didn't think Harding would learn any more than I had. Tim and Jessie would be on alert now for anyone they didn't know. I hoped that would help.

✦ ✦ ✦ ✦

They were all complaining about being questioned a second time before I left for a risk management meeting later that day. I sure had plenty of risks to manage, I

252

wanted to announce, but the serious tone of our guest speaker, a local lawyer, hadn't encouraged comments. After the meeting I returned to a still-upset staff.

Even Jessie, who was usually placid and seldom made a fuss, greeted me with annoyance. "What do they think? That we murdered a patient? We're nurses!" she said, tapping her pen on the stack of charts in front of her.

Tim pulled some charts off the rack. "What I want to know is how someone could get in here and attack a patient. Even Laura would have noticed someone strange going into a patient's room."

I had to agree.

"We ain't criminals," Ruby moaned, rolling her chair closer. "I weren't even here that day."

"They're just trying to find out how this could have happened," I told them all.

"Monika, do you think someone got in and did this here?" Jessie asked seriously.

I shrugged. "It sure looks that way. I just can't figure out how."

The phone rang. It was for me, Ruby told me.

"I found something." Her voice was soft, but I recognized it.

"What?"

"I have to go."

"Wait."

A click. The line was dead.

I tried to access the file to look up her number but our computer network seemed unusually slow. I slammed my hand down on the counter just as the chart appeared on the screen. I dialed the number. It was busy. Impatiently I pushed the redial button. Still busy.

An alarm went off. Automatically, I glanced toward Hannah's room, forgetting momentarily that she'd gone home the day before.

"It's a code," Tim yelled over his shoulder, sprinting into the patient's room as Jessie grabbed the crash cart and I followed to run interference.

I forgot about the call.

Chapter 24
Thursday, 29 March, 1415 Hours

I had just grabbed a sandwich in the cafeteria when Ruby paged me. It was after one when we'd finally given up trying to resuscitate Mr. Ritenour. His wife, a fixture on the unit for the past few weeks, had remained calm throughout the code. When it was over, she had picked up the plastic bag filled with his belongings and walked out dry-eyed.

I went into the hall outside the cafeteria and called Ruby back.

"It's the other Shepheard sister. She's been admitted. It looks bad. You better get up here."

I sagged against the wall; I should have tried to call her again. Did the murderer figure out that it wasn't Hope who had been killed in the hospital, so now he was after her again?

"An accident," Jessie told me as I came through the doors. "Hit and run, they say."

"How is she?"

Jessie shook her head. "Not conscious. Too soon to tell. Lord's in there now."

Hope's parents were standing by the desk, arguing.

"I told them to take her to Memorial. I don't want another daughter of mine in here," Mr. Shepheard said, looking at me.

"We don't have a say," Mrs. Shepheard said, her voice whiny. She clutched what looked like Hope's black leather bag to her chest.

"Mr. and Mrs. Shepheard, why don't you come with me?" I pointed toward the door.

"Why?" Mr. Shepheard asked.

"We can talk better in the waiting room."

"We don't want to talk to you," Mr. Shepheard said. "We want to talk to someone in charge." He glanced around at the activity. "Where's the doctor?"

Staff were running in and out of the injured girl's room bringing equipment and supplies as needed. A lab tech came in to draw blood for a stat analysis.

"He's in there with your daughter," I told the Shepheards as Jack came through the swinging doors. "They should be out in a few minutes. You go on down to the waiting room, and I'll send him to you as soon as they're finished."

"You all need to wait outside," Tim told them.

"Finally, someone who knows what he's doing," Mr. Shepheard said.

"You mean has a penis," whispered Serena.

One of the new nurses giggled.

Jake Lord came out of Hope's room.

Mr. Shepheard lunged toward him. "Not him! Keep that monkey away from my daughter!"

I heard a sharp intake of breath from Ruby behind me and for a moment no one moved. Lord's face was frozen in a mask of anger.

"Hold on," Jack said, grabbing Mr. Shepheard's arm.

"And you," he said turning to Jack, "you don't care, do you? You don't want to make them pay for killing my daughter!"

A large group of visitors banged through the door with Bud behind them. Jessie tried to tell the group that only two at a time were allowed in the room. A middle-aged man was arguing with her, insisting that they hadn't driven all the way up from Springfield to wait outside when Serena came out of Hope's room and gave a short yelp of surprise.

"Serena, what is it?" I asked her.

She shook her head and disappeared into the med room.

The group of visitors left except the argumentative man and a woman who looked to be his wife. Jessie ushered them into their niece's room. Tim scooted the Shepheards out the door, assuring them that their daughter had the best doctors. He didn't say anything about the nurses.

Serena peeked out of the med room. "Are they gone?"

"Serena, what's going on?"

She shrugged. "I thought he looked familiar, that's all."

"Who?" I barked.

"The tall one." She said as she headed into Hope's room.

"You jumpin' on everbody," Ruby complained.

I sank into a nearby chair. "I know, Ruby," I sighed. "It's getting to me."

Jessie came out of Hope's room, followed by Serena.

"How is she?" I asked.

"Lord said she has a closed head injury and some soft tissue damage but nothing's broken."

I rubbed my still-sore neck in sympathy.

"Will she be all right?" Serena asked.

"We'll have to watch for a subdural hematoma, bleeding that can swell, press on the brain," Jessie explained to her.

"Would it kill her?"

Jessie nodded. "It could, yes. But she'll probably be just fine." Jessie smiled encouragement. "It's just too soon to tell."

"Is she awake?" I asked Jessie.

"She can be roused." She pulled a ballpoint pen out of her pocket and showed it to Serena. "You run this—unopened—up the sole of her foot to see if she reacts to the stimulus."

"Did she?" Serena asked.

Jessie nodded. "And she didn't like it, but she dropped back asleep right away."

"What happens next?" Serena looked worried.

"We wait," I told her. "And watch."

Chapter 25
Friday, 30 March, 0745 Hours

The next morning the rain had stopped and the sun was peeking through the clouds. I'd scheduled myself for the afternoon shift so I could pick up my glasses and go to Mass for Good Friday. Now I needed a walk and the time to think.

Who could have killed Charity? Who would have wanted to kill Hope? BJ said it was usually about money. Jack couldn't have known Hope was pregnant, and he appeared to genuinely love her. But Bud had said Jack had a life insurance policy on her. Certainly people were murdered for less than a hundred thousand dollars. I didn't know where he was when Charity had been killed, but I thought Harding should be able to find that out now that he was motivated to do some serious investigating.

I considered the other family members, starting with the father. BJ said it was Mrs. Shepheard who hit him, although I'd seen evidence of his temper. But what reason would he have to kill his daughter? Because she'd "sinned?" He'd have to be some kind of nut to sacrifice her life just to wash away her sins, but nut he was, according to Hope, the neighbor and what I'd seen.

The mother was too self-absorbed to care much about anything but herself from what I'd seen. Could she want to harm her daughter just to get sympathy? Some parents have made their children sick to get attention, but not killed them.

It couldn't have been Hope's husband, Jack, because he was on the Army post when they called him. What about Hope? She'd said they were competitive but it was difficult to imagine her actually killing Charity. She said she'd been on the bus to Savannah, but had she? But then why did she try so hard to find out who killed her sister? What had she found that she'd called me about? And what had happened in the hit-and-run? Had someone tried to kill her?

Maybe Charity was the intended victim after all. She and Bud were separated so he might have a motive to kill Charity if he had known she had switched places with Hope. He might inherit part of the gun shop if his wife died, although I didn't think the father would let that happen. Then there was the preacher with his cloying looks and hands, allegedly. Could he have been involved with one or both of the women and be afraid of the consequences? He certainly possessed an arrogance that led me to believe he considered himself above the petty affairs of normal human beings.

Jake Lord wasn't a suspect by any stretch of the imagination because Hope had said she'd gone to a back-street doc. That only left the staff. No one on my staff had a motive. And all of them had been too busy that day to murder anybody anyway.

Ruby had complained that everything happening at the hospital had started when Judyth arrived, hinting about unexplained deaths in the Chicago hospital, but Ruby's habit of embellishing facts made her tale suspect. Our budget cuts occurred about the same time Judyth came. That was the only coincidence.

Rounding the corner at the park, I noticed it was unusually quiet. Then I remembered that Catholic schools were out for Good Friday.

One school kid, though, was bike riding early. Even without my new glasses I recognized him. I could taste the anger as it rose in my throat. He was a long way off and pedaling slowly, unconcerned.

I looked around the park. The storms of the last week had loosened dead tree branches, scattering them about on the ground. I scooped one up as I swerved through the grass. I had to hurry now. He was getting closer and as he saw me, he grinned. I looked around casually as if I were enjoying the budding trees and bright sunshine, carefully avoiding meeting eyes with the oncoming rider still several yards away. I stepped into the street, glancing both ways as if I planned to cross. He wheeled his bike away from the curb and straight toward me. He was less than a yard from me when I dropped down, seemingly to tie my shoelace. I could hear his breath as he pumped the last few pedals to my side. As his arm dropped down to touch me again, I shoved the stick into the spokes, and his front wheel twisted to the side as the bike came to a sudden and complete stop. The boy was tossed over the handlebars and into the street. When I heard the thud, I felt a moment of panic. What if a car came along and hit him? I jumped up and ran over to him. One side of his face was scraped and pieces of gravel were embedded in some of the open sores—road rash, we nurses call it. It would heal, but before that it would hurt. He would hurt a lot, I thought, with satisfaction.

"My bike," he said, pulling his legs out of the tangle of wheel and handlebars. The twisted front wheel and the handlebars faced in opposite directions. "My new bike." He brushed at tears on his face, smearing dirt into his wounds.

I felt a tiny bit guilty.

"You're lucky that's all that's broken," I told him, my anger returning. "Listen to me." He looked up in surprise. "If you ever . . ." I said, my words slow and measured, ". . . ever . . . touch a woman again, I'll come after you worse than this." He didn't say anything, but his face registered understanding. I turned and sprinted toward home. At the corner, I glanced back. He was still staring after me, holding his broken bike by its bent handlebars.

Damn, it was a Good Friday.

Chapter 26
Friday, 30 March, 0930 Hours

The light was blinking on my answering machine when I got home. I punched the play button, remembering I hadn't checked for messages the night before. I listened as I peeled off my sweaty clothes.

Her voice was so soft I didn't catch the beginning. When she'd finished, I dialed a familiar number. BJ's voice clicked on, tersely telling me to leave a name and number.

"Wake up, BJ, I need you," I shouted into her machine. I said it two more times and then waited for her to pick up. But she was either sound asleep or gone. I told her to call me at work ASAP. I had something to tell her.

✦ ✦ ✦ ✦

I stopped Serena as she came in the door. "What was going on with you yesterday? Who'd you think you recognized?"

"I don't know. He looked so different." She ran stubby fingers through her spiked white-blond hair.

"Who are you talking about?" I asked her quietly, not wanting to rattle her.

She rubbed a silver stud stuck in the side of her nose. "It was one of the guys in here yesterday. The tall one. But he was wearing a lab coat last Saturday. I thought he was a doctor."

"When?"

"Before she died. The twin."

"Serena, which man?"

Detective Harding and his partner came through the door. "What's going on?" I had left him a message earlier, telling him it was urgent.

I nodded toward Serena. "She saw someone the day . . . of the incident," I said as a family came through the door.

"Oh?"

Serena looked around as if she wanted to escape.

I gently took her arm. "Let's go in the conference room." I nodded toward the open door behind us.

"Just her," Harding said, taking Serena's other arm.

"But I have something to tell you," I said.

"I want to talk to her first. Alone."

BJ came through the door while I was waiting on the phone for the lab. I handed the phone to Ruby to wait for the report and led BJ out into the hall. I told her Harding was talking to Serena as we headed for my office.

"Listen to this," I said, scooping the mess off my chair. I set the small tape player I'd grabbed from home on my desk. "I tried to get Harding to listen to it but once again he had other ideas." I pushed the play button.

Hope's voice was hesitant. "I'm sorry I hung up on you." She was quiet, seeming to gather strength. "He did it. He killed my sister." She took a breath. "I found something from the hospital." She choked. "I think it's blood." Silence. Then she went on. "I called you, but he drove up and I got scared. Monika, I'm going to bring them to the hospital. Maybe you can have it tested." There was silence on the line and I thought she'd hung up, but just before I pushed the rewind button, her soft voice continued. "I'm so scared."

"Damn her. Why didn't she call the police?" I asked.

"Can I talk to her?"

"Not yet, BJ, she's not really awake and we don't know when she will be. You can never tell with head cases."

"They know who did it?"

I shook my head. "Hit and run."

"Where do you think she stashed whatever it was she found?"

"I don't know. We could ask the family, but . . . who do you think she meant? He? Serena said the same thing—'he.' Serena thought she saw the same man here yesterday, someone she saw the day Hope—well, Charity—died."

"Who was it?"

"I don't know. We had a bunch of visitors all at once."

"What did that tape say?" BJ pointed to the tape player. "About a weapon?"

I rewound the tape, and we listened again. "She said them. More than one?"

"What could it be?" BJ asked, frowning.

"Max said it had to have been a long instrument of some kind that reached up through the vagina and cut through the artery."

"What do you have here like that?"

I thought. "Forceps. Scissors."

BJ frowned. "I thought you said they had to be long."

"There are some scissors twelve to fifteen inches long. Used in surgery."

"But where would someone get those? Do you have them up here?"

I looked around. "No."

"He couldn't get into surgery, could he?" Her eyes narrowed. "Unless he was a doctor."

"Maybe the ER."

"They'd have them?"

"Sure. They do lots of procedures."

"But they wouldn't just be laying around for anyone to pick up."

"Let me check." I looked at my watch. "I need to catch up with Max in the lab, too. I can run down there now." I stood, knocking the budget file to the floor.

She picked up the scattered pages and replaced them on my desk. "Maybe Harding's found out something from your nurse."

"Student. She's not a nurse. Not yet."

But the two detectives had gone.

"Where's Serena?" I asked Jessie.

"I sent her home. She was too upset to be any good."

"Did she say anything?"

Jessie frowned. "About what?"

"Whatever she told the detective."

Jessie shook her head and focused her working eye on me. "She was crying. She just left."

"I'll take this with me," BJ said, slipping the tape of Hope's message in her jacket pocket.

"I can't believe Harding left without talking to me," I said to BJ. "I'll let you know what I find out," I told her as we rode down on the elevator together. "Will you ask Harding to call me if he knows something we should know?"

✦ ✦ ✦ ✦

It didn't take long to find out everything. Max had read the report on the drug analysis and confirmed what we suspected. Charity had had high levels of narcotics—both Amytal and codeine—in her blood. Enough to knock her out for a long time, Max had said. And to sleep through her own brutal murder.

✦ ✦ ✦ ✦

An old friend from nursing school was temporarily running the ER. She was glad to tell me how bad their staffing cuts were. When I asked her if she could remember anything unusual about St. Patrick's Day, she threw her hands in the air.

"I threw a holy fit that day, Monika," Wanda said.

"What happened?"

"That Saturday morning I came in early to catch up on some paperwork. There's no time to get it done during the week, you know."

I nodded.

"I found the trash cart and a tray of dirty instruments sitting in the hall. From the night before! I called housekeeping, but no one was there, of course, so I tracked one of them down emptying trash in the lobby. The guy mumbled something, and I told him to get to ER pronto. When I came out of my office an hour later, it was still there! This time he was drinking coffee in the cafeteria! I just blew up!"

"What'd he say?"

She shrugged. "He was mad because he was supposed to have help but no one ever showed up. And they'd already doubled his workload."

"Like all the rest of us."

"Yeah."

"Did you notice what else was on the cart? Something long and sharp like surgical scissors?" I spread my hands about a foot apart.

She shook her head. "I didn't, but if so they'd be dirty ones. They'd have been used on someone else."

✦ ✦ ✦ ✦

Jake had been in and Hope had not improved by the time I went into her room after lunch. I was stowing an extra box of tissues in the drawer of her bedside table when I saw her black bag on the shelf. I glanced around. Machinery whirled and low voices sounded from several rooms, but I was alone in the curtained cubicle with an unconscious Hope. I dropped to the floor, took the bag and released the snap on top. I squinted into it but couldn't make out anything in the dim light. I reached inside and pulled out a hairbrush, a billfold with two driver's licenses with identical photos, a set of car keys, a small makeup bag, some loose tissues, a tiny address book, and a tube of hand cream. I turned the bag upside down and a half-eaten Hershey bar dropped out.

No long scissors. No weapon of any kind.

I pocketed the address book and her car keys and was stuffing the other contents back in the bag when I heard Mrs. Shepheard's voice.

"Wait," she said. "I need to go to the restroom."

Her footsteps clicked away. The curtain was pushed aside and Hope's father stood in the doorway. I stayed kneeling on the floor, wishing myself anywhere but there, but he didn't notice me. The light surrounded his head like a halo, and his eyes, focused on his daughter, shone with emotion in the half-light. My leg started to cramp, and I shifted slightly.

His tear-filled eyes slid over me, unseeing, as he made his way to his daughter's bedside. "My baby," he whispered softly. His eyes never left Hope's face.

I stood and silently slipped out.

✦ ✦ ✦ ✦

Jerry Wagner had reluctantly agreed to station a guard outside Hope's room overnight, complaining that he'd have to cut down on patrolling in the garage. The young recruit was leaning back in his chair reading a book called GUNS FOR FUN AND PROFIT when I went in to check on her one last time before I went home. He didn't look up as I closed the curtain to her room nor did he look up when I came back out. As I passed him I bumped his chair that was balancing precariously on only two legs.

"Hey!" he yelled, jumping up as the chair crashed to the floor.

"Shhh," I told him in a stage whisper. "Sick people in here." I kept my face neutral.

He righted the chair and grumbled about "damn nurses" as I rounded the corner and pushed open the swinging doors. It was unfair to take out my frustration on a poorly-paid and even more poorly-trained security guard, and I felt a prickling of guilt as I swung my car out of the garage and onto the street.

I drove more carefully than usual. It was Friday night, traffic was heavy and Black Beauty was newly repaired. The rain had quit, leaving clean-washed streets that reflected the lights of the city. I decided to treat myself so I headed west toward the old Route 66 for a frozen concrete from Ed Krewe's.

At the next stoplight I unlocked the top and slid it back over my head and gazed up at the inky sky thick with stars. Honking behind me brought me back to reality. I moved ahead as a large black van sped around me and into the lane in front of Black Beauty and slammed to a stop at the corner. My brakes squealed as I slid to a stop inches from its bumper. My heart sank back in my chest as the van took off again in a spurt of gasoline fumes. I started up slowly to give it room to move ahead. It was soon out of sight.

I turned on the radio to KFUO to hear the end of Dvorak's Symphony No. 7 as I caught a yellow light at the next cross street. I stopped, for once foregoing the thrill of trying to beat the red.

A motor revved next to me. The same black van had just pulled up next to me. I sat very still, trying to control the fear prickling my neck.

The radio extolled the latest exhibit at the St. Louis Art Museum, but I cut it off in mid-sentence.

The light turned green and I made a quick right.

The van crossed the lane in front of a honking car and followed me onto a side street.

I sped up.

The van kept pace.

I looked up at the sky peppered with stars, but this time I felt exposed, vulnerable. I couldn't put the top up without stopping the car and getting out. We both pulled up behind a line of cars at the next intersection. The van sat next to me, like a large, black predator, quiet, menacing, waiting to pounce. The arrow turned green for a right hand turn and I slid around the corner. A glance back told me the van was stuck in the middle lane while other cars in the right lane followed me. I let out a long-held breath and came to another stoplight. Slowly I relaxed my shoulders and flexed my hands.

I turned the radio back on and let the wind blow in my face as I listened to a Beethoven concerto. After a few more blocks I swung back toward home. I had lost my appetite for ice cream. I was nearing my neighborhood when bright headlights bounced off my rearview mirror. I tried to see who it was but the lights blinded me. Fear caught at my throat.

I slowed as the light ahead turned yellow and nearly came to a complete stop but, just as it turned red,

Twice Dead

I stepped on the accelerator and zipped past two cars that had started into the intersection. I glanced back. The black van stood waiting at the light, fuming, it seemed.

I was in my house, with all the doors locked, within five minutes.

Chapter 27
Saturday 31 March 0655

"Did you get a license number?" BJ asked as she poured herself a cup of coffee at Uncle Bob's the next morning.

"I didn't think of it. I was too scared."

"That's what they count on." BJ stirred her coffee with a bent spoon. "What did he do exactly?" She was using her police officer voice.

"He just followed me." It didn't sound like much of a threat. "And showed up later back on Hampton."

BJ frowned. "Are you sure he was after *you*?"

"I don't know, BJ. I thought he was but—"

"But he didn't really do anything, did he?"

"Nooo. Not really."

"Keep an eye out for the van. And I'll let some of the guys who patrol that area know about it. Maybe they can get a license number and we'll see who it is." She reached across the table and patted my hand. "It'll be all right, Monika."

"Just catch our killer. Then I'll be all right. What do you know about the investigation? What's Harding doing? Do you think Hope's accident had

273

anything to do with her sister's death? What'd Harding find out from Serena?"

"Hold on there, kid. I don't know anything yet. I left the tape for Harding but he was out and we got busy."

"This is important!" I said.

"More than you know. It's a murder investigation now. Not manslaughter. That's what they thought they were investigating after they found out the dead twin wasn't pregnant."

"What if she had been?"

"They probably would have called it accidental death."

"And no one would be blamed?" I asked, surprised.

"Not if they didn't mean to, and not if they didn't do anything wrong."

"But we'd get sued for malpractice."

"They could but that's civil; it's not criminal. Remember OJ?" BJ glanced at her watch. "Gotta go. I'll check with Harding when I get in." She reached in her pants pocket and pulled out a dollar. She tossed it on the table. "I'll call you when we know something."

I gave her a salute. "You take care."

She pulled on her jacket and slid reflective sunglasses over her blue eyes. "Will do," she said, patting her side where her revolver lay hidden in its holster. I watched her make her way through the restaurant, walking erect.

◆ ◆ ◆ ◆

I stopped at the pay phone on the wall on my way out and dialed the number I'd looked up at home. No answer. Maybe Serena would be at the hospital when I got there.

As the manager, I was off on weekends, but I sometimes went in to catch up on paperwork that I was too tired to do at the end of the day. That Saturday I wanted to check on Hope.

Jessie reported that she was awake and oriented. I went in to see her.

Jack was leaning over her, his back to the door.

"What are you doing?" I grabbed his arm, spinning him around. He stumbled, then caught his balance, knocking a vase of roses to the floor. The vase shattered. He stepped back, slipping in the spilled water and sat down hard.

"Are you okay?" I asked a startled Hope.

"Jack!" Hope pushed herself up in the bed.

He got up and brushed splinters of glass off the seat of his khaki pants, getting tiny lacerations on his hands. I handed him the tissue box as I looked closely at Hope.

"What'd you do that for?" she asked me, her voice weak.

I felt foolish. Obviously, she was fine.

"I'm sorry," I said to both of them. "I guess I'm just jumpy."

"I know. You're worried about her," Jack said, smiling at Hope. "We all are."

I stooped down to pick up the roses, pricking my finger. I sucked at a tiny puncture.

"I need to go home and change." Jack kissed Hope goodbye as I laid the roses on the bedside table.

"What did you find? And where is it? Why didn't you call the police?" I asked while I washed my hands.

She moaned as she reached the hand tethered to an IV up to her head, stopping the flow of fluid in the tubing.

"I don't know."

"You don't know!"

"Ouch. Don't shout. Please." She clutched her head. "All I can think about is Charity—what she went through."

"She didn't know what happened to her, Hope. She slept through it." I took her hand and lowered it to the bed. The IV fluid began flowing again. "But what did you call me about? You said you'd found something with blood on it."

She took a breath, seeming to fight for strength. "I don't know." She tried to raise herself on the bed. "What time is it anyway?" She looked up on the wall at the large numbered clock that we use in all the rooms to help orient our patients who never see daylight.

"It's Saturday."

"Saturday? No, it can't be."

"We talked Wednesday night. On Thursday you left me the phone message that you'd found something from the hospital. Was it the . . . murder weapon? You were bringing it—or 'them,' you said—to me to be tested, when you had the accident. They think you hit your head on the car's doorframe when you were rear-ended. You've been unconscious since yesterday."

She frowned. "I don't remember."

"You don't remember calling me? Or finding a weapon?"

She shook her head, slowly this time. "Nothing. The last thing I remember is driving over to Charity's apartment." She rubbed her forehead. "I can't remember anything after that."

Retrograde amnesia. Not uncommon with closed head injuries. No way to tell when and if she'd regain what she'd lost.

As I reached up to adjust her IV, uncoiling the tube that had been hung incorrectly, I felt, rather than heard, the curtain move behind me. Hope let out a sharp yip and I turned to her: fright was written on her face in dark, frozen creases. I swirled around as the curtain swished closed. The ace and queen disappeared beneath the curtain.

"Stop!" I yelled. "Stop him!" I tried to run, but I was tangled in the IV tube.

"They're in the Miata," Hope cried, grabbing my lab coat. Seeing him had jogged her memory. "He must have found out they're missing! Scissors he killed her with, big scissors!" She still held on to me.

I pulled free easily. "I've got to stop him! Call security!" I yelled.

A woman visitor stuck her face out from behind a curtain but the nurse's station was empty. Ruby only worked weekdays, and, for once, no one was at the desk charting or on the phone.

I ran to the phone and punched in the emergency code for security. The operator answered on the first ring and I heard the familiar click of the recording tape. "Tell Wagner to stop the man with cards on his heels— he—" Several visitors had come out of patient rooms and were listening. I lowered my voice. "Blond hair, six feet, skinny, and wearing cowboy boots. And get that guard back up here!"

"Everything's fine," I told the visitors. "He forgot something, that's all." I pushed through the doors and slammed into an empty gurney that was backed up to a housekeeping cart brimming with trash and dirty laundry. Brown paper towels tumbled onto the floor and a blood- and feces-stained sheet slid out of the contaminated laundry bag. Not wanting to wait for the elevator, I ran down four flights of stairs to the front entrance.

"What's the matter with them!" I said out loud, stamping my foot when there were no security personnel in sight. "Where the hell are they!" I said out loud to Wagner as he came off the elevator.

"Shhh, Monika, this is a hospital!"

"I know it's a hospital," I said, "and one with a . . ." I glanced around at the crowded lobby. ". . . person we need to catch," I added lowering my voice. "Did you get him?"

Wagner shook his head.

"Did you try?"

"I didn't understand what you said."

I shook my head in frustration. "I described him right down to his card-playing cowboy boots! Damn!"

"All right now, Monika, that's enough." Wagner grabbed my arm, pulling me toward the stairs.

"Let go of me!" I jerked my arm free.

Mr. Haslett, our CEO, came around the corner trailed by a young city police officer. "You," Haslett said, pointing to Wagner. "Come with me. Now." He left no doubt he meant it.

"Wait," I said as the men moved off with Jerry between them. Haslett waved me off as they rounded the corner.

I couldn't seem to think what to do—keep Hope safe? Follow Bud? I wiped sweaty palms on my scrubs and tried to slow my pounding heart.

An elevator swished open at the end of the lobby. I ran toward it as a throng jostled their way out. I glanced at the line waiting to get on, sprinted to the door and, taking two steps at time, ran up one flight. I stopped to catch my breath on the landing. I had to keep calm, I told myself, think clearly. Had Bud heard Hope say the scissors were in the Miata? I had to get them before he did.

I went back down the stairs, slamming the first floor door open and bumping a woman on crutches. I mumbled "sorry" as I pushed the door to the lower level open. I passed the hospital's basement entrance and ran through into the garage. Then I remembered that my car was on the top level. Fortunately the garage elevator door was just opening. I pushed past a couple getting off and then had to wait for the doors to close. When I reached the top I tried to shove the doors open faster— to no effect—and then ran down the aisle to my car. I slipped my hand under the left front fender, feeling for the magnetic key holder.

It wasn't there! Had the accident jarred it loose? I took a breath and slid my hand forward. There it was!

Black Beauty squealed around the corners of the garage descending to the entrance and we barely missed one car as it was starting to back out. I slipped my key card into the slot in the exit gate and fumbled in my pocket for the address book I'd grabbed from Hope's purse.

At the first stoplight, I looked for the address. It was there, under C. At the next light, I pulled my map out of the glove box and found the street. About ten minutes away.

My insides felt like jelly, quivery, but I held tight on the steering wheel, knuckles white. I took a breath and closed my eyes at the next stop light, but all I could see was the dead twin's blood, and two playing cards bouncing out of the room, much like they must have done two weeks before as I was watching Irish dancers jig to the tune of bagpipes at the parade.

A horn honked behind me. I jumped. The light had turned green.

I made one wrong turn, going south on Kingshighway off Chippewa instead of north but found the address a few minutes later. It was a two-story apartment building probably built in the fifties with an outside stairway and a balcony running around the three sides. It looked its age with cracked and split weathered siding, broken steps, grass growing through cracks in the sidewalk. A black van, its windows blacked out, sat behind Hope's Miata looking like a black panther about to pounce on the small red car.

I drove slowly past the building, found a parking spot, and watched in my rearview mirror for signs of activity. I tried my cell phone but, as usual, it wasn't working. I'd rather be doing this with sirens, badges and guns.

I took a deep breath, opened the door and closed it quickly, then scooted out into the street in order to approach the vehicles on the street side, hoping I'd be less visible to anyone looking out of the apartment windows. The Miata was in front of the van, the trunk and bumper folded into a V that rested behind the driver's headrest. The black van had red paint streaks on its slightly dented silver bumper.

I dropped down to the ground, took a breath, and moved around the Miata to the curbside. The door was locked. I fingered the keys I'd taken from Hope's purse as I went around to the street side, this time standing up and walking naturally, realizing I looked pretty suspicious creeping around. The largest key opened the door and I slid into the seat as if I were contemplating a casual ride with a driver yet to arrive. A pickup truck passed by with two men talking animatedly in front.

I opened the glove box. It contained only the owner's manual and Missouri state inspection certificate. I reached under the front seat and pulled out a plastic grocery bag, unprepared for the sight and the odor. Stale, sickly sweet. There were two clear plastic bags inside, one held a bloody towel—still damp with blood, another a pair of long surgical scissors crusted with dried blood. I checked under the seat again and found another bag. A blood-splattered lab coat was wadded up inside.

As I cracked open the car door to get some air, I heard a door slam.

Bud came out of an apartment on the top floor, strolled along the balcony and bounced down the stairs, cowboy boots clicking on the concrete. He was carrying an overstuffed duffel bag.

I ducked down and stayed perfectly still. And waited. Was he headed for the Miata? I reached for the bag with the scissors.

The engine started behind me, and the black van pulled out and zoomed off down the street. I raised my head just as the van skidded around the corner.

I sat there, paralyzed. Bud was running away, I was sure of that. I knew, now that I saw the van, that he had followed me the night before, trying to frighten me, maybe do something worse. I was frightened and now. I sat in the dead girl's car unable to move.

Then I thought about Bud getting away, and I slid over the console, catching my leg on the gear shift, swore, and stuck the key into the ignition, firing up the Miata. I turned the corner and spotted the van two lights ahead. A pickup truck was between us. When the light changed and Bud took off, the pickup truck turned right. I tried to drop back, but the light ahead had turned red just as Bud reached it. I had nowhere to go. I slid up slowly behind the van and watched his side view mirror. He wasn't looking at me.

The car behind me gunned its engine.

Bud looked up at the sound and spotted me in his mirror. He took off while the light was still red.

A dark blue Buick was already in the intersection. The scream of metal against metal split the air, and pieces of black van and blue Buick flew up, tumbling over and over as if in slow motion, dropping one by one to the ground.

Cars from all directions screeched to a halt. I jumped out.

The Buick's driver had been thrown clear. Blood streamed from multiple cuts on his face and dribbled out of the corner of his mouth as he lay on the pavement. I detected a weak, thready pulse in his carotid. People were gathering around. I yelled for someone to call 911 and asked if anyone had a blanket. A man returned with one and said that someone had called an ambulance. I covered the man and then went to see what had happened to Bud.

"I can't feel anything," he moaned. "Down below." He lay in the street, his head pressed against the curb. His legs were twisted beneath him. "I can't move," he said, his voice coming in gasps.

I told the bystanders not to move Bud.

Sirens screamed in the distance.

I returned to the other driver but he had expired. I pulled the blanket over his face as people gawked openly at the dead man.

An ambulance pulled up. I directed them toward Bud, explaining that they were too late to help the other victim.

Bud was screaming. "I can't feel anything! Do something!"

"You'll be all right," the female EMT told him, stabilizing his neck and back before sliding him onto the gurney. "We're on our way to the hospital."

"Where're you taking him?" I asked her, as they slid the gurney into the ambulance.

"St. Teresa's," she said, slamming the door. "It's closest."

A police car squealed around the corner and screeched to a halt beside the curb, its siren whining to a stop. BJ jumped out of her patrol car and sprinted over the grass to me.

"What are you doing here?" I asked her as two more patrol cars skidded to a stop.

"Harding figured out that Bud Burke was the guy Serena had described and wanted to question him. I was on my way to meet him at Burke's when I heard this call. What are you doing here?"

"I had to follow him. He came to the hospital and . . ." I stopped, needing to catch my breath. "Hope remembered everything. So I had to get them before he did. And I did."

"Found what?"

"Surgical scissors with blood on them, a towel and a lab coat. It's all in Hope's—Charity's—car." I pointed to the small car parked awkwardly at the curb. "Under the front seat."

"Did Hope tell you it was him?"

"Not exactly. But he came into her room when I was there and she looked terrified. Then, when he ran—
"

One of the officers yelled for BJ. She told him she'd be right there.

"He'll never walk again."

"Huh?"

"He's paralyzed. His legs, at least, maybe more. Lots more," I added. "Maybe no more sex. He's the one seduced Hope, then killed her sister—his own wife—thinking it was Hope."

She unhooked the radio off her belt. "I better call Harding and then get reports on this. You'll have to come down to the station for a statement."

She looked at the man from the Buick being loaded without hurry into another ambulance. "Vehicular homicide, too." She slipped the notepad into her jacket. "And your security guy. He's the one causing all the accidents. We got him down at the station crying like a baby." She laughed. "Said he needed more money for security and he thought if they saw what happened, they'd cave."

"He did what?"

"The bomb threat. The broken equipment. He even stirred up the protesters, telling them the hospital wanted trouble so they could fire your doc. He's feeling bad, I'm glad to say, he didn't mean for anyone to get hurt." She looked at me. "You okay?"

I felt just like I had after my accident the week before, shaking so hard I couldn't talk.

"Hey, you better sit down," she said, moving toward me. She held my arm as I collapsed onto the grass, and then she gently moved my head between my knees. I wasn't sure if I was going to faint or vomit. I did neither and in a moment looked up into BJ's concerned eyes. "You okay?"

I smiled. "I am now."

Chapter 28
Sunday 1 April 0930

Easter Sunday dawned bright and clear. I stepped out the door for church and saw that the rain had washed the streets and sidewalks clean, making them look like newly poured concrete. Sunlight sparkled on the grass and trees. The world felt new and fresh, and I felt cleansed. Black Beauty was poised and ready to roll.

Bud's preliminary diagnosis was trauma to the spinal cord at L5—prognosis— paralysis, permanent.

He'd confessed, BJ'd told me later that night, after being admitted to the same room in ICU in which he'd killed his wife, thinking she was Hope.

When he found out about the money his wife was going to get when the gunshop was sold, he was afraid Hope would tell her sister about the two of them. And he was afraid of Jack and his buddies. He had just wanted to talk to Hope, he'd said, when he came to the hospital. He'd grabbed a lab coat off a hook coming through the ER. The scissors were a handy afterthought. Maybe to frighten her. When Hope (he thought) wouldn't wake up, it occurred to him to use the scissors to put an end to his problem.

286

He'd done it before, he'd bragged to the officers. His girlfriend got pregnant and he'd tried to help her abort it. When she'd passed out, he got scared and left her to bleed to death on her parents' garage floor.

He heard Illias working in the next room so he'd wrapped the scissors in a towel and tried to toss them in the trash, but Illias saw him and yelled at him. So he just turned and left, taking the scissors with him.

He had just found out that Hope was still alive when he'd seen her jump into Charity's car. He'd rammed the car and left, leaving an unconscious Hope behind.

In his closet the detectives had found another box. It held an assortment of women's underwear—bras and panties—and T-shirts. Each item had a girl's first name written on it in pen. Hope's name was on the label of a drab-green Army T-shirt. Momentos of his conquests.

I shivered, thinking about Charity, the twin I'd never met except in death, grateful her sister had survived.

I was going to Mass with Hannah and her family, then we were planning to have dinner with Hope and Jack, who were leaving the next day for Georgia. Hope had agreed to join us, saying she'd had enough of self-righteous religion; she wanted to spend Easter with a nice Catholic family.

Driving down Hampton, I passed a church. A sign outside read, EASTER IS ABOUT HOPE; MORE THAN SOMETHING TO DYE FOR.

I couldn't stop smiling.